TITANIA HAS A MOTHER

To
THORP
(formerly "T" of *Punch*)
Colleague and Friend

*

Titania has a Mother

Doris *Cardine* Abrahams

CARYL BRAHMS
&
S. J. SIMON

"A poet who should now make the whole action
of his Tragedy depend upon enchantment of super-
natural spirits, would be censored as transgressing
the bounds of probability, be banished from the
theatre to the nursery, and condemned to write
Fairy Tales instead of Tragedies."

DR. JOHNSON

London
MICHAEL JOSEPH

First published by
MICHAEL JOSEPH LTD.
26 Bloomsbury Street,
London, W.C.1
NOVEMBER 1944
SECOND IMPRESSION AUGUST 1950
THIRD IMPRESSION APRIL 1965

Printed in Great Britain by
The Hollen Street Press Limited London W1

CONTENTS

★

A grey day in fairyland. Clouds like bats' wings obscured the sky. Castles were carved out of cobweb instead of cornelian, and even the palaces looked like slate rather than crystal.

" Turn on the technicolour," said the gnome, shocked.

*   *   *

Little Bo-Peep, trudging dismally along in search of her sheep, brightened at once. The sun, one beaming smile, had swept away the clouds. Birds were shaking out their feathers, ready to flash from branch to branch, flowers were opening up their petals and swaying on their stalks in a colourful symphony of encouragement and she wouldn't have to send her dress to the cleaner's after all. Why the stripes on her petticoat were as bright as the day Mr. Disney had painted them!

On the top of a hill a palace carved out of crystal was glittering like anything. The turrets were tiled with rubies—real rubies— each one worth a King's ransom, the domes were ballooning sapphires, and the doors were made of emerald and ivory with pearls for handles. It will be seen that the King of Boxing Night Land was reasonably rich.

To-day you could see his palace flashing and glittering from even further off than usual. For to-night it was to be the scene of a ball of unrivalled splendour.

From the foot of the hill the old woman who lived in a shoe looked up at the Palace and sighed. She wondered how the Queen had managed it.

*   *   *

The Queen hadn't.

In fact she was at this moment bending over a cradle.

" The herring loves the merry moon," she sang tenderly.
" The mackerel loves the wind.
  But the oyster loves the dredging song
  For he comes of a gentle kind."

" Oysters," said the King. " Will twenty-seven barrels be enough ? "

But the Queen was counting her baby's toes. They were all there.

" Stop crooning," said the King. " Concentrate. Don't you realize we're giving a ball of unrivalled splendour ? "

" Yes, dear," said the Queen. She kissed the baby's knuckle.

" All the fairest in the land," said the King. " And a conjuror." He picked up an invitation fronde. " Gold leaf." He fluttered it. " Do you think the wording's all right ? " He peered.

" Mumble, mumble," he said. " You are commanded to attend, mumble, mumble, on the occasion of the christening of their daughter, the Princess Aurora, yes . . . yes . . . quite . . . unrivalled splendour, dot, dot, dot, um, R.S.V.P., broomsticks at eleven, excellent, excellent."

" Broomsticks! " The Queen woke up. " Then you've asked the witches ? "

" And the fairies," said the King. " Must. Remember what happened to King Cophetua."

The Queen stiffened. " If you've asked her," she said, " I'm not coming."

" See what I mean," said the King. " Cophetua was a good fellow. Nothing wrong with Cophetua. " But," he waggled a finger, " never offend a fairy. . . ."

In his study in a fashionable mews a middle-aged young man in a polka-dotted dressing-gown pushed aside a bundle of contracts. Three plays, his personal appearance in one of them for a very limited season, his biography, and the film for the Ministry of Reconstruction could wait. He was going to write a pantomime. So far he had never written a pantomime. Overlooked it. Sheer carelessness. They were beginning to whisper he couldn't do it. He'd show them. Already he had his opening set.

" *Opening Chorus*," he wrote. " *Never Offend a Fairy*."

He settled down to find a rhyme to cretinous.

The telephone rang.

" Tony," the middle-aged young man winced. " Nice to hear you! Lunch at the Ivy ? I'd love it. Right away!"

He dressed humming his new tune.

. . . An apologetic cough was making itself heard at the King's elbow. It belonged to the Chamberlain.

" Your Majesty," he said. " The list of guests."

He unrolled a parchment. . He began to read. . . .

" No," said the Queen violently. " Not Scheherazade."

" . . . Cinderella, Sindbad, and all the fairest in the land," ended the Chamberlain an hour later.

" Excellent. Excellent," said the King. " Now are you quite certain you haven't forgotten anybody."

" I've been right through Who's Whose," said the Chamberlain virtuously. " Sat up all night," he pointed out.

" What about the fairies ? " asked the Queen. " I wouldn't like to offend a fairy. No one must have hurt feelings, to-night of all nights.

CHAPTER II   What they wore

" . . . How you can consider going to a ball of unrivalled splendour to which your mother has not been invited. . . . Your own mother, who's brought you up, who's sacrificed her life . . . all her best years. . . ."

It was the Fairy Carabosse speaking. Her feelings were definitely hurt.

. . . " A list of invitations as long as a crooked mile. All the fairest in the land invited. Everyone but your poor old mother. It's a deliberate affront, and they've done it on purpose! And how you can think of going when your poor old mother, who's sacrificed everything for you, has been insulted . . ."

" But, mother," said Titania mutinously, " you said I could go."

The Fairy Carabosse took out a handkerchief. She was a wicked fairy. She waited till her daughter was looking at her. She wept.

Poor Mother! Why was the world so cruel to her, all the time ? Perhaps it was because she was a widow. Poor father!

Titania was a good fairy. She put her arms round her mother.

" Don't cry, darling," she said. " I'll stay at home with you. I won't have my mother insulted." Anyway, she was thinking, I can wait till mother is asleep and fly out of the window.

But the Fairy Carabosse had been putting in some quiet thinking, too. Invited or not, she would go to the ball and spite them, unrivalled splendour and all. But she wouldn't tell her daughter yet. Sympathy was sweet and Titania had not always been sympathetic of late. Indeed, there had been moments when the dear child had been very nearly brusque.

" No dear," she said. " Mother doesn't want to spoil your enjoyment. Run along and have a good time. I'll be quite happy with my knitting." She held up a shred of gossamer. " See—it's coming along nicely."

Titania kissed her mother. She was a little puzzled. " Oh, thank you," she said. " I'll come straight home the moment I've given my present."

Present! The Fairy Carabosse thought of something. She smirked. " What are you giving the baby princess ? "

" Virtue," said Titania.

Serve the brat right, thought the Fairy Carabosse. But aloud she said " Very suitable."

This point settled, Titania hugged her mother and returned to her toilette. And the Fairy Carabosse, that point settled, too, watched her with a mother's pride. She might have envisaged a fearful revenge for later, but at the moment she was here to make certain that her daughter arrived at the ball of unrivalled splendour more resplendent than any of 'em.

" Too much star dust on your wings, child. Come to mother and let her brush it off. There now—let me look at you."

Titania advanced, turned, and spread her skirts. The Fairy Carabosse relaxed into a fond beam. No prettier chitling in all fairyland. A little of her mother's character and all her father's charm, blast him! She'd be the sensation of the season and perhaps end up by marrying the King of Fairyland. Certainly she should marry the King of Fairyland. She'd like to see him try to stop it. Her mouth fell into its accustomed lines of severity.

" Don't you like it, mother ? " asked Titania.

The Fairy Carabosse remembered. Praise went to Titania's head all too easily. Just like her father, drat him!

" Skimpy," she said. " Not enough of it."

" But, mother," said Titania, " Oliver Messel designed it for me himself. It couldn't be more the fashion."

" If you'd listened to your mother you'd have gone to Bakst,"
said the Fairy Carabosse. " I wouldn't be dressed by anyone else
if you paid me." She plumped out her quiltings. " Still," she
said, " what's cut can't be uncut, and I daresay you'll be the
prettiest fairy there."

Titania flushed with pleasure.

" And that reminds me," said the Fairy Carabosse. " Be nice to
Prince Oberon."

" Prince Oberon ? " Titania pouted. " Why ? He's a fright-
fully bad dancer, mother. His lifts! " She shuddered.

" He's the direct heir to the Throne of Fairyland," said mother,
" and that's more important than dancing. Not your dancing,"
she amended, " but his."

" But he's a Warwickshire fairy," argued Titania, " and everyone
knows how rustic they are."

" Rustic or not, he's royal," said mother. " And if he invites
you to a *pas de deux*, just follow as best you can."

" But mother," said the despairing Titania. " Be reasonable.
He'll be doing a folk dance."

" What if he does," said mother, " he's still heir to the throne."

Titania kicked over an acorn. " Corduroy trousers," she muttered rebelliously.

" Trousers or no trousers, folk dances or folk songs, Oberon is
Queen Mab's son," said mother. " And if you don't dance with
him if he asks you, I'll spank you."

" If he asks me," said Titania.

" And if he doesn't ask you," said mother, " I'll want to know
the reason why."

Titania knew when she was beaten. " All right," she agreed,
" he'll dance with me." She turned to a more attractive theme.
" They tell me," she said, " that some of the prettiest mortals are
coming. Goldilocks, Snow White, Little Red Riding Hood . . ."

" A brunette." The Fairy Carabosse waved her away. " It's
the men mortals you've got to watch. Can't sight a fairy without
asking for three wishes. And all of them for one thing," she added
cryptically. " Though not lately," she finished with faint regret.

" I've never met a mortal," said Titania.

" Just as well," said the Fairy Carabosse. " Remember Prince
Florizel." She sniffed. " Another rosebud on your ballet shoe,"

she said. " Five more spangles on your frock." She sprinkled.

" I've never met a man," said Titania. " What are they like ? "

" Like your father," snapped the Fairy Carabosse. She tweaked the crown straight.

" But wasn't father a fairy ? "

" That's just what I'm complaining about," said the Fairy Carabosse bleakly.

Titania gave it up. She picked up her wand, straightened the star and tossed off thirty-two fouettées on a silver thimble top.

" Keep your hips in," said the Fairy Carabosse from force of habit.

⋆   ⋆   ⋆

" How do we look ? " asked the fairest in the land, turning expectantly to their mothers.

" Skimpy," said the mothers in unison.

Mr. Messel had been awfully busy. All over Fairyland people were getting into his creations. No matter how these balls of unrivalled splendour went off he, at least, was always sure of a personal success. Photographs were trickier. Poor Cecil!

Never had there been such an expectancy of preparation. As usual.

Never had there been so much sprinkling of stardust, such shimmering of spangles, such glistening of cellophane wings. As usual.

Never had there been so much speculation about who Prince Oberon would dance with. Pure routine.

In short, the whole of Boxing Night Land, fairies—good and evil—witches and wizards, gnomes and goblins, elves and dwarfs, pixies and leprechauns, animals in human form and human animals were looking forward to an evening of unsurpassed magnificence.

" No," said Cinderella. " I'm not going."

Prince Charming passed a weary hand over this thinning hair.

" Darling," he said, " do come. You'll have the smallest foot there."

" I'm tired of parties," said Cinderella. " I'm going to stay at home and get on with my jam-making."

Prince Charming sighed. " You used to like balls once. You made quite an effort to go to one—remember ? "

" Oh, if you're going to get sentimental . . ." said Cinderella. She turned her back on him.

Prince Charming looked at her. Still beautiful. Still the smallest foot in Fairyland, but oh, that garment of provincial respectability she had gathered around herself!

Their first year of marriage had been one of ecstatic admiration, with Cinderella marvelling at the strange new world and Prince Charming as the man from Cooks. How pleased she had been with his palace. The arches carved out of amethyst. The resplendent throne. The bevy of attendants straight from the Cone School and Conti's, liable to rush on in a body at any moment and go into an energetic routine keeping strictly in line. How she had gasped in the gardens, and wondered at her wardrobe and worn her jewels when they were dining alone. How she would fear that she had offended him if any one day passed without his singing to her the song that he had first sung that night as he looked at her left-behind slipper in the privacy of the limelight :

> " If I could plant a tiny seed of love
>   In the corner of your heart, pom, pom."

Prince Charming sighed again.

But the second year she had taken her surroundings for granted. And by the third she had begun to alter them. The throne might be glittering, but it collected dust in the crevices. Amethyst arches might impress visitors, but they let the draughts in.

And all those stairs!

Living in a Palace was all very well, but what she wanted was a home.

And Cinderella set about to make it one.

How well she had succeeded. Prince Charming winced. Anti-macassars everywhere, and that confounded hearth-brush. The banqueting hall turned into a damned cold hygienic nursery where he was expected to gargle before he kissed his own child—baby Dorothy Ward.

" If you must have atmosphere," Cinderella had said, " there's always your den."

At the thought of his den Prince Charming brightened. He

dwelt with warm approval on the stained-glass windows, the circle of gauze inserted in the wall through which varying visions beautiful could beckon to him, the dummy books, the desk with the drawers jammed, the trick chair, Widow Twankey's washing basket left over from last year, the whitewash bucket and the step-ladder, and the broker's men tumbling all over the place.   A snug little corner.   Just as the Melville Brothers had created it at the dear old Lyceum.

It was nice of Cinderella to leave his sanctum undisturbed.

" Darling," he said.   " Do come to the Ball.   You'll have the smallest foot there . . ."

*   *   *

All over Fairyland people were dressing for the ball of unrivalled splendour.

" Where the hell are my boots," snarled Puss.

" I like myself in red," said Snow White defiantly.

" Censored," cried Little Boy Blue exasperated.

Out in a barn ten little nigger boys were dressing themselves in an assortment of coloured cottons.

> " I gotta a shoe," they sang.
> " You gotta a shoe.
> All God's chillun got shoes . . ."

In his rocker Uncle Rochester shook a warning finger.

" Now youse chillun be mighty carefu'—mighty carefu'," he repeated, liking the words.   " Doan' you forget dem lines in de book or sho' as daylight somefin' turrible is goin' ta happen."

He opened the book.   He read.

" Ten little niggah boys went out to dine,

One went and choked hisself and den "—Uncle Rochester paused eerily, " dey was nine."

Nine little nigger boys nodded solemnly.

" Me! " said the tenth little nigger unimpressed.   "Choke myself! " . . .

*   *   *

Up above the world so high the little star was twinkling like anything.   No need to ask it how it was.   Twinkle—twinkle—

shining out of the velvet sky brighter than all the diamonds in Mr. Cartier's window.

But not so bright as the diamonds in Fairy Dark Diamond's coronet.

Worth all the money Haroun-Al-Rothschild had paid for it, reflected Fairy Dark Diamond complacently. And she had kept her bargain with him. She had appeared wearing it and very little else in his sealed palace at midnight with all the doors locked and all the slaves' eyes bandaged.

" But you sent him to sleep with a potion, you cheat," said a fruity chuckle in her ear.

It was Puck. He found great delight in hovering around Fairy Dark Diamond and whispering. Not that he was alone in this. But his sentiments were different. The Fairy Dark Diamond had social ambitions and he would not willingly miss a single wobble of her climb. Starting with the kindness to a swineherd, unerringly diagnosed as a Prince on sight, he had been at her elbow, counselling, chiding and chuckling, until now she was ready to reach for the highest prize in Fairyland—Prince Oberon himself.

" Titania," said Puck, " is looking very lovely to-night. And she's limbering up like anything."

" Titania dances very well," said the Fairy Dark Diamond, plying a lipstick. " I give her full points for her pirouettes."

Titania was her best friend.

" A pity that the girl is socially oblivious," she continued. The things she does. Did you know that the other day she was seen at," her voice dropped with the shame of it, " Banbury Cross ? "

Even Puck was slightly shaken. " She probably only wanted to get rings on her fingers and bells on her toes," he suggested charitably.

" But to go to Banbury Cross for them," repeated Fairy Dark Diamond despairingly.

" Don't be so smug," said Puck. " Soon it won't matter where Titania goes. She'll make it the fashion just by going there."

" Titania! " The Fairy Dark Diamond sprayed herself with Chanel.

" Titania," said Puck, " is going to marry Prince Oberon."

" You're babbling," said Fairy Dark Diamond. She sniffed

appreciatively at her own shoulders. " Oberon is going to marry
me. You're just saying that to be malicious."

" Me! " said Puck. " Malicious! I'm only telling you for your
own good. Her mother has just decided that's what she wants."

The Fairy Carabosse! Dark Diamond paled. She turned to
her mirror and patted in some more rouge.

" Titania and Oberon," she said. " Don't be so silly. I happen
to know she can't stand his Warwickshire accent."

Puck bristled.

" What's wrong with a Warwickshire accent ? " he demanded
truculently. He stuck his chin out.

*   *   *

In his dressing-room in an adjoining kingdom King Gullible
the Astute was striding up and down in his royal underwear. He
was in a fever of impatience. Here was the ball of unrivalled
splendour practically at its height—at any rate, it would be starting
soon—and here was he, Gullible the Seventh, puissant monarch of
Goose-feather Land, waiting for the new Royal robes of dazzling magnificence and seventy leagues to go after donning
them.

At the thought of the new robes King Gullible hugged himself.
They would be a sensation! No mean achievement to wear a
robe that would create a sensation at a ball where sensations were
taken for granted. And not only were the robes to be woven of
gold-flame and silver thread and colours that the rainbow had never
even thought of, but they had a magic property as well. They
were robes of high moral purpose. Only those worthy of the
position they held could see them. The tailors said so. The
unworthy would see nothing at all. Serve them right, thought
King Gullible the Astute. He gave a little skip of anticipation.
But they ought to have been ready hours ago. He paced up and
down again.

From the palace he could see across the gardens to a little tilted
street where, cross-legged on a table, in a lighted window, the
tailor of Gloucester was stitching busily. A little man in spectacles
with a pinched face and old crooked fingers.

" No breadth at all and cut on the cross," he was muttering.
" It's no breadth at all ; tippets for mice and ribbons for mobs for
mice! " said the tailor of Gloucester.

Time was when he had cut for the King himself, and very fine clothes they were, too. The stitches of the button-holes were so small—*so* small—they looked as if they had been made by little mice. But no magic properties. King Gullible clicked his tongue. Still, at least the Tailor of Gloucester had been punctual. He stamped his foot.

"Have patience, Your Majesty," said the Chancellor. "The new robes are well worth waiting for. I," he swallowed, "have seen them in the piece."

"So you have," said the King. He brightened and the little gnaw that had been trying to get at him through his excitement subsided. If that old dodderer could see the material, what doubt could there be that he, King Gullible the Astute, the cleverest of the seven—everybody said so—would be able to feast his eyes, too.

"Mind you," said the Chancellor, "they'll make a great dent in the budget."

The gnaw came back. A man worthy of his position, the new tailors had said. Well, it didn't seem to take much to be a Chancellor. But to be a King. Here was a test indeed. Well, he would prove worthy of it. No doubt of that. And in order to set his mind at rest he would go down and look at the material on the loom.

He clapped his hands. "Call out the bodyguard," he ordered, "I am going down to the workshop."

The King's bodyguard marched smartly across the square. Their chests were out, their hips were in, and everyone, except the Chancellor, was in step. But their eyes wore a worried expression. Might as well face it. It was not everyone who was worthy to be a member of the King's bodyguard.

In the workshop a thousand candles were shining bright as daylight, revealing the busy backs of a hundred tailors singing as they bent over their looms :

> "Hey diddle, dinketty, poppety pet
> The merchants of London they wear scarlet.
> Silk in the collar and gold in the hem
> So merrily march the merchant men."

In a corner a tailor was sitting cross-legged stitching at nothing.

You could see his needle flashing up and down.   Only the needle.

The Captain of the bodyguard paled   This was a judgment on him for juggling the mess accounts.

The tailor twisted a thread.   It was invisible.

The Chancellor nodded sadly.   Ah well, he had known it for three days now.

" What workmanship," he said hopefully.

The tailor finished his stitching and held the garment to the light.   You couldn't see a thing.

King Gullible paled.   Mustn't breathe a word about this.   He put his finger to his lips.   He remembered and took it quickly away.

" I hope it fits," he said severely.   And he crossed to the looms where the spinning figures were busily manipulating nothing. Tentatively he approached the head tailor.   If he had not been a King you could have sworn he was a coward.

" Er," he said.

" So merrily march the merchant men," sang the head tailor. He stopped the loom and ran his fingers delicately under nothing.

" Your Majesty deigns to approve the pattern ? " he asked.

King Gullible blinked.   " A little complicated," he managed, " but it'll do."

Were the eyes around him sceptical ?   The King shivered.

" See how the colours glow," said the head tailor.   " The blue and the orange.   The crimson and the amethyst."

The King thought of something.   Not for nothing was it that they called him the cleverest of the seven.   This would throw dust-storms into their tea-cups.

" Amethyst ? " he said.   " I would have called it purple."

This shook the tailor.   Just for a moment he peered at nothing. He recovered.   He turned to the Chancellor.

" What shade would you say it is ? " he asked.

" Excellent," said the Chancellor quickly.   " Excellent. Excellent."

The tailor smirked.   He was himself again.

" Where in the whole of fairyland," he boasted, " could you find such good material ? "

In his study in the fashionable mews the middle-aged young man was frowning at the script of his pantomime.

A bit thin for the Coliseum. And it would sound singular on the gramophone records. Distinctly singular.

With a gesture of impatience he pushed aside the script and strode into the night. He wandered aimlessly through Mayfair and even Pimlico, further and further, cudgelling and cudgelling, and emerged suddenly into a little tilted street where, sitting cross-legged in the candlelight, the Tailor of Gloucester, worn to a ravelling, was stitching busily and singing in a little cracked voice:

> " Four and twenty tailors
> Went to catch a snail.
> The best man amongst them
> Durst not touch her tail.
> She put out her horns
> Like a little Kyloe cow,
> Run, tailors, run, or she'll have you all 'een now."

Expressive, thought the middle-aged young man, but unlikely to carry in a big house.

But there, across the courtyard, stood a palace, madly Harker Brothers, and clearly just the thing for a panto. And there, next to it, were the Royal Workshops. He could hear the looms spinning. The very thing.

He strode in.

Before a mirror, strutting and turning, was a Fred Emney type in some really revolting underwear. All round him tailors were patting, adjusting and tweaking at nothing at all, while the Court stood festooned around in ecstasies of admiration.

" No material here," said the middle-aged young man crossly.

He strode out.

CHAPTER III   **The Final Touches**

For a ball of unrivalled splendour the first essential is a splendid ballroom. The King of Boxing Night Land had not overlooked this fact. Benois 'imself had been summoned to design the décor, and though 'e 'ad not come, Rex Whistler has made a very credit-able job of it at twice the price. But never would you have imagined this from looking at it now—unless, of course, you had a great deal of experience at this sort of thing.

The marble staircase has been folded up like a concertina and pushed into the wings. The crystal walls are flapping halfway between Hell and the flies, the Throne has got itself all heaped up with alabaster pillars, the banquet is even now being set on the next revolve, and the bejewelled cradle from Hamley's has not yet arrived.

At the switchboard someone is whistling grand opera. Jo, the electrician, is experimenting with his ambers. The rays fall on a small bent figure in a trailing dressing-gown and a pointed hat with stars on it. It waves a serpent-stick over the littered stage.

Hey presto!

The crystal walls are firm and come right down to the ground —though of course you mustn't lean against them. The pillars are upright and quivering slightly. The marble staircase looks solid enough for Maison Lyons. And a man from Carter Paterson's is saying " Sign 'ere " for a crated but bejewelled cradle in the centre of the floor.

You can say what you like about State Sorcerers, but you have to admit that they do economize in stage hands.

Perhaps this is as well, for were it otherwise, it is doubtful whether this particular State Sorcerer could have held down his job much longer. When you have been State Sorcerer for nine hundred and ninety years, staging marvels for at least that number of balls of unrivalled splendour, you are apt to repeat your effects. If there was one thing Abra Cadabra dreaded, it was the stigma of repeated effects. Nothing puts a sorcerer on the retired list quicker.

He looked with distaste at the props provided for his magic to-night.

Another marble staircase! He shuddered. There was nothing more he could do with a marble staircase—except to make it vanish during the descent of the guests of honour, and the King would be against that. No sense of humour.

He looked at the alabaster pillars. How the Queen had screamed when he had turned them into serpents—two-headed—at her wedding feast. Ah, those were the days!

He looked at the aspidistra, a useful stand-by. You could do things with an aspidistra—why it was funny before you even started on it. Seven hundred years ago he had turned one into a Christmas tree of insulting presents that had caused a war, and a century or so before it had become a sudden, very powerful fountain and drenched all the guests except Fairy Bea Lillie, who had come in a flower-pot and a mackintosh. How the guests had laughed! Or had they?

Abra Cadabra ran a crabby hand through his beard. If not the aspidistra, then what? Music out of nowhere? Commonplace. Showers of golden sovereigns from the King's mouth? Expensive. The baby's cradle? Out of bounds.

It would have to be the aspidistra again. Now what could be done with an aspidistra? He concentrated.

* * *

Mab, Queen of Fairyland, stood in front of a cheval glass and surveyed herself. The image in the mirror nearly curtsied. But the fairies-in-waiting grouped in a ring around her indulged in no coos of admiration—attitudes of ecstasy were frowned on in Warwickshire circles—though pride in their Sovereign was reflected on every face.

Every inch a Queen—all two and three-quarters of them.

The Queen signed to the First Fairy-in-Waiting. The Fairy Peaseblossom advanced. With the pride of one performing an inherited duty she cupped the Starinoor in her hands and placed it gently upon the Fairy Queen's brow.

Her moment had arrived. This was the time when the Queen spoke to her. Or didn't.

"Ah, Peaseblossom," said the Queen, "there is something I wanted to ask you."

Fairy Peaseblossom flushed with pleasure. A direct question! She must be in high favour indeed to-night. She curtsied. It was as though a ramrod had slipped down one notch.

"Tell me," said the Queen, "how are the Babes getting on?"

Fairy Peaseblossom's face fell. What a pity the answer had to be unfavourable. She shook a regretful head!

"Not out of the wood yet," she said.

Queen Mab frowned. "Speak to Tom Arnold at once." She made a gesture of dismissal.

The Second Fairy-in-Waiting caught the Royal eye. She brought forward the ribbon of the garter.

" Well, Cobweb," said the Queen, " are you afraid of the Big Bad Wolf ? "

Fairy Cobweb shivered. " No, Your Majesty," she managed.

" Spoken like a soldier's daughter," said the Queen. " There's my own good fairy. From now on," she bestowed a favour, " you are godmother to the three little pigs."

Between tears and pride Fairy Cobweb withdrew.

Her place was taken by the Third Fairy-in-Waiting. Fairy Moth came apprehensively forward, carrying the Royal pearls. She had not been as good a fairy as she might have been.

The Queen spoke not a word. The pearls were fastened in silence. Indeed she inclined her head so little that Fairy Moth had to stand on tip-toe to fasten the clasp. And the Royal gaze looked steadfastly away from the slight singe that no amount of stardust could conceal on Fairy Moth's wings. And yet Fairy Moth was made only too well aware that an appointment with the Court Doctor had been fixed for her at dewfall to-morrow. No hope of a changeling now. No hope at all.

There was a distinct chill in the atmosphere as Fairy Moth took her five steps back to join the group. She sniffed furiously. At all costs she must hold back her tears until the Fairies-in-Waiting were dismissed the Presence.

And now fairy after fairy advanced to complete the Royal toilet. They tied the Queen's sash, they put on her shoes, they showed her a selection of cloaks (she chose the third best). And now the last Fairy-in-Waiting advanced for the final duty of all—to hand Queen Mab her wand. Fairy Mustard-Seed's eyes were as bright as the Star in the wand she tendered. The girl took a pleasure in her work. Queen Mab melted a little. She had only meant to say ' Good evening,' but now she changed her mind.

" If I remember aright," she said, " you are in charge of Old King Cole."

As expected, Fairy Mustard-Seed flushed with pleasure. How kind of the Queen to remember. And what a memory she had! All those fairies and all those charges, and not one but wasn't in some predicament.

" King Cole is in my charge, ma'am. Thank you, ma'am."

" And how is His Majesty ? " asked the Queen, spoiling her.

Fairy Peaseblossom was looking livid. Two whole sentences! Currying little minx!

" If you please, ma'am," said Fairy Mustard-Seed, " he's doing nicely. He's just going to listen to some music."

Fairy Peaseblossom felt better. That last piece of information was both unasked for and unwarranted. The Queen could be trusted to deal with it faithfully. Wait for it! She rubbed her hands.

But the Queen was smiling indulgently, almost reminiscently.

" He's such a merry old soul," she said. . . .

> Old King Cole was a merry old soul
> And a merry old soul was he.
> He sent for his pipe, and he sent for his bowl,
> And he sent for . . .

The Palace was in an uproar. Everybody was dashing wildly around looking in corners, cupboards and cricket pavilions. And all of them had their fingers in their ears. For the merry old soul was roaring his head off.

" Where the hell is that third fiddler ? " he was bawling. " Where is he, the demned, lazy, scraping, good-for-nothing, bow-legged, addle-pated, drunken . . ." He stopped himself. " That's it," he said. " Drunken. Go look for him at the Bull and Goblin."

The whole Court turned as one man. " Yes, Sire," they threw over their shoulders.

" Oh no you don't," snarled the merry old soul, " I'll go myself."

. . . But entirely unaware of her charge's present objective, the Fairy Mustard-Seed withdrew the regulation five paces pink with pleasure, the happiest fairy in Warwickshire.

" I am ready," said Queen Mab. " Fanfaronade," she commanded, " summon my son."

* * *

PRINCE OBERON!
Prince Oberon!
Prince Oberon !

" Oh, where has he got to ? "

As the voice of Fairy Fanfaronade died away, the Fairy Moth trailed wearily into her apartment. She flung herself face downward into her thistledown bed and wept into her mistletoe pillow. It was her voice that should have been calling frantically down the corridor. It was her voice that should have been dying away in despair. Another proof of the Royal displeasure. Oh, why had she done it ? And how had the Queen found out ? How did the Queen find everything out ? The poor girl sobbed again.

Tap! As urgent as a dwarf's pick in a gold mine. Tap on the window-pane. There it was again. Tap!

" Non! Non! Non, je n'irai plus au bois," sobbed the Fairy Moth.

But it was only a silver pigeon with a scroll in its beak and its head expectantly tilted awaiting the approving pat.

The Fairy Moth unlatched the window and let the pigeon in. Listlessly she unrolled the scroll and looked at the pointed and enraged lettering with lack-lustre eyes. It read:

> Madam :
>> Georgie Porgie, pudding and pie
>> Kissed the girls and made them cry.
>> Kindly keep your charge in better order and oblige.
>> Mother Goose.

The Fairy Moth let the scroll fall from her hands. Her wings drooped. This made the day quite perfect!

She remembered herself. She patted the pigeon.

* * *

Not in the counting-house, not in the council-room, not on the roundabout.

Where could Prince Oberon be ?

Not in the courtyard. Not by the lily pond. Not in the dairy. This was serious!

Not in fresh fields. Not in new pastures.

Oh dear!

The Fairy Fanfaronade fluttered her wings in agitation. Where hadn't she looked ?

Not on the high way. Not on the low way. Not by the way-side.

Did you ever!

Not on the battlements. Not on the drawbridge. Not in the moat.

A pity.

Not in the strawberry-beds. Not in the chicken-run. . . .

From the stables came the sound of a baritone. It was not a very true baritone, but it was definitely a vigorous one:

> " At Brill-on-the-Hill
> The wind blows shrill
> The cook no meat can dress.
> At Stow-on-the-Wold
> The wind blows cold.
> I know no more than this."

" . . . Tra-la-la, I know no more than this," carolled the baritone.

Got him!

The Fairy Fanfaronade hurried towards the stables.

*   *   *

At the Palace of Boxing Night Land all was hither and thither. The whole of the personnel from Lord High Chamberlain to low-down scullion were rushing about, putting last minute touches to those of the minute before. As for the King, he had got himself into the kitchens and was counting the sugar plums.

" Good heavens," he said, " there won't be more than two apiece."

In his horror he ate one.

As for the Queen, she was weeping.

" There, there, ma'am," said the old nurse. " Don't take on so. Babies often cry," she assured the distraught mother. " Good for the lungs," she encouraged her.

The Princess Aurora agreed.

" I mind back to when I was nurse to Jack the Giant Killer. How he howled! " said the nurse. " And look what a fine strapping fellow he grew up to be."

The Queen shuddered.

" Mind you," said the nurse, observing this, " because they howl it doesn't mean they're all going to be strapping fellows and kill giants. Come to think of it, Tom Thumb made quite a noise, too."

" As much as my baby ? " asked the Queen.

" Oh no, ma'am," said the nurse quickly. " This is the lustiest baby I ever tended."

The Queen beamed.

" And now, ma'am, why not go downstairs and take a look at the nice decorations," urged the nurse. She had to get the brat dressed some time. " I am told," she tempted, " that their splendour is unrivalled."

Like a child that has been comforted and given something else to think about, the Queen went away.

" Now!" said the nurse to the suddenly silent baby. . . .

In the ballroom the old Chancellor was waddling happily about admiring everything. His heavy work for the evening was over. All he had to do now was to keep himself clean and usher the guests towards the Throne, which he could do in his sleep, and frequently did. How well he had discharged his onerous duties. All those invitations, all in his best handwriting, and not a single name forgotten. Though, mind you, some of the fairest in the land were by no means as blond as he'd like them to be. The ten little nigger boys! He shook a doubtful head and wandered over to the aspidistra. It reminded him of the Court Sorcerer. He wondered what corny gag old Abey had thought up this time. If it had anything to do with a red hot poker, or an aspidistra, he'd put him on the retired list and chance the consequences. And this time he meant it.

In the vaultiest cellar of them all, Abra Cadabra was already busy on his spell.

" You can't go wrong with an aspidistra," he exhorted the lanky apprentice, peering into the cauldron.

" Yes, Mr. Cadabra," piped the Sorcerer's Apprentice. " May I put in the frog's legs now ? "

" No," said Abra Cadabra forcibly. " How many more times must I tell you no frog's legs in this spell. Beetle's wings and moth balls only. Frog's legs would be fatal." He took down a flagon from the shelf. He dipped into a bin of vervain. He sprinkled it into the cauldron.

> " Vervain and dill
> Keep witches from their will,"

he chanted and stood aside for the apprentice.

The apprentice drew himself up. He fumbled in his pocket and drew out the white hair of a Unicorn born under the Hunter's Moon. At least, he hoped it was a unicorn. He cast it into the cauldron.

" Devil, devil, I defy thee," he incanted in a squeaky wobble.

" Stop! " screamed the Sorcerer. " Stop, blunder-wit! "

But the apprentice was oblivious.

" Magpie, Magpie, I go by thee," he finished gaily.

The Sorcerer pushed him to one side. He got busy with both hands—flasks, filters, flagons and all.

" Double, double, toil and trouble," he complained, juggling frantically. " Fire burn and cauldron bubble. Now, you young fool, come here and help me to stir. Nearly ruined the whole thing," he mumbled crossly as the fire flared up and the cauldron bubbled like a geyser.

" It's wizard," said the Apprentice admiringly.

The Magicians took up two large wooden spoons. They dipped them in.

" STIR," boomed the Sorcerer.

" Stir," piped the Apprentice.

" STIR," boomed the Sorcerer.

" Stir," piped the Apprentice.

" STIR."

" Stir."

They stirred.

*　　　*　　　*

In the ballroom the aspidistra shivered.

*　　　*　　　*

In the Royal Cowsheds of Fairyland a calf has been born. It lay on the straw and blinked its little eyes at a Royal figure in corduroy breeches that was bending over it. On the straw beside her the mother lay back panting but well pleased. As good a midwife as ever she'd had.

Mother and child doing well. The Royal figure straightened itself. It burst triumphantly into song :

> " Dance to your Daddie,
> My bonnie laddie,
> Dance to your Daddie, my bonnie lamb!
> You shall get a fishie,
> On a little dishie,
> You shall get a herring when the boat comes hame! "

he promised.

" Prince Oberon! Prince Oberon!" The Fairy Farfaronade flew in. " Oh, Your Highness, I've been looking for you everywhere. From the heavens to the haystacks. From the sea-shells to the stars. Your mother," she said, as one expecting the news to start a panic, " is waiting for you."

" Cooming," said Prince Oberon. He bent over the calf again.

> " Dance to your Daddie
> My bonnie laddie,
> Dance to your Daddie, and to your Mummie sing!
> You shall get a coatie,
> And a pair of breekies,
> You shall get a coatie when the boat comes in! "

he told it encouragingly.

The Fairy Fanfaronade fluttered despairingly around the stables. " You don't understand," she quavered. " You can't have heard," she suggested. " The Queen is waiting."

" Cooming," said Prince Oberon again. He tickled the calf's ear.

*　　　*　　　*

" STIR," boomed the Sorcerer.
" Stir," piped the Apprentice.
" STIR," boomed the Sorcerer.
" Stir," piped the Apprentice.
" STIR."
" Stir."
They stirred. . . .
" Well," said the Sorcerer exhausted, " I'll just leave you to watch it now. And, mind, don't take your eyes off it," he cautioned, " or it'll start boiling at once."

" Not if it be seven times seven," swore the Apprentice. " I'll watch it, Mr. Cadabra, sir, never fear."

" Good lad," said the Sorcerer. " And when the hour glass runs out," he instructed, " sprinkle in seven sunflower seeds and stir again."

" Widdershins ? " asked the Apprentice.

" No, sunwise," said the Sorcerer. " And repeat the curse."

" Obley, obley, my first go ? " asked the Apprentice.

" No," said the Sorcerer. " Obley, obley onkers—my first conkers."

" I'll remember," said the Apprentice.

Satisfied, the Sorcerer hobbled off. In the doorway he delivered a final warning.

" Remember," he said severely, " don't improvise."

" Improvise ? " said the Apprentice, shocked. " Me! "

He looked wistfully at the mandrake.

*   *   *

Useless to wait any longer. Over the moat and through the courtyard the Fairy Fanfaronade fluttered against the wind. That calf would be a cow before Prince Oberon had finished crooning at it. And the poor Queen, never a minute late in her life—except for her wedding. Up the stairs and through the corridor. Oh woe was her! Woe was her! Through the ante-room and into the Queen's apartments.

" Well ? " said Queen Mab.

Fairy Fanfaronade dropped a ramrod curtsy. If she had not been Warwickshire born she never would have risen from it.

" If you please, ma'am," she said, " he says he's coming soon."

" Soon! " said the Queen. With awful calm she sat down.

*   *   *

With awful calm the Fairy Carabosse closed the book of curses. What she had found there would do quite nicely and make Boxing Night Land rue the day it had insulted Titania's mother.

Not invited, forsooth! And Ali Baba asked!

She picked up her magic moonstone. She breathed on it. She turned it three times—widdershins. The mist dissolved and there was the Sorcerer's Apprentice, gazing fixedly into the cauldron.

The Fairy Carabosse sent her will through space.

The Apprentice reached out a hand and took down the mandrake.

He opened the bottle and poured the contents into the cauldron.

> " I last night lay all alone,
>   O' the ground to hear the Mandrake grone ;
>   And pluckt him up, tho' he grew full low
>   And, as I had done, the Cock did crow."

> " He who gathers the Mandrake shall die
>   Blood for blood is his destiny,"

he piped as one possessed.

Great Merlin! What was he doing ? He looked at the empty bottle in his hand. Perhaps it was as well he had no idea. He kicked it under the cauldron.

The hour glass had run out. Now for the incantation. Onkers, not obley. He got ready.

The moonstone clouded over and cleared again. The Fairy Carabosse concentrated.

> " Obley, obley,
>   My first go,"

piped the Apprentice.

Oh dear, what had he said ? He hoped it was all right, but his heart misgave him. He picked up the wooden spoon and started to stir.

The moonstone clouded over. " Now ! " willed the Fairy Carabosse.

The apprentice was stirring like anything. " Stir—stir—stir—stir," he encouraged himself.

Far away in her solitary bower the Fairy Carabosse smiled evilly and laid down the moonstone.

The Apprentice came to with a click. Great Merlin! He had been stirring Widdershins.

CHAPTER IV   **Through the Night**

And now the hour was drawing near. The sun had gone down, the moon had come up, the Princess Aurora was growing older every minute, and all the world was on its way to the ball of unrivalled splendour. Fairies had summoned their thistledowns, goblins their grasshoppers, and from far and near carriages, coaches and other conveyances were converging on the crystal palace.

From North, South, East and West, up and down and sideways, came the stream of guests. Golden coaches drawn by milk white horses, silver coaches drawn by jet black horses, jet black coaches drawn by silver-horses. Not a pumpkin growing in the land but had not been purloined and turned into an equipage. Not a mouse but was marvelling at finding it had become a horse.

Indeed, there had not been so great a drain on transport since the wedding of the Widow Twankey—and all that laundry late!

And in the air the fairies were sliding down on moonbeams, gliding in on falling leaves, whipping up their butterflies and whizzing by on shooting stars. While behind the witches buzzed angrily on their rather slower broomsticks. And Haroun-al-Rothschild, setting out confidently on his magic carpet, found himself caught in a traffic jam and didn't get there till morning.

And now the stars shine bright and the music changes to Mendelssohn. Here comes Titania wrapped warmly in rose petals and chirruping to her white butterfly. All around her, school friends and elder cousins throw her a laughing greeting and wish her well. In contrast, the Fairy Dark Diamond, whipping her bumble-bee, sees but a disapproving succession of turned backs while Puck, under his own power, keeps catching her up to say annoying things:

> " The bat, the bee, the butterflee
> The cuckoo and the swallow,
> The kittiwake and the corncrake,
> And all the rest may follow,"

he mimics in his best falsetto.

" Oh, go eat an acorn," says the Fairy Dark Diamond crossly.

Down below King Gullible the Astute is shivering. A King feels mighty cold when all he is wearing is a canopy. And of course the magic robes of the material that the unworthy could not see—or feel for that matter. King Gullible sneezes. A

B

mistake, he reflects, to have had his overcoat made out of the stuff as well.

He looks with envy at the wrapped-up Chancellor. He blows on his fingers.

*   *   *

High in the high heavens, travelling down the long silver streak of a very solid moonbeam, Mab, Queen of Fairyland, progressed to the party. The Royal coach was a simple buttercup of solid gold drawn by a posse of milk-white unicorns, each no bigger than a firefly. None of your modern motor-moths for the Royal house. Unicorns might be slow, but they got you there. Besides, the Royal coachman, a well-fed frog whose mouth was twice as large as his circumference had been with the Royal family since Queen Mab had been a budding Princess—travelling would never be the same without him. As a matter of fact, he was a wicked Uncle who, long long ago, had been turned into a frog so that someone or other might live happily ever after—but now he would have been heartbroken if anyone had turned him back again.

With slow paces, in perfect rhythm, and with no regard for the lateness of the hour, the unicorns high-stepped through the stars. All around them the other travellers cleared a respectful path for the ram-rodding Queen with the sulky Prince Oberon beside her.

" Son," said Queen Mab, out of the corner of her mouth. " I shall have much to say to you later. But for the moment, pray remember you are a Prince, so smile and acknowledge the cheers of the multitude." She inclined a gracious head to a Castle in the Air, floating as near to her as it dared.

Prince Oberon kicked moodily at the buckles of the shoes his mother had sent him back to put on.

" Moother," he asked, " how soon can we leave ? "

*   *   *

" Sister Anne, Sister Anne! " The plaintive voice of Blue-beard's seventh wife came floating up to the turret. " Do you see anybody coming ? "

Sister Anne took a deep breath. . . .

*   *   *

And now the overture is ended. Outside all is darkness and expectation, but inside the folds of the fourth wall the ballroom is flooded with light.

It is to-day at 2.30.
Rap-rap-rap.
The curtain rises.
A round of applause for the décor, please, and . . .
Here comes the Corps-de-Ballet!

CHAPTER V   **The Christening Gifts**

The ball of unrivalled splendour has begun.

The glass floor is a kaleidoscope of revolving figures, and the music is playing *con brio*. Here are all the fairest in the land assembled to do honour to the baby Princess, and not a care in the world among them—or very nearly.

What a charming gathering they are as they glide, turn and chassé under the swinging chandeliers. Jack Frost and the Sugar Plum Fairy, Snow White and the Grand Old Duke of York. Little Boy Blue and his milkmaid, a little overawed by her surroundings perhaps, but ever so Dresden. See how she quirks her little finger. There, in the centre of the floor the Lady of the Lake is dancing with the Man in the Moon. How strange that their steps should match! While on the outskirts the ten little nigger boys, like gingerbread shadows, are dancing ring o' roses all around them.

Here and there are some distressing incidents. Behind the throne the Little Girl with the little curl right in the middle of her forehead is tugging Shock-headed Peter's mop, and over there in the corner Little Lord Fauntleroy is swopping old school stories with Eric, Little by Little. Glowering at them is Little Jack Horner. Usurpers!

But all these things pass unnoticed in the general merriment.

The walls of the glittering ballroom are lined with elders—shrill dames, bankrupt barons and Uncles, good, wicked and repentant. Between them, juggling and tumbling, come the butlers, harlequins and broker's men, and all of them playing to the gallery like anything.

Over by the buffet, sipping their glasses of port, linger a group

of benevolent old gentlemen talking in many tongues but saying
much the same things, and nodding approvingly at the antics of
their children. This is their evening, and they are entitled to
enjoy it.

They are Hans Andersen, the Brothers Grimm, Charles Perrault
and Poushkin.

At a distance a middle-aged young man in a polka-dotted
dressing-gown is eyeing them wistfully.

All those revivals!

*　　　*　　　*

And now a fanfare rings out and twelve plump little girls,
dressed as twelve plump little boys, march sturdily across the
clearing floor, their trumpets raised, their streamers fluttering.
Almost you might think that they were playing.

All eyes are focused on the portals through which the Royal
cradle is about to appear.

Here it comes now, only you can't see it for Duchesses acting
as nursemaids. Patience! For later, when the privileged have
grouped themselves, the remainder of the fairest in the land will
be able to gaze their full at the Royal Princess, at the moment
howling with rage at a tummy-tickling Duchess.

" Don't do that," said the Queen, upset. " Count her toes,"
she urged. " She likes that."

And now, at long last, the Duchesses have consolidated into a
group, perfectly poised and a pleasure to look at. All except the
fifth Duchess from the left, whose fourth position is perfect only
not in line.

Pained, the Chamberlain hobbled over to her.

" Go back behind your pillar," he hissed, " where Petipa put
you."

" Petipa! " said the Duchess. " I spit me of Petipa."

She stayed where she was.

The fairest in the land crane their necks and stand on tip-toe
trying to catch a glimpse of the infant in the cradle. But all they
can see are the swaying headdresses of the Duchesses, and all they
can hear is a thin continuous wail like a new-born banshee.

Emboldened by her curiosity, Mrs. Thumb, the sturdiest lovely
in the land, pushes her way through the craning courtiers and

bankrupt barons, by-passes a broker's man or so, and here she is in the front row. She manœuvres to an angle of vision between the Duchesses and triumph!—there is the Baby Aurora!

Mrs. Thumb inspected her. She sniffed.

"A simple smock," she said. "Why, my baby had a shirt of spider's cobweb."

"You don't say," said the broker's man on her left, impressed.

"I do say," said Mrs. Thumb sharply. She closed her eyes in reminiscent ecstasy. "Why, I can see him now. Hose and doublet of thistledown, a hat made of a beautiful oak leaf, and stockings from the peel of a delicate green apple."

"Must have cost a fortune," said the Bankrupt Baron on the other side of her.

The Baby Aurora stopped crying and kicked its legs.

"Bare feet," said Mrs. Thumb with terrific disapproval. "My baby had shoes made of the skin of a little mouse, and most curiously tanned."

She craned again and was just about to tell them about Tom Thumb's garters (made from the finest little hairs plucked from his mother's eyebrows) when another fanfare rang out.

The twelve plump little girls dressed as twelve plump little boys marched across the ballroom and flung open the windows.

In flew the fairies—one after the other, glinting, shimmering, and waving their wands. They circled the room under their own power, and as the Duchesses, dropping low curtsies, made way for them, alighted in perfect formation all around the edges of the cradle. An instantaneous coo of admiration issued simultaneously from a flock of fairy throats.

"Gentille." "So little." "Ten toes."

And the Baby Aurora gurgled and smiled at them as though she'd never shed a tear in her life.

The Fairy Dark Diamond nudged Titania.

"Pink-faced brat," she said, smiling deliciously at it.

Titania couldn't have been more shocked. Darkie was a darling, of course, and everybody knew she had had a very hard life, but even so. . . . A new baby was like a crumpled rose-leaf. Every nice girl knew that!

The fairies' fourth positions were getting a little strained. Here they were all ready to go into their enchainement and present their gifts, and Queen Mab had missed her entrance.

"Extraordinary," fluted Fairy Bird-Song. "Why the Queen has never been late in her life except," she remembered, "for Prince Oberon's christening."

With a little wriggle in her fourth, Titania looked round the ballroom. Her first ballroom! What a lovely room! How the lights shone and quivered. What a perfect floor! Her toes tingled to get at it. What a shame to be standing here in a silly old fourth waiting for the Queen, when one might be dancing with a mortal.

And even as she looked the guests, like flowers caught in a drifting wind, broke from their ranks and swung on to the floor. One by one the fairies peeled off from the sides of the cradle, smiling graciously at their mortal escorts, until presently Titania stood alone and watched with beating heart as a Crêpe Beard bowed at her.

"May I have the pleasure?" asked the Crêpe Beard confidently.

"Oh yes, please," gasped Titania, and floated blissfully away in his clutch. Poor chit—how was she to know she was dancing with a Wicked Uncle?"

As Titania danced by, laughing radiantly at the jokes the Crêpe Beard was reeling off, the Fairy Dark Diamond nudged Aladdin.

"A good-natured girl," she said. "But no social sense."

"Ah, but so beautiful," said Aladdin. He sighed heavily. The Princess Baldroubador had been putting on weight.

Titania's merry laugh rang above the throng causing Old Mother Hubbard to smile indulgently, and just for a moment forget her dog's reproachful face.

"Yes, yes," said the Crêpe Beard, chuckling fruitily. "That's the answer. When it's a jar."

"I wouldn't have guessed it in a bunch of daisies," said Titania happily, as they danced past the doorway. Through it was coming a glorious mortal in a brocaded waistcoat and silk leotards. His smile dazzled Titania. Poor chit—how was she to know that his hair was thinning and his agent, once all cigars, now kept him waiting in the outer office.

"Who is that wonderful being?" she breathed.

The Crêpe Beard cast a casual glance. " Oh him," he said. " That's young Charmin'. Nice fellah." He danced on. " When," he asked, " is a cat not a cat ? "

But Titania was not attending.

" And who," she asked, " are those two elegant women who have just joined him ? "

The Crêpe Beard lit up. " Those," he said, " are the Ugly Sisters. Cinderella's," he explained. " Those gals go everywhere. Have a wonderful time. Don't believe poor old Charmin' would ever get asked at all if it weren't for his sisters-in-law. A dullish dog, you know."

" Oh," said Titania. She wouldn't believe it. It couldn't be true. Not with that fair curly hair.

" But the gals," said the Crêpe Beard. He ogled them. " Smartest pieces in town. Look at those gowns." He ran an approving eye down them. " Made by their godmother, the Fairy Schiaparelli, you know. She did a charmin' turn-out for Cinderella once—remember ? "

Titania was thinking. " They're very smart, of course, and Schiaparelli's a darling, but I don't think I'd like her to dress me."

" She wouldn't take you on," said the Crêpe Beard. " You're not the type. What," he changed the subject, " did the earwig say as he fell off the edge of the tea-cup ? "

" I think," said Titania, " one of the Ugly Sisters is smiling at you."

" Is she, by Jove! " said the Crêpe Beard, excited. " Maybe she'll give me a dance. That'd be one in the eye for Sindbad the Sailor."

He waltzed her over.

" All right, Alcazar," said the First Ugly Sister, " you may dance with me."

Elated the Crêpe Beard jigged off.

" Sorry, Ali Baba," said the Second Ugly Sister, " but I've promised the supper dance to Robinson Crusoe. I'll take a turn with you now if you like."

They shook away, and Cinderella was left alone with the most glorious mortal she had ever met. Such teeth.

It is said that admiration is communicable. At any rate, Prince Charming knew that this delightful wisp of fairiness approved of

him—nay, more—admired him. His chest swelled out, he
flounced his fichu, his charm was hardly tired at all.

" May I," he asked, " have the honour of a rumba ? "

The twelve plump little girls dressed as twelve plump little boys
raised their trumpets for another fanfare. The guests stopped
dancing and waited in a readiness of curtsies for what must be the
arrival of Queen Mab.

See, round the door comes the exploratory head of a lady-in-
waiting looking exactly like a frizzled sheep. She comes into the
room. Stay, she is a frizzled sheep looking exactly like a lady-in-
waiting. What is this ? More sheep follow her in. A flock of
them, fanning round the room and bleating like Maids of Honour.

Furious, the King turned on the Sorcerer. " You did this
three years ago," he snarled, " and it wasn't funny then."

The Sorcerer wrung his hands.

" Sire," he said, " it isn't me. It's Bo-Peep."

" Ah," said the King. He lost interest.

And so the sheep snuffled and wandered round the room and,
after that, they wandered into the corridor, and the fairest in the
land laughed and resumed their dancing as though nothing had
happened, as indeed it hadn't. And the sheep wandered down
the corridor and inspected the Royal Apartments, and peered into
the torture chamber, and ended up in the banqueting hall.

There, sitting up at the table, nine little nigger boys were eating
very carefully. Uncle Rochester's warning voice rang in their
ears, and they filleted each sardine.

But the tenth little nigger boy didn't care. He had surrounded
himself with lemonade, roast goose, and water-melon, and was
tucking in. Let's face it—he was gorging!

The sheep bleated. It was probably envy, but nine little nigger
boys heard the voice of Uncle Rochester. " One over-ate hisself
and den . . ." With a shudder they pushed aside their sardines
and climbed down from their places.

But the tenth little nigger looked up blearily and tried to focus.
An ecstatic smile spread over his face.

" Baa baa, black sheep, have you any rhum ? " he enquired
hopefully. . . .

*   *   *

In the ballroom the fairest in the land are rising from their deep curtsies. Queen Mab has arrived at last.

She is an hour and three-quarters late, but you would never think it to look at her.

" Let the revels continue," she said graciously, and allowed herself to be escorted to the cradle.

" So this is the Baby Aurora," she said. " Wooji-wooji-wooji! Ten toes! " She turned to the Queen. " You have a lovely baby. My congratulations."

" It was nothing," said the Queen, confused.

But, of course, Queen Mab did not hear this. She was surveying the ballroom through her lorgnette.

" A charming gathering of guests," she said.

" The fairest in the land," said the Queen, smugly.

" Not a single name forgotten," said the King. " All here," he pointed out. " Though whether there'll be enough pat-a-cakes, tut-tut-tut, well, well, well—we'll have to wait and see. . . ." He trailed himself off.

Queen Mab surveyed the shimmering ballroom. Little Red Riding Hood's grandmother must be better, for there was the grand-daughter, and she couldn't be enjoying herself more if she were a water baby. The six dancing princesses pirouetted past— very pretty. And—good gracious!—could this be Snow White wearing red! Queen Mab shook her head. A sign of the times.

She turned to the Fairy Peaseblossom.

" Where," she enquired with the forced cheerfulness of one resigned to being gracious, " is our little debutante? I hope," she frowned at the wiggling behinds on the floor, " she is not doing this curious dance."

Fortunately Titania had left the rumba some time ago.

" There she is," said Fairy Peaseblossom. " On the kissing chair, talking to a mortal."

" Which mortal ? " said the Queen sharply. " This is impor-tant." She raised her lorgnette and peered. " Prince Charming," she said. " Well, it might have been worse."

She raised her lorgnette again and resumed her inspection.

" She's grown," she announced. " Her dress is a little skimpy perhaps, but in these days that is inevitable. And I like the way she is sitting—several inches away from him. Yes, the girl has manners. Alas for this age when they have become a virtue to be mentioned!"

"Quite so," said the Fairy Peaseblossom virtuously.

"Not Warwickshire," said the Queen regretfully, "but quite a good French family—as French families go. Her father . . . well, he's dead, and her mother has brought her up strictly."

"Top of her class at finishing school," said Fairy Peaseblossom. "But she failed in algebra."

"I will overlook the algebra," said Queen Mab. "A fairy who has inherited a crooked sixpence has no need to pass in algebra."

Fairy Peaseblossom sighed. She knew the Binomial Theorem and how much good had it done her? Just as well she hadn't bothered with Einstein.

"Yes," said Queen Mab. "Yes, I think she will do."

Fairy Peaseblossom tingled with interest. The Queen confiding in her! A very good thing she hadn't bothered with Einstein.

"You don't mean, ma'am . . ." she breathed.

"Precisely," said the Queen. "She will make an excellent wife for my son. It is high time he married."

She looked round for him. But, of course, he was nowhere in sight. She beckoned the Fairy Fanfaronade.

*　　　*　　　*

On a kissing chair Prince Charming was talking to Titania, and Titania was gazing at him entranced. What a distinguished and unusually intelligent mortal he was.

"My wife," Prince Charming was saying wistfully, "doesn't understand me."

"Oh dear," said Titania, sorrowing with him.

"Of course she's got the smallest foot in the world," said Prince Charming, "but," he faced it, "that isn't everything."

Titania brooded. "It isn't the foot that counts," she decided.

"How right you are," said Prince Charming. "How perceptive. Do you know," he said, gazing intently at her, "I think you are the only person I've ever met who really understands me."

"Am I?" said Titania softly. Poor chit, she went on thrilling while Prince Charming, gathering tempo, reeled off one platitude after another as though he had invented them all. And as he talked his technique came back, his thinning hair was forgotten, and his paunch was no longer a frown on his dresser's face. Once again he was coming down a marble staircase at £200 a week and extra if they flew him.

But even as he was manoeuvring for a long row on the lake next Sunday, Peter Pan, dancing by, turned to his partner.

" Who," he asked in the piercing tones of the elderly determined to stay young, " is the old boy talking to Titania ? "

" Oh him," said Goldilocks. " That's Cinderella's husband."

" A punt," said Titania, already seeing herself among the cushions. " How exciting. I've never been in a punt."

But the damage had been done. Prince Charming was now feeling five hundred if a day. Cinderella's husband. . . . It was The End. However, he made a gallant effort.

" Tra-la-la ! " he said. " Tra-la-la, tra-la-la ! "

But somehow it lacked conviction.

* * *

Not in the corridor. Not in the pantry. Not in the transformation scene.

" Oh dear," said the Fairy Fanfaronade.

Not in the practice room. Not in the green room. Not in the wings.

" Might have expected it ! "

Not in the library. Not in the enchanted garden. Not in the First Act finale.

" Who drew up his contract ? "

* * *

And now, in the ballroom, Tchaikovsky has replaced Cole Porter. The Fairies go through their variations, *pas de bourré*-ing, arabesquing, and rotating. Each one smiling as though she had never been cursed in the classroom by the Fairy Ninette and would not, in fact, be cursed again almost immediately after this performance.

And now Queen Mab, flying with as much dignity as though she were walking, alights on the edge of the cradle and signs to her subjects that they may advance and present their gifts.

Fairy Breadcrumb of the twirling fingers darts up. " Honesty," she announces and twinkles away again.

There is a coo of approval from the hall and a dubious shake of the head from the Chancellor of the Exchequer.

Now Fairy Song-Bird flutters over. " Gaiety," she says.

The Queen is delighted, but the Court Jester looks glum.
" Dew on her face in the morning," offers the Fairy Rosebud.
Nanny shakes her head.   She can't see the point of this.

     *   *   *

Not in the solarium.   Not in the aquarium.   Ah, the conser-
vatory!   Two figures by the Japanese lily pond in close embrace. . . .
No, they weren't!
" You're a Beast," said Beauty.   She slapped his face.
What a disappointment.   Ah well!
Not in the billiard room.   Not in the buttery.   Not . . .

     *   *   *

The presents were coming along nicely.   Health, wealth,
happiness, modesty, pride, and so on.   And yet the King was
looking worried and nudging the Queen frequently.   No one had
given the Baby Aurora obedience.
" Sophistication," pronounced the Fairy Dark Diamond, " and
may you know no other jeweller than Cartier."   She streamlined
off.
And now it was Titania's turn.   Unaware of the Queen's eye
on her, she wrinkled her nose at the baby.
" Virtue," she said, and whisked right back to Prince Charming
to demand his approval.
Prince Charming looked depressed.

     *   *   *

Not in the apple orchard.   Not in the cherry orchard.   Not in
Tchekov.
Just as well!

     *   *   *

Puck is hugging himself with glee and nimbling round the room
like quicksilver touched to excitement.   Soon he will be presenting
his gift.   Everyone knows what it is going to be, and nobody
likes it, for it means trouble for all of them.   But nobody dares
stop him, and he knows it.
" Thrift," donates Fairy Peaseblossom.
" Thirty-two fouettés," says Fairy Mim Rambert with the air
of one conferring a blessing.
But the King doesn't think so.   He plucks the Queen's sleeve.
" No one has given her obedience," he whispers urgently.

     *   *   *

Not in the summer house. Not in the hothouse. Perhaps in the Turkish bath. . . .

" It's warm in here," said the Snow Maiden meltingly.

*   *   *

" Mud in her eye," beamed Fairy Mustard Seed.

*   *   *

Not on the Band waggon!

*   *   *

" Mischief," said Puck. He cocked an eye at the King.
" Very nice, I'm sure," said the King absently.

*   *   *

Not in the bulrushes.

*   *   *

" Tact," said the Fairy Tinkabell, and the King groaned aloud. She was the last fairy of all except, of course, Queen Mab, and she always gave the Royal Cipher in diamonds. Ah well! Better buy some birches at once.

*   *   *

The Sorcerer was concentrating on the aspidistra. As soon as the Fairy Queen had made her presentation and the applause had died down, he must be ready with his new astonishment.

Queen Mab was in the fifth position about to make her classic bow. Time to start mumbling.

Good gracious! The spell was starting ahead of schedule. Already the aspidistra had risen six feet into the air. It had no business to rise. Already the leaves were streaking lightning— they ought to be drooping away. A roll of thunder rent the air. In the wings someone was banging a tray like anything. Confound it—it should have been Music While You Work.

Darkness enveloped the stage, and when the lights went up again the Sorcerer had his eyes firmly closed. Queen Mab's, on the other hand, were tight open.

For there, in a chariot drawn by eight little boys turned into mice, was Titania's mother, the Fairy Carabosse, glaring at the Conductor.

Not at all what the Sorcerer had planned.

*   *   *

For a moment you could have heard a dew drop. There stood

the Fairy Carabosse, glaring malignantly around her, and there
stood the Fairest in the Land, shrinking back.

" So glad you could come," said the Queen faintly.

" Pleased to see you," said the King.

" You're late, Carabosse," said the Queen of Fairyland. " Why?"

The Fairy Carabosse bobbed a curtsey. You could not quite
put your finger on what was wrong with it, but it was definitely
impertinent.

" Why ? " asked Queen Mab, and the chandeliers shivered at
the ice in her voice.

But not the Fairy Carabosse. " I have not been invited, ma'am,"
she said. She turned to the King and Queen. " I have not been
invited," she announced more loudly. She turned to the Fairest
in the Land. " I have not been invited," she screamed.

A Fairy had been offended.

There was a commotion round the throne. Someone was
pushing the Chancellor forward. It was the Sorcerer.

" Pumpernickel," said the King sternly. " Is this thing true ? "

The Chancellor bowed his head. " Can't think how it happened," he mumbled. " Went through the list three times . . .
own handwriting."

" Go forward and beg her pardon," commanded the King. He
pushed.

" Do hurry," urged the Queen. She helped.

Holding herself in, the Fairy Carabosse waited.

" Down on your knees," she ordered.

The Chancellor knelt.

" Kiss the hem of my garment."

The Chancellor kissed.

And then the rage of the Fairy Carabosse burst its bounds. She
fell on the grovelling Chancellor. Her long fingers tugged at the
venerable head and tore off great handfuls of his hair until his pate
was as bald as Moussorgsky's mountain. She turned him into a
cat, a rat, a hedgehog. She left him like that.

" You! " she turned on King Gullible. " Go home and dress
yourself!"

She crossed to the cradle and cackled evilly at the Baby Aurora.
She saw Titania looking at her. She remembered she was a
mother.

" Enjoying yourself, child ? " she asked indulgently, and went back to her cradle cackling.

The Queen advanced fearfully. " What are you going to do ? " she asked.

" Do ? " said the Fairy Carabosse. " I have not been invited, but I hope I know my manners. I am going to give the Baby Aurora my christening gift just like all the other fairies."

The King brightened. " Obedience ? " he asked hopefully.

" No," said the Fairy Carabosse.

That was flat. The King withdrew.

" Take good care of the Princess Aurora," intoned Carabosse. " Take good care of your only child. Remove all sharp things from the nursery. Pluck every thorn from your rose bushes. For," her voice became a hiss, " if ever she prick her finger and a drop of her blood be spilt, then she will fall asleep into the deepest sleep of all sleeps."

" No," said the Queen. " No! "

But once again the aspidistra darted lightning and thunder was heard in the wings.

The curse of the wicked fairy had been spoken.

" Where," demanded Carabosse, " is the buffet ? "

For some moments you could have heard a leaf flutter. The Fairest in the Land were downcast. The Queen, too late to do any good, had taken her baby out of the cradle and was hugging it. The fairies fluttered around shrugging helpless wings. The King was stowing away a nail file into a deeper pocket.

To prick a finger and to sleep the deepest sleep! What a dreadful doom for a new-born babe. And how little the poor mite recked of what had happened to her.

" Gug," she was saying. " Gug-gug."

But at that precise moment when every hand was reaching for every handkerchief, Queen Mab spoke.

" Dry your tears," she said, " for I have not yet given my gift."

" Wassat ? " The Fairy Carabosse swung round.

" Obedience ? " asked the King listlessly. What did it matter now ?

" I cannot, of course, remove the spell," said Queen Mab, " but I can extend it. After Aurora has slept her deep sleep for a hundred years there shall come one, the seventh son of a seventh son, who

shall wake her with a kiss, and they shall be wed and live happily
ever after."

The Fairest in the Land brightened and cheered their Fairy Queen
to the echo. What was a hundred years in Fairyland ? Not even
long, long ago.

But the Queen of Boxing Night Land was weeping.

" My poor baby. How lonely she will be when she awakens.
We will all be dead. There will be no one she knows except this,"
she sniffed, " seventh son."

" Take comfort," said Queen Mab, " and when it comes to
pass (and if you are careful there is no reason why it should) I will
be at hand to help you. When the Princess Aurora falls asleep
all those around her within seven miles, crooked and straight, shall
fall asleep too and awaken with her."

" What a lot of seventh's sons we'll need," said Fairy Peaseblossom muddled.

Queen Mab waved her away. " That is all," she said. " We
will now resume the revels."

And walking straight past the quivering, vengeful Fairy Carabosse she helped herself to a pat-a-cake.

" Delicious," she said.

The Incident was at an end.

Beside herself the Fairy Carabosse strode to her coach. She
waved her wand over it and straddled herself on the result.

" Home, James," she hissed, " and don't spare the broomstick."

She was gone.

Titania turned to Prince Charming.

" Oh dear," she said, " mother has been impulsive again."

*   *   *

Not in the parlour. Not in the pantry. Try, try again.

*   *   *

Outside the palace it was cold—so cold. The little match-girl
pressed her nose to the palace window. She had heard so much
about the Ball of Unrivalled Splendour that she had trudged all
the way from Denmark and held up Hans Andersen for a couple
of sentences just for the hope of a glimpse.

And how worth while it had been. The shine of a thousand
candles lighting the scene with some strange bits of amber and
surprise pink she couldn't quite account for. The shimmering of

the Fairest in the Land, their flashing jewels, their radiant smiles. And the music they moved to, ringing out like the chimes of all the bells in the great white world on New Year's Day.

The little match-girl turned and lit a match to warm her hands. Then she turned again and glued her nose to the window.

These must be the happiest people that ever were born.

But in fact, inside the Palace, the party had gone flat, though the guests were still dancing, for Queen Mab had commanded it. The orchestra was playing listlessly, the floor no longer tempted, and even the pat-a-cakes had lost their savour. The conversation of the chaperones was punctuated by yawns and no one felt the personal success they had been earlier in the evening.

Another half hour of this and the ball of unrivalled splendour would trail off into a definite flop.

But Queen Mab had given the sign to ignore the incident. Let the revels continue, she had said, so continue they must.

The King whispered to the Queen. The Queen nodded. And presently there was a fanfare.

"Ladies and gentlemen, take your places for the Paul Jones," proclaimed the hedgehog.

*   *   *

Not in the schoolroom. Not in the pool-room. Not in the tilting yard. And if he was in the maze, how did that help?

CHAPTER VI   **Tell Mother**

"Good night, my child," said the Fairy Carabosse.

"Good night, Mama," said Titania. She snuggled under her lily-leaf. "Oh dear," she sighed, "I have had such a lovely time."

"That's right, daughter," said the Fairy Carabosse. She rubbed her hands. "So did I."

Titania went dim. The Fairy Carabosse changed the subject quickly.

"Did you dance every dance, child?" she asked.

"But yes," said Titania. "Every one on the card and many more."

"There's your mother's daughter," said the Fairy Carabosse, well pleased. "And how did you fare with Prince Oberon?"

"Well, Mama," said Titania, "the Prince arrived and then he disappeared and no one saw him again.* Wasn't it funny?"

"Very," said the Fairy Carabosse, not so pleased. "Then who did you dance with?"

"Oh, mother," said Titania. She looked at the ceiling. "The cleverest, kindest, handsomest mortal you ever dreamt of."

"H'm," said the Fairy Carabosse. "Sounds like Prince Charming."

"It was," sighed Titania. "However did you guess?"

"H'm," said the Fairy Carabosse, "it's a good thing you've got a mother." She turned down the firefly. "Good night, daughter."

"Good night, Mama," said Titania starily.

"H'm," said the Fairy Carabosse. She went out.

INTERMISSION

A beautiful night in Fairyland. The grass was hung with diamonds, and on fairies and witches, fauns and leprechauns, the lover and his lass, the moon shone benevolently.

But the moon, though benevolent, wore if anything an expression of surprise.

In a farmyard a cow landed with a thud. It was sweating in every pore.

From the tiles a cat surveyed her incuriously.

"Well?" she conceded.

The cow shrugged. "Not worth the effort."

---

* Not in the cuckoo clock. Not in the Minuscule. Not in a nutshell . . .

CHAPTER VII

In which a Bargain is made

And so time passed and all things in Fairyland flourished. Good was rewarded, evil was punished, wicked uncles were turned into tadpoles by the dozen, and people lived happily ever after all over the place.

As for the Princess Aurora, she had outgrown her knitted bottines for white kid shoes with pom-poms, and was waddling about the palace preceded by a bodyguard of pin-picking-up Duchesses, and followed by a retinue of noble tidy-uppers. While outside the palace little tin soldiers had been posted at every entrance to keep a look-out for sharp practice. Visitors were searched and their valuables, if pointed, taken from them, and only restored upon the production of a receipt when they left for home. Diplomatic immunity went for nothing, and a war nearly started every time King Nebuchadnezzar, who never went anywhere without his spiked breastplate, was asked to take it off. And every morning an army of gardeners fell upon the meadows and tore from them the innocent thistles that had grown up in the night.

It will be seen that the King of Boxing Night Land was taking no chances. Fond as he was of his after-dinner nap, no good could come of overdoing it.

In spite of this and the hundred and one other precautions, fond and far-fetched, that the Queen kept on thinking up, the Princess Aurora had already had one or two narrow escapes. The trouble, as the King said, was that Baby, though she had gaiety, beauty and thirty-two fouettées, was not obedient and, though she was now two years old, could not even be relied on to obey the most important of her many instructions : " Never pick up anything until somebody else has picked it up first." The Court had not yet recovered from the awful shock when she had picked up a kitten. . . .

Ding-dong, Bell!

Hard on poor pussy, but it was the one safe place!

But the greatest danger of all lay not in accident but in the fell designs of the vengeful Fairy Carabosse. Although no one knew in what guise she would arrive to fulfil her dread purpose, everyone was certain that arrive she would and the sorcerer was kept busy night and day transforming ambassadors into gargoyles in case they weren't, and failing to turn them back again although they were. Unaccountable. And the Cabinet was flooded with strong notes of protest from surrounding countries demanding the return of their envoys or else! and the stock excuse of the Big Bad Wolf they must have run into on their way back was wearing very thin.

Difficult times.

*   *   *

In a raftered room at the top of a palace a beautiful maiden was weeping. Perhaps she wasn't so beautiful, but she was certainly crying like anything. All around the room were great heaps of flax, and if all of it were spun into gold by morning she would be a queen and live happily ever after. The King of Stoney Land had said so. But if it wasn't it wouldn't be nearly so nice. The King had mentioned this, too.

At the moment prospects were bad. The maiden had no idea how to weave flax into gold. In fact, she didn't even know how to begin to set about it. She picked up a handful and let it slide through her fingers. Why, oh why had mother boasted so, and why, oh why, was the King of Stoney Land so credulous—even though he was second cousin to King Midas? Why, oh why, had he believed mother? And why, oh why, hadn't mother said that she could play the piano, or skate, or manage the servants, or something! But no—mother had to say her clever daughter could weave flax into gold, and here she was, waiting to have her head chopped off in the morning.

" Why are you weeping, my pretty one ? " chirruped a goblin. " More or less," he added inspecting her from the doorway.

She told him.

" No need to cry," said the goblin. " I can spin that into gold for you in a jiffy." And he sat down at the spinning wheel. Whir-whir-whir. Chink-chink-chink. Clatter-clatter—and there was a pile of gold on the floor beside him.

" See," he said.

The beautiful maiden cheered up at once. In fact, she looked very nearly pretty.

" Oh thank you," she said. " Please do go on."

But the goblin shook his head. " First," he said, " we must agree our terms. Business is business."

" Anything," said the maiden. " Even though it be half my kingdom when I get it."

But this, it appeared, was not the goblin's rainbow. What he was after, and what he found a certain difficulty in putting into words was what in other books is called a Fate Worse Than Death. When at last he had made his meaning clear she shrank from him.

" All right," said the goblin crossly. " No more spinning."

The beautiful maiden began to cry again. She looked a lot plainer. The goblin relented.

" I will give you a chance," he said. " I will turn your flax into gold, and if by the time I have finished you have guessed my name, I will go away and think kindly of you, and you will never see me again. But if you don't guess my name then you shall marry me," said the goblin, and stuck out his chest.

For his name was Rumpelstiltskin, and there didn't seem to be much risk.

The maiden wiped away her tears. " What a lovely condition," she said.

They shook hands on it. " And I'll never see you again," she reminded him.

" A bargain's a bargain," said Rumpelstiltskin reassuringly. " Guess my name and you won't see me again."

And he sat down at the spinning wheel.

Chink-chink. Whir-whir-whir. Clatter-clatter.

The maiden eyed him fondly. How nice to think he soon wouldn't be there. All she had to do was to guess his name. Not even where the thimble was hidden!

" Is it Winken ? " she asked.

" No," said Rumpelstiltskin. " That it isn't."

" Is it Blinken ? "

" No," said Rumpelstiltskin. " No, indeed."

" Is it Nod ? "

But the goblin rubbed his hands and shook his head. " No," he said. He certainly had her guessing.

Whir-whir.　Chink-chink.　Clatter-clatter.

* 　 　 * 　 　 *

How truly has it been said that trouble begets trouble. For the woes of Boxing Night Land had their repercussions in the neighbouring countries, and the curse on the Baby Princess had upset the balance of power in Fairyland.

" It's no use arguing," said Gullible the Astute. " You will never convince me that it is to the advantage of Goose Feather Land to enter into a long term alliance with a country liable to fall asleep at any moment for the whole length of the agreement and a bit over."

The hedgehog bowed his head.

" As for encirclement," said King Gullible, " tcha! We've been encircled before."

The hedgehog tried to think of an answer and couldn't. He felt at a disadvantage arguing with the well-dressed King Gullible. His own spikes had been clipped so that the Baby Princess could stroke him with safety. He wasn't looking his best and he knew it. It wasn't fair of the King to send him on a delicate diplomatic mission. He was all wrong for it mentally.

" Cheer up, old man," said King Gullible. " Soon be asleep."

The hedgehog made a final effort. " Your Majesty will regret this," he said. " Awake or asleep, we are still a better proposition than Old King Cole."

* 　 　 * 　 　 *

Old King Cole was a Merry Old Soul.

He was doing his accounts to Music while he Worked, and he didn't like the items, and he didn't like the answers, and he didn't like work, and he didn't like the music.

The fiddlers fiddled themselves into a fanfare. It sounded terrible.

" His Excellency, the Chancellor of Boxing Night Land," announced a flunkey.

The hedgehog came in.

He had tied ribbons on his blunted spikes. He bowed.

Old King Cole looked at him. He purpled.

" Sire," said the hedgehog, " I have come to propose an alliance between our two mighty kingdoms."

" Oh," said Old King Cole. " You have, have you ? "
He picked up an inkpot.

*   *   *

" Solomon Grundy.
Born on a Monday.
Christened on Tuesday.
Married on Wednesday.
Sick on Thursday.
Worse on Friday.
Died on Saturday.
Buried on Sunday."

" And that," said Fairy Peaseblossom thankfully, " was the end
of Solomon Grundy."

Queen Mab frowned. " Very sudden. Lace my stays, Peaseblossom."

Fairy Peaseblossom applied herself.

" Not so tight," said Queen Mab.

Clearly she was in a carping mood.

" Did you go to the funeral ? " she pursued.

" A Jewish funeral ? " said Fairy Peaseblossom, shocked.

" You can say what you like about Jewish funerals," said Queen
Mab, " but the food is always excellent." She dismissed her.

Fairy Moth came forward. There were no signs of scorching
on her wings now. The Court Surgeon had seen to that. But
the Queen had not spoken to her yet. Yesterday, however, she
had looked through her, and that was encouraging. At least she
had not looked past her.

" Moth," said Queen Mab sharply, " I don't care for the rosebuds
on your garters."

Highly elated Fairy Moth proferred the jewels. At this rate
she would be forgiven in a month of Sundays. Rehabilitation!
She must get to work at once on Polly Flinders and cure the girl
of her Bad Habit before the Queen enquired after her.

" And what," asked Queen Mab evilly, " is little Polly Flinders
doing now ? "

The old bitch jolly well knew!

*   *   *

" Chink-chink. Whirr-whirr. Clatter-clatter.

" Peregrine," guessed the beautiful maiden.

" Cold," said Rumpelstiltskin.   " Very cold."

Chink-chink.   Whirr.

" Ambrose ? "

" Not by a long stalk," Rumpelstiltskin chuckled.

Chink-chink.   Whirr-whirr.   Clatter-clatter.

" Geraldo ? "

" No," said Rumpelstiltskin.   He looked offended.

Chink.

*   *   *

At Court the Ladies-in-Waiting were sniffing. Queen Mab
had carped with them faithfully one and all.   But she was feeling
no better, for she had many things on her mind.

For the first time in her reign a fairy was defying her.

The Widow Carabosse.

True nothing had been said, but the atmosphere was electric
with je-m'en-fouism.

Carabosse knew perfectly well she disapproved of the curse.
Carabosse must have known it the instant her Queen had sailed
past her and helped herself to a pat-a-cake instead of waiting to
have the plate passed to her.   Carabosse was perfectly aware that
an incident was being ignored.

And yet she had not lifted the curse.   She had not even applied
for an audience to discuss the matter.   Carabosse would have to
be summoned and told very firmly what was expected of
her.

It was a pity she could not be told plainly as well, but it was
out of the question for a democratic Queen to make a direct request
about a Fairy's spell.   These things had to be implied.   Queen
Mab had every confidence in her power of implication.   But it
galled the Queen even to have to do that.   Carabosse should rue
this even after she had consented.   And that for one moment the
Queen could have thought seriously of marrying her only son to
that creature's daughter!   A pretty chitling, all the same.

" Mustard Seed," she said, " take a look in the mirror and tell
me what little Titania is doing now."

STIR.

Stir.

STIR.

Stir.

" No, you ninny," said Queen Mab. " Not that mirror. My private mirror."

Fairy Mustard Seed picked up the dewdrop on the dressing table. She concentrated.

" Oh," she said. She blushed scarlet.

" H'm," said Queen Mab. " Prince Charming ? "

" Yes, ma'am," said Fairy Mustard Seed. She gazed again.

" Put down that mirror," said Queen Mab. She snatched it. " A mortal. Poor Carabosse," she said with steel in her voice. " A married mortal. How we mothers suffer."

*　　　*　　　*

Not in the sitting-room. Not in the scullery. Not in the soup. Heigh-ho!

*　　　*　　　*

> " If I could plant a tiny seed of love,
>   In the corner of your heart, pom-pom,"

sang Prince Charming, while the punt swayed lazily under the trees and the birds scattered wildly in all directions.

Titania looked at him starrily. What a brain! What a soul! What head notes!

*　　　*　　　*

Deadlock. Utter deadlock.

Fairies-in-Waiting, peering through a plentitude of keyholes, trembled for the Fairy Carabosse. Really, how she had the nerve to stand there, bold as a bodikin, and let the Queen go on hinting for ten minutes and answer directly what was said instead of what must not be spoken . . . how Carabosse could behave like that . . . it took their breath away. They bent down and peered again.

" I do not agree," said Queen Mab, and was the royal voice a trifle testy ? " that unstinted sleep is good for mortals." And if the hint was perhaps a trifle blunt, Carabosse had asked for it.

The Fairy Carabosse pretended to consider. " What about Rip van Winkle, ma'am ? " she produced. " Did him no harm! "

It was maddening. Queen Mab had no desire to discuss old men who nodded for twenty years. She wanted to discuss a baby liable to fall asleep for a hundred—and a whole kingdom with her. She wanted the spell lifted. But tradition must be respected. She could not say so outright.

" That ninny Moth," she observed, " pricked herself this very morning, making a white petticoat for little Nancy Etticote."

" Easy to prick yourself," said the Fairy Carabosse. " There seems no way to guard against it," she pointed out smugly. If she had not been in a fourth position she would have rubbed her hands.

Queen Mab flushed. No getting away from it the creature was not going to humour her. But had she but known it, behind her defiant stance, the Fairy Carabosse was badly shaken.

It was all very well to come to the Palace with a set plan of defiance and then, the firmness of her intention well and truly established, to pass on to make her bargain. But ten minutes of defying Queen Mab had proved an even greater strain than she had anticipated, and the confidence with which she had seen herself laying down conditions to the Queen was fast ebbing away.

For, of course, it was etiquette that any condition must not be laid down but implied, and how did one imply that one would lift the spell on the Princess Aurora, the day the Queen's son married one's daughter ?

" My daughter," said the Fairy Carabosse, " is a great comfort to me."

Queen Mab's eyebrows shot up. Clearly no more was to be gained from this interview.

" No doubt," she said, " you wish to return to her. My son will be here shortly to see you to your broomstick."

*   *   *

Not in the dazzle. Not on the razzle. Not in the morning after!

*   *   *

But at last the conversation was going nicely. Indeed, Queen Mab had rung for tea, and the haggle, though oblique, was in full spate.

" It would be tragic," Queen Mab was saying, " if the marriage of the fictitious pair we are discussing should be marred by any shadow hanging over this kingdom we have created."

" It would be unthinkable," said the Fairy Carabosse, shocked. " The humble subject we have just thought of would of course have to lift the spell."

" The greatly concerned Queen we have been envisaging," said

Queen Mab, " could then see no obstacle to the union.   A cake-ling ? " she passed the plate.

" Thank you, ma'am," said the Fairy Carabosse.   She nibbled. " Shall we then," she traced a coy pattern with her toe, " consider our fictitious couple plighted ? "

" Very nearly," said Queen Mab, " but I think, don't you, that our imaginary Queen would insist that the tragic spell we have improvised should be lifted before the banns are published."

The Fairy Carabosse rubbed her chin.   " I do not think that is quite in character, ma'am, with the story that we are weaving. The humble subject, as we have depicted her, would never trust a Queen, however kind, to remember a promise once the incentive for making it was gone.   She would have so much on her mind."

The atmosphere grew chill again.

" Are you implying," asked Queen Mab, " that the Queen, the imaginary one," she caught herself, " would in any circumstances break her word ? "

" Not break, ma'am," said the Fairy Carabosse.   " But forget it."

" Same thing," snapped Queen Mab.

It was freezing.

" Can it be," snapped the Fairy Carabosse, " that this gracious Queen of ours suspects the humble subject will double-cross her once the wedding has taken place ? "

" She does," said Queen Mab shortly.   " No spell or else no wedding bell."

The Fairy Carabosse sighed.   " Before everything," she said, " our humble subject is a mother.   She will lift the spell, but she must be given royal assurance that the match will be announced immediately afterwards."

Queen Mab relaxed.   " That's very nice," she said.   " I'm so glad the little story we have concocted has had a happy ending."

Outside the Fairies-in-Waiting had broken into excited little knots.

A love match!   A love match!   A love match!

Inside the mothers were setting the details.

" I shall tell Oberon to-night," said Queen Mab.

" And I shall tell Titania," gloated the Fairy Carabosse.

" There is just one thing," said Queen Mab.   " Titania has been very rash of late.   She must stop it."

" Titania ? " said the Fairy Carabosse.

" And Charming," said Queen Mab.   " It won't do, Carabosse,
my dear.   It must stop at once."

" It shall," said the Fairy Carabosse.   " I'll turn him into a Bank
Manager right away."

" No," said Queen Mab.   " Charming's my god-child.   Give
your girl a sound wigging, and see it doesn't happen again. . . ."

*   *   *

Whirr-whirr.   Chink-chink.   Clatter-clatter.

" Robin Hood ? " guessed the maiden hopefully.

" Never was," said Rumpelstiltskin.

" Rasputin ? "

" Wrong again."

" Robinovitch! "

" You're not even trying," said Rumpelstiltskin in disgust.

*   *   *

" Mother," said Titania, " why mustn't a Fairy marry a Mortal? "

The Fairy Carabosse put down her candlestick.   She had waited
till Titania was in bed for that hour of confidences when a mother
kisses her daughter and sits on the edge of the bed to prolong the
truce ; she had meant to dazzle her with the news of the impending
match, interspersed with a few tears of gladness, after which Prince
Charming's gosling could have been cooked in a couple of sentences.   But this was a different kettle of fishlings.   She sought
quickly for an attitude.   Wordly wisdom softened by mother-
love.

" Why do you ask, child ? " she said gently.

" A fairy I know . . ." said Titania, gazing at the ceiling.

Oh hell, thought the Fairy Carabosse.   More pretending.   " Go
on, child," she said in a level voice.

" Well, this fairy," said Titania, " the one I know, is in love with
a mortal."

" Imagines she is," said the Fairy Carabosse, worldliness to the
fore.

" Oh no, it's the real thing," said Titania raptly.   " He is the
most wonderful, the most intellectual, the most considerate mortal.
And he's in love with her, too."   She wriggled deliciously.

The Fairy Carabosse looked at her flushed daughter.   " That I
can understand," she said smugly, mother-love foremost.   " But

are you sure your friend knows her own mind ? It is so easy to be fascinated by a mortal."

" How understanding you are, mother," said Titania. " The most understanding mother in the world." She snuggled up.

Better, thought the Fairy Carabosse. She put an arm round her. " You know," she said, " that all mother cares about is your happiness."

A tactical mistake! Titania had heard this one too often, and usually in the middle of a scene. She shrank away.

" But this girl I know," she said, " is very grown up for her age." Carabosse smiled.

" She is a modern fairy. Clear sighted, unconventional, and a straight thinker."

The smile died out. Blast that Charming! If only she could turn him into a toadstool! . . .

" She faces facts fearlessly."

. . . An octopus! . . .

" And she must work this thing out for herself."

. . . A bus stop! . . .

" But why doesn't she ask her mother's advice," said the Fairy Carabosse. " After all a mother . . ." Motherhood surged up again.

" Well, that's just it," said Titania. " This girl I know is willing to face up to all the rest, the scandal, the ostracism, the shame— perhaps even poverty. But she is afraid that mother might be hurt. And she doesn't want to hurt her mother."

" She would be," said the Fairy Carabosse, back on firm ground. " It would break her mother's heart, which, I am sure, cannot be very strong after all she has gone through." From force of habit she clawed at her left side.

" Oh mother," said Titania irrelevantly, " I'm so glad you've got a heart like a steam engine."

The Fairy Carabosse sat up. " Who said that ? " she snapped.

. . . A Home Guard! . . .

" But, mother," said Titania, " why shouldn't a fairy marry a mortal ? "

Back to the beginning.

The Fairy Carabosse stood over her daughter. For the moment she had forgotten both worldly wisdom and mother-love.

" I'll tell you why you're not going to marry a mortal, my chit," she said. " You're going to marry Oberon. Mother has arranged it."

Titania put her hand over her mouth. " I can't," she said. " I can't. I won't."

" And why not ? " said the Fairy Carabosse dangerously quiet.

Titania looked at her mother. It was like a butterfly looking at a stoat. And there was no comfort in the stoat's expression.

" Mother," she said, " I cannot deceive you any longer. I must tell you the truth." She gulped. " There isn't a girl I know. She's me."

She burst into tears and pulled the goose-feather over her head.

" There, there," said the Fairy Carabosse, patting the sobbing lump and thinking furiously. " There, there, there ! "

*   *   *

At the Palace, Queen Mab, in a poplin night-cap, a red flannel dressing-gown girded firmly across her practical nightgown, walked, candle in hand, through the corridor towards her son's apartments. She had been waiting for that time when a mother kisses her son good night and sits down on the edge of the bed to prolong the moment. She meant to break the news to Oberon of the impending match, to dazzle him with Titania's beauty, interspersed with a few tears of gladness, after which he could be persuaded to swallow his mother-in-law in a couple of bites.

She knocked, a gentle knock.

" It's mother," she said. " May I come in, son ? "

There was no answer. She knocked again, still gently but a little louder.

" May I come in, son ? It's mother."

Silence still.

Queen Mab brushed off a flutter of annoyance. She was glad the boy slept soundly. She would tip-toe in, turn up his bedside glow-worm with the shade carefully adjusted to shield his dear eyes from the light, and sit on the edge of the bed to wait for his awakening, just like any other mother. And she would make a very nice picture to linger in his memory when he opened his eyes.

She adjusted her nightcap and went in.

The glow-worm was already turned up. In fact, none of the

lights were out. Extravagance! The *Agricultural Times* lay on the dressing table, and a spade with a gob of mud still sticking to it was propped in the corner.

But the bed was empty.

Queen Mab looked round. " Oh dear," she said. " Gone out without his overcoat."

She willed.

Fairy Fanfaronade, her hair in plaits, appeared rubbing her eyes.

" My son," said Queen Mab.

" Yes, ma'am," said Fairy Fanfaronade.

Suppressing a yawn, she fluttered off.

* * *

" But, Titania, you foolish chitling, reflect a minute. Don't you want to be Queen of Fairyland ? " The Fairy Carabosse looked pleadingly at her daughter. " Don't you want to have every fairy obeying you, copying you, envying you ? " And all the mothers envying her mother, she suppressed.

" Better a supper of herblings where love is," said Titania starrily.

. . . A Kangaroo! . . .

" Titania," the mother's voice took on a deeper note, " there is a subject that you and I have never talked about—a subject that I never meant to talk to you about. No, not that subject. You'll hear about that in due course," she assured her.

Titania suppressed a faint twinge. But this was not the moment to tell Mamma that it would not be necessary.

The Fairy Carabosse leant against a buttercup and folded her hands.

" I am going to talk about Prince Florizel," she said calmly, and, in spite of her misery, a thrill of anticipation ran through Titania.

For this was the name that must never be spoken, not even in the dormitory after lights out, when all sorts of things were mentioned. Though the broad outlines of the case were known well enough throughout the seven times seven Kingdoms of the Fairy Realm.

Prince Florizel, heir to the throne of Fairyland, had abdicated, married a mortal, and gone off to live happily ever after.

And that is all anyone was permitted to know. For when the

deed was done, Queen Mab had plucked her eldest son from her
heart, and her hair had gone quite white, and she had decreed
that all that happened to him henceforth must not be mentioned,
and, more difficult, all that had preceded it must be forgotten.
And she had made her younger son the heir to the throne, and
she tried never to remember that he was not her eldest born, and
she hoped for the best.

But, though no newspaper ever printed a word of Prince Florizel
and the younger generation grew up in ignorance of him, there
were always the birds of the air to carry tidings, and the elders
knew very well all that was happening to him, and took much
malicious pleasure therein.

" Prince Florizel," said the Fairy Carabosse, " met a mortal at a
ball of unequalled splendour—just as you did. She was Scheherazade's sister, and they fell in love—just as you did. And they met
in secret and went for rows on the lake—just as you do. And
then one day they were seen together—taking tea at Fairy Ann's
pantry, and the scandal was out.

" Perhaps," said the Fairy Carabosse, " if the whole thing had
been ignored it might have faded away and no more harm would
have been done, except to Scheherazade's sister. But there I think,
though it's not for me to judge her, our dear Queen made her first,
her only, mistake. She created a scene," said Titania's mother with
strong disapproval, " and the upshot was an ultimatum."

" The Queen made Prince Florizel an ultimatum ? " gasped
Titania.

" No," said the Fairy Carabosse. " Florizel made the Queen
one. Where so far he had rather avoided dwelling on the future,
he now insisted on marrying at once. And he did," she said.
" And, of course, he had to abdicate."

" Many waters cannot quench love," said Titania, loyal but
muddled. " And I'm sure he's never regretted it for an instant."

" On the contrary," said the Fairy Carabosse " he's regretting it
all the time. It is one thing to love a mortal—it is quite another
to spend your life with one—and all her friends—for no fairy will
call on you." The Fairy Carabosse shook a doleful head. " Prince
Florizel misses his own kind, his own land, his heritage. He was
heir to the throne of Fairyland and was not fitted for any other
walk in life. And now, he is merely odd fairy out among mortals,

and even they are used to him, and as he follows his wife through the streets to market not a single head turns to look."

"But at least they have each other," said Titania.

The Fairy Carabosse controlled herself.

"As to that," she said, "you are right. They are fond of one another still, so you see this was real love, and much good has it done them! For she spends her time wishing he were more like other men, while her inability to perform even the simplest miracle, once so charming, now irks him beyond measure. She cannot even discuss anything with him, for he knows what she is thinking before she speaks. And so they live, denizens of two worlds, not happy in either. Do you think," said the Fairy Carabosse, having reduced herself almost to tears, "that I should permit my only daughter to share a fate like that?"

"But they have each other," said Titania. "It's worth it! And he can sing to her." She gazed raptly at the ceiling.

Suddenly it was too much. The mother surged up in Carabosse. She snatched off the goose-feather, she plucked her daughter out of bed, she put her across her knee, and she spanked her.

She had been wanting to do this for months.

*   *   *

In a cabin, with the candlelight streaming into the darkness, and the gentle thrum of plantation songs rising from all around, nine little nigger boys had spent a happy evening at play. And now Uncle Rochester rose from his rocker chair, took out a massive silver hunter, shook it to make sure it was going, and waved a finger at his piccaninnies.

"It sho' is getting late," he said. "Time all little niggah boys wurz in bed."

Eight little nigger boys rose from the floor, put away their toys, and exchanged their coloured cottons for white nightshirts. Eight little nigger boys knelt to say their prayers, and scrambled into one large bed. Uncle Rochester kissed eight little nigger boys good night.

He frowned. The numbers were wrong.

At a table in the candlelight the ninth little nigger boy was sitting immersed.

Uncle Rochester peered. "Uncle Tom's Cabin," he observed. "It sho' is a mighty good book. But it's time to go to bed, Suetonius."

c

The ninth little nigger boy looked up and produced an angry babble of oppressed races, colour bars, and equality of opportunity.

" Now don't you worry about that," said Uncle Rochester. " Tings is different now. We all dun got de same education. Now, Tonius, you run along and get your sleep and I'll tell you about dem communists in de morning."

But the ninth little nigger boy had gone back to his book. He read on. Indignation welled up in him.

" Son, son," grieved Uncle Rochester, " done you be forgetting what it says in de Book ? " Without even opening it to refresh his memory, he quoted :

" Nine little niggah boys sat up very late.
One overslept hisself and den,"

Uncle Rochester's voice sounded the bass knell of doom, " dere was eight."

Eight little niggah boys on the brink of sleep, shivered and pulled the blankets over their heads.

But the ninth little nigger boy went on reading.

CHAPTER VIII   **Schemers All**

A summer's day in Fairyland, so sunny, so shady, so warm, so cool, so songful, so quiet, so dazzling, so shimmering, so radiant that never would you have suspected it could contain hearts heavy with care. But in spite of the wishing wells and the Emperor's nightingale there were furrowed brows in Fairyland that day.

In her garden Mary Mary was sitting among the cockleshells sobbing her heart out. Round her the silver bells were tinkling dismally and the pretty maids all in a row had hung their heads.

" How contrary you are, child," said Fairy Cobweb exasperated. " Haven't I just given you your biggest social success ? Hasn't the King of Spain's daughter been to see your herbaceous borders ? "

Mary Mary buried her head in a Canterbury bell.

" But she didn't look at it," she sobbed.

She didn't look at it! This was serious.

" Now pull yourself together, Mary Mary," scolded Fairy Cobweb, " and tell me all about it."

Mary Mary choked back her tears. She sought for words.

> " I had a little nut tree and nothing would it bear
> But a silver nutmeg and a golden pear."

She pointed.

> " The King of Spain's daughter."

Her eyes filled with tears.

> " . . . came to visit me.
> And all for the sake of my little nut tree."

She burst into tears again.

" Not for my silver bells, not for my cockleshells." She stamped her foot. " Not for my pretty maids, though I got Zinkeisen to dress them. No! No! No!" She clenched her fists. " All she'd look at was that stupid old tree left behind by the last tenant."

She plucked a pear and flung it at Fairy Cobweb. Then she lay down on the ground and kicked her heels in the air.

*   *   *

And just a few thatched cottages away little Bo-Peep was pacing up and down her living-room in a frenzy of mounting depression.

" I've left them alone for a long time now," she told grannie, " just as you advised. And what's happened ? "

" Leave them alone a little longer," advised grannie, " and they'll be here, tails and all, see if they're not."

There was a bleat outside the door. Bo-Peep rushed to open it. Even grannie looked over the top of her spectacles.

Outside stood a lamb, a little lamb of course. All by itself in the sunlight. Its fleece was white as snow, and already there was a faithful expression in its eye.

" Oh hell!" said Bo-Peep. " So now I'm little Mary."

*   *   *

A lovely day. A day to lie in an orchard and not tell the time by the dandelion clock. A day to lie by the stream and watch the sky in the water. Certainly not a day for disputations.

Yet by a river, not seven crooked leagues away, a cat was arguing with its master.

"Do as I tell you, master," pleaded Puss. "Take off your clothes and jump in the river. And I'll bet my boots," said Puss, "it'll be all right."

"That's all very well," said the miller's third son, who was as fond of a swim as anyone. "But where's it going to land us?"

"Patience, master," said Puss. "I have planned this act to impress the King."

"I'm sick of impressing the King," said the miller's third son. "You've already impressed him with two pheasants and a rabbit, which I could have eaten very nicely myself. I'm hungry."

"So am I," said poor Puss. "But am I complaining?"

"You didn't take that mouse to the King, I noticed," said the miller's third son.

"It wouldn't have impressed him," said Puss. "Now do as I tell you, master. Jump into the river."

"What am I going to see for it," asked the miller's third son obstinately.

"Leave it to me," said Puss, "and you'll see a nice new suit of clothes."

"Promise?" said the miller's third son suspiciously.

"On the word of a cat," said Puss.

"That's different," said the miller's third son.

He stripped and plunged.

*   *   *

A lovely day. One of the many, many lovely days since the Fairy Carabosse had spoken to Titania and Queen Mab had failed to speak to Prince Oberon. And every day the Princess Aurora grew just a little older; in fact, one day she grew five months older, and was quite a big girl for her age, though not at all obedient.

And every day Titania still refused to give her heart to Prince Oberon, and every night her mother worked on her for her own good, trying tears, kindness and stark brutality—all with no effect. The most she could extract was a promise that Titania would make a serious effort to pluck Prince Charming from her heart, but she would not even promise to stop seeing him while she did the plucking.

Poor Carabosse! Defied by her daughter and forbidden by the Queen to transform her godson into some less lovable shape.

. . . A mangle! . . .

So all that the Fairy Carabosse could do was to create obstacles in Prince Charming's way to make him late for his appointments in the hope that Titania might tire of waiting for him. But even though he turned up four days late (swimming a stream that widened as he stroked), Titania met him lovingly and, slightly muddled, swore that it had seemed like no time at all.

Something was happening to the chit. She was more than a daughter defying her mother, and so the whole world. She was a Valkyrie receiving reinforcements.

As a matter of fact, Titania had the Fairy Dark Diamond right behind her.

" Oh, Darkie," said Titania on that lovely day, " you are such a true friend. You give me courage. I don't know what I'd do without you, indeed I don't."

" It's the least I can do," said Dark Diamond, polishing her nails with cherry blossom. " After all, we were at school together."

" I could never have gone on defying mother without you."

" That's what I thought," said Dark Diamond. " Without me you'd have given in and been married to Oberon by now. And I'm determined to stop that," she added truthfully.

Titania sighed. There was only one tiny cloud in the sky, but the sun had gone behind it.

" It's no use, Darkie," she said. " Mother is breaking her heart and we're not getting anywhere. What's the good of going on ? "

" Come, come," said Dark Diamond, slipping easily into her daily pep talk, though each day she had to talk a little harder. " You can't give him up now. Think of Prince Charming," she exhorted. " Think of his love. Think of his profile."

" He sings the most beautiful songs in the world," said Titania. " Sometimes I think if he came and sang them to mother . . ."

" No," said Dark Diamond firmly. " That's not a good idea, Titania."

" There you are," said Titania. " You see it's hopeless. Quite, quite hopeless. We'll just go on and on and get nowhere."

Fairy Dark Diamond did not like the turn the conversation was taking. She tried a new line.

" Think of that woman," she said. " What's her name—Cinderella. Think of the life she leads him. All those antimacassars." She giggled.

"She doesn't even begin to understand him," said Titania indignantly. "Just because she's got a small foot she thinks that's all that's required of her. But a wife needs more than a small foot," she argued hotly.

"Especially a wife with as sensitive a husband as Prince Charming," said Dark Diamond.

From a cowslip bell came a hoarse chuckle.

Puck, drat him!

Dark Diamond turned to Titania. "Let's snuggle in that rosebud over there where no one can overhear us," she suggested, "and I'll tell you what you're to do next."

"Oh, Darkie," said Titania. "Have you got an idea?"

Their arms round each other's shoulders, the girls flew away.

"Heigh-ho!" said Puck. "I wish I knew which side I was on."

*   *   *

And now, believe it or not, Fairy Fanfaronade has found Prince Oberon and, not leaving his side for an instant, has clucked him into the Royal Presence.

"Morning, Moother," said Prince Oberon. "Lovely morning. Just off to harvest the wheat. Bushels and bushels of it!" He turned to go.

"Come back, son," said Queen Mab. "Sit down. I'm a gardener myself," she pointed out, "but there are more important things in life than gardening."

Prince Oberon looked dubious.

"Marriage," said Queen Mab.

"Surely, Moother," said Prince Oberon politely.

"Your marriage."

"Eh!" said Prince Oberon.

Queen Mab waved to her ladies-in-waiting, palpitating to a fairy.

"Fairies," she said, "you may withdraw."

"Blast!" said Fairy Moth under her breath. But the Queen was a lip-reader. Poor Moth.

But that was later.

For the moment the Queen was concentrating on her son, who had launched himself on to a one-track conversation.

"But I doan't want to wed, Moother," he was saying for the fifth time.

" You will be King," said Queen Mab, " and Kings have a duty to their subjects. You must provide a Queen for them to curtsey to. You know that perfectly well."

" But I doan't want to wed, Moother," said Prince Oberon.

" I have given you every opportunity to select a suitable wife for yourself, son," said Queen Mab. " You have shown no signs of even looking."

" Well, it's like this," explained Prince Oberon. " I doan't want to wed, Moother."

" So," said Queen Mab, " I have made the match for you."

Prince Oberon changed the record.

" And who be she, Moother ? " he asked.

" She is Titania," said Queen Mab.

Another record went on.

" But, Moother," said Prince Oberon, " she has a moother."

Queen Mab sighed. " I know she has, son. The widow Carabosse. Still, you can't have everything. And Titania is very beautiful, and very well brought up ; indeed, she is a girl who would grace any Court."

" Can she milk coo, Moother ? " asked Prince Oberon, not impressed so far.

" She can learn," said Queen Mab without batting an eyelid.

A greenhorn ! Prince Oberon concentrated furiously. If only he could explain !

" Moother," he said. " You see it's like this. I doan't want to wed ! "

*   *   *

A lovely day. The sun was shining on the sea. Little children made castles of sand, while their elders clapped their hands over their stomachs and took their naps under striped umbrellas.

Somewhere on the beach eight little nigger boys were guzzling their last large slice of water-melon, while Uncle Rochester, his hat passed round for the last time and his banjo put back in its case, was packing the picnic basket and counting the spades and buckets.

" Well, chillun," he said, " it sho' is time to take the train."

" Ready, Uncle Rochester," chorused seven little nigger boys in close harmony.

But the eighth little nigger boy grabbed a spade and bucket and made off, all by himself, to a shallow pool.

Uncle Rochester looked aftcr him fearfully. The lines of the
Book welling up in his mind.

> " Eight little nigger boys, travelling in Devon,
>   One said he'd stay there and then . . ."

Was Babbacombe in Devon ? Why had he dun not asked ?
Without any hope he made his way towards the pool.
" Auriculus, Auriculus," he called. " It sho' is time to be going
home, Aurie."
The eighth little nigger boy dabbled his hands in the water and
clawed deliciously among the rocks for crabs.
" Doan wanna go home," he said defiantly. " Ah likes it here."
He popped a seaweed. . . .

* * *

A lovely summer's day.
" And that," said King Gullible, dropping his arm as the last
tin soldier eyed-right and marched away in a swirl of dust, " is
our glorious army."
Old King Cole was a merry old soul. He sniffed.
" Toy soldiers," he said disdainfully. " Now I've got some
mounted cossacks."
" Mercenaries," said King Gullible. He glared.
There was a clucking behind him. The Chancellor was tugging
at his sleeve to remind him that King Cole was on a friendly visit
with a view to forming an alliance.
It was not for nothing that Gullible was called the Astute. He
reminded himself of this as the royal coach drew up. His manners
became perfect.
" After you, my friend," he said.
" Erch-cher," said Old King Cole, and heaved himself in. He
took up the whole of the back seat, and King Gullible had to sit
with his back to the cheering populace and nearly twisted his head
off bowing his acknowledgments along the route. It was quite a
relief to reach the open country.
" Our mountains," said King Gullible, waving a hand in the
direction of the snow-capped peaks. " Excellent defensive
positions," he pointed out.
" That's as may be," said Old King Cole.

"Our forest," said King Gullible, waving his other hand. "Impenetrable," he boasted.

They drove into it.

King Gullible tried again.

"Our brook," he said. "Babbling," he pointed out.

"In my country," said Old King Cole severely, "brooks never speak till they're spoken to."

"Oh," said King Gullible.

They drove on.

Through the trees on the edge of the impenetrable forest was a dazzle of blue like Juno's eyelids and all the bluebells of Scotland.

Old King Cole brightened. "A river," he said. "Let's go fishin'."

King Gullible fidgeted. It was the one thing his Ambassador had warned him against. When Old King Cole went fishing he either caught nothing or a cold, and, whichever happened, came back in no mood to sign treaties.

But how to put it tactfully? He would have to think quickly, for already Old King Cole had alighted and was looking at a worm.

"Help! Help!"

An agitated figure was gesticulating from the bank.

"Help! Help! Help!"

At first sight it looked just like a pair of top boots. But from nearer to you, could discern a cat inside them.

"Help, help!" said Puss. "My master is drowning."

"Who?" asked Old King Cole.

"My master," shouted Puss. "The Marquis of Carabas."

"By Jove!" said King Gullible, "we must do something. Fellow sends me game. Remember that pheasant you had last night?"

Old King Cole did. "Let him drown," he advised warmly.

"Oh no," said King Gullible. "Very decent sort of chap. Nice cat, too. Most respectful. Well, Dickery," he turned on the coachman, "what are you waiting for?"

Resigned, the coachman climbed down from his box. Tenderly he took off his top hat, dived into the pool, clutched the miller's third son by the scruff of his neck and began lugging him towards the bank.

"Stop!" cried Puss. He faced King Gullible. "A terrible misfortune has befallen my master," he announced. "While he was swimming some robber stole his clothes." He pointed to an empty boulder.

Old King Cole was a merry old soul. He roared with laughter.

But King Gullible was greatly concerned. " Poor fellow," he said, " you shall have the finest suit my wardrobe can boast." He turned to his outrider. " Up, Jenkins," he said. " Off to the Palace with you and see to it that you bring back my choicest raiment."

Up-Jenkins raised an eyebrow. " That one ? " it said.

" That one," said King Gullible's lower jaw.

" Atchoo! " said the Marquis of Carabas.

*   *   *

The Master of the Wardrobe flung open the Royal Cupboard, pushed aside the ermine-trimmed velvets, the paduasoy waistcoats, the pink silk tights and, with great care, took down a coat-hanger. He took nothing off it and passed it to the valet. The valet spread nothing carefully on the ironing board. The hot iron passed smoothly over thin air.

Perfect!

The Master of the Wardrobe kissed his fingers. Then he picked up nothing from the ironing board, folded it carefully, and put it over Up-Jenkins's arm.

" Be careful not to crush it," he said severely.

*   *   *

" Atchoo! " said the Marquis of Carabas.

" Atchoo! " said the coachman.

Up-Jenkins galloped up and reined in.

" There you are," said Old King Cole testily. " And about time, too."

He had found a worm long ago, but he hadn't caught anything yet.

King Gullible advanced to the horseman and with the greatest care in the world took nothing from him.

" There you are, my dear fellow," he said to the shivering Marquis, and with his own hands helped him into the matchless raiment. " Button it well at the neck," he advised.

" Atchoo! " said the Marquis of Carabas. He tried to catch Puss's eye, but Puss wasn't playing.

" A cat can look at two Kings," he was thinking. " So what! "

★   ★   ★

It was a lovely summer's morning. The next lovely morning. The Fairy Fanfaronade was fluttering all over the home acres.

. . . Not in the orangery. Not in the apple tree. Not in season. . . .

Indeed, the only figure in sight was a swineherd chewing a straw, while his piglings nuzzled around his gaiters. He was propped up against a kissing-gate, gazing at something on the other side of it—no doubt a cow. How like Prince Oberon the swineherd was!

Fairy Fanfaronade pursed her lips. Apeing their betters! She fluttered off to look beneath the magic carpet. So easy to sweep under!

The swineherd went on gazing. There was a cow in the meadow and a cush cow at that, but he was looking past her. He was gazing at a vision picking its way daintily among the dandelions and coming nearer to him every instant. A milkmaid up with the lark and to bed with the nightingale. As fresh as cellophane and as dainty as Dresden. Raven black hair, a simple sprig dress and shoes with silver buckles. Definitely huggable.

" Heigh-ho," said the swineherd. For he was no ordinary swineherd. He was in fact Prince Oberon determined not to be found by Fanfaronade this morning.

. . . Not on the thirty-nine steps! Phew! . . .

The milkmaid tripped nearer. She carried a striped milk-pail with ribbons tied on it. She also carried a beribboned crook which became her mightily. She had such poise and so much lipstick that had she not been a milkmaid you would have sworn she was the Fairy Dark Diamond. And how right you would have been!

The incognitos impinged.

" Where are ye going to, my pretty maid ? " said Prince Oberon, shifting the straw to the other corner of his mouth, a concession.

Dark Diamond bobbed a curtsey.

" I'm going a-milking, sir . . . zur," she said.

Prince Oberon pointed to the cush cow.

" Well," he said. " Git on wi' it."

*   *   *

A lovely summer's morning. Prince Charming on his way to a rendezvous with Titania looked at the sky.

" Tira-lirra," he sang. " Tira-lirra! "

But suddenly the light was snatched from the sky by great branches that had sprung up all around him. And his horse whinnied and would have bolted had there been room.

" Quiet, my trusty steed," said Prince Charming. " Your master has more trouble than you wot of."

For how could a lover be punctual to his tryst when impenetrable forests kept on growing up like this. No wonder Prince Charming was seven days late.

But at least he could sing to keep his courage up.

" There's a long, long trail a-winding . . . "

*   *   *

" Cush cow, beauty, let down thy milk
And I will give thee a gown of silk.
A gown of silk and a silver tree,
If thou wilt down thy milk for me."

The cush cow considered. There was little hope that the milkmaid would keep her promise, but you never knew. She wondered how Ferdinand would like her in a gown of silk.

Milk poured from her.

The swineherd took the straw right out of his mouth! What a milkmaid!

For Dark Diamond had whipped out a three-legged stool with ribbons on it, put it down nowhere near the cush cow, and wheedled. And dear old Buttercoop, not worth the milking these seven seasons, was giving a yield to put the United Dairies to shame.

"Well done, lass," said the swineherd. "Well done, indeed."

The milkmaid's eyes sparkled. "Do you think," she said, "that Prince Oberon will be pleased with my milking?"

So she liked him for himself alone! The swineherd's chest came out.

"Surely, surely," he said. "You be the best milkmaid seen in these parts these seven seasons coom Michaelmas."

He vaulted the stile, put an arm around her, and tried to draw her to him.

"Oh no," said the milkmaid. She disengaged herself.

"Don't you luv me?" said the swineherd, pained.

"My face is my fortune," said the milkmaid firmly, "and I can't afford to squander it." A bitter memory came surging back. "Listen," she said, "and I'll tell you a story."

Prince Oberon squatted. He was as fond of a story as anyone in Fairyland.

"Once upon a time," he prompted.

"Not so long ago," took up Dark Diamond, "there was a beautiful Princess. She had virtue, wit, and a *pas de bourrée*. But she was spoilt and selfish. Suitors came for her from far and near, but mainly from far, for those near knew her too well, and the Princess Thundercloud spurned them all, rich and poor, especially the poor," said the Fairy Dark Diamond.

"Normal so far," said Prince Oberon. "Go on."

"One day," continued Dark Diamond, "a Prince came to the Palace and he brought a red rose to the Princess and he offered her his heart. The rose was the rose of happiness, but the Princess was insulted by anything less than orchids. She threw it at him."

"Shouldn't throw flowers," said Prince Oberon. "Bain't grown for that."

"So," said Dark Diamond, "the Prince went sadly away. And in the forest he met a poor swineherd with only two pigs."

"Bain't poor with two pigs," said Prince Oberon. "Not if you breed well." He whistled to his rooting family, who came immediately and rooted round Dark Diamond.

" This poor swineherd," said Dark Diamond, shooing them
away, " had a platter. It was a magic platter. Little bells were
hung around it which tinkled prettily, and played an old, old
melody.

She sang it. " Ach du lieber Augustin . . ."

" Alles weg, weg, weg," finished Prince Oberon strongly.

" You know it," said Dark Diamond.

" Who doesn't ? " said Prince Oberon.   " Go on, lass."

" So," said Dark Diamond, " the Prince bought the platter for
a purse of silver, and he put on the swineherd's old jacket and his
weather-beaten hat, and he went back and stood outside the Palace
walls and the platter played the ancient tune."

" Ach du lieber Augustin," sang Prince Oberon, entering into
it and tattooing time on a pigling's back.

" And the Princess came out of the Palace," said Dark Diamond,
" and she demanded the platter from the swineherd.

" ' Oh no,' said the swineherd. ' You must buy it from
me.'

" She threw him a bag of gold, but he threw it right back again.

" ' The price of the platter,' he said, ' is one hundred
kisses.'

" ' Why not," said the Princess.   ' Fenella,' she beckoned.

" ' Not a maid of honour,' said the swineherd. ' The Princess
herself.'

" The Princess considered. She wanted the platter very much.
The bells played beautifully. So," said Dark Diamond,
" before Prince Oberon could burst into an ' ach,' she extended
first her hand and then her cheek, and eventually her lips. And
the swineherd kissed her and the Court counted."

Prince Oberon was enthralled.   " Hussy! " he said.

" But," said Dark Diamond, " just as they got to seventeen her
father, King Gullible, looked over the wall to see what all the
commotion was about.   And when he found out he flew into a
rage and shut his daughter out of the Palace.".

" Was it snowing ? " asked Prince Oberon.

" Inches deep," said Dark Diamond obligingly. She resumed
her story. " And then the swineherd took off his weather-beaten
hat and he put on his golden crown.

" ' You would not take the rose of happiness,' he said, ' but you would buy a toy. You would not wed a Prince, but you would kiss a swineherd.'

" And he went sadly back to his kingdom.

" ' What,' said the Princess, ' is to become of me now ? ' And the trees were still and the snow fell around her."

Dark Diamond was silent.

" And what did ? " asked Prince Oberon.

" Oh, Gullible took her back," said Dark Diamond. " But that's not the point. What I'm coming to is that some time later I met a swineherd myself. And he had a silver platter which played . . ."

" Ach," guessed Prince Oberon.

" It did," said Dark Diamond. " So of course I was nice to the swineherd. I was very nice indeed. And what do you think ? " she said indignantly. " He was just a swineherd."

" Eh ? " said Prince Oberon.

" The Prince," said Dark Diamond savagely, " had given him back the platter."

The swineherd thought it over. He threw away the straw.

" Well," he said, " you're loockier this time."

He cuddled up.

*   *   *

Here he was at last. And here was she trembling as usual. The effect he had on her!

" Sorry I'm a fortnight late," said Prince Charming, dismounting, " but my horse got turned into a tortoise." He pointed.

The tortoise kicked its heels and galloped off. It was a horse again.

" You've got to hand it to mother," said Titania with unwilling admiration. " Always considerate to dumb animals. The moment a spell has served its purpose she takes it off."

" Tira-lirra," said Prince Charming with, perhaps, less enthusiasm than usual.

They settled down on a bank whereon the wild thyme blew, and the newts and the blind worms watched and did no wrong, and Prince Charming sang " Keep the Home Fires Burning," and they were very happy. They drank tealing from a thermos flask, and they tried to make plans for the future, and they grew more and more depressed.

"The whole truth of the matter," said Prince Charming moodily, "is that you don't love me."

"How can you say such a thing?" said Titania. "After all, the times I've waited for you."

But Prince Charming only sighed. "If we go on like this," he said, "you'll be just a memory among my souvenirs."

He sang it.

Titania burst into tears. "I can't bear it," she sobbed. "I don't want to be a might-have-been."

From an overhanging tree a little boy alighted with a thud.

"That's my copyright," said Peter Pan coldly. He flew off.

Prince Charming clicked his tongue. "That boy will never grow up," he said severely. "Not even when he's Fay Compton."

"Someone should take him in hand and teach him manners," said Titania.

"Can't keep up with him," Prince Charming shook his head. "Runs for ever," he said enviously.

He put his arm round Titania.

"Darling," he said, "what's the use of going on like this? You must make up your mind. Take the plunge. Burn your bridge. Cut the caper."

"Oh dear," said Titania.

"We could be at the blacksmith's forge to-morrow," urged Prince Charming. He remembered something. "Barring impenetrable forests and such," he added.

"But you haven't got your divorce from Cinderella yet," said Titania.

He hadn't thought of that. Prince Charming stroked his chin.

"How would it be," he suggested, "if we got married first and told—er—my wife afterwards. More irrevocable," he argued.

"But, darling," said Titania, "that would make me a bigamist. And I hate to think," she added, "what mother would make you."

"Oh," said Prince Charming, "that's different. Perhaps we had better wait a little longer."

"And in the meantime," said Titania, and there was just a shade of mother in her voice, "you can divorce your wife."

Prince Charming mooched. "That will take a long time," he muttered, "and while we're waiting you won't be growing any younger, and neither," he faced it, "shall I."

" But, darling," said Titania, " you wouldn't want me to be a bad girl, would you ? "

This was exactly what Prince Charming had been working for—the cad.

" Not bad," he said. " Broad-minded."

Titania looked at him. " Same thing," she said mutinously. " What's the difference ? "

" My dear child," said Prince Charming, embarking on difficult waters. " being broad-minded is being fearless, untrammelled, modern, facing facts bravely—in fact," he went on in a burst of inspiration, " being exactly like you. Being bad," he hesitated, " is—well, just being bad." He waved it away.

" Darling," said Titania, " how well you put it. I feel much better now."

" I'm so glad," said Prince Charming. He made a grab.

" But all the same," said Titania, turning her cheek, " if you don't mind I'd rather be married first—to please mother," she excused herself. " It's not that I'm not untrammelled, only . . ."

No use rushing things.

" Darling," said Prince Charming, and let her go. " I'll wait for you." He leant back and put his hands behind his head in the attitude of one prepared to sit there for ever.

" Darling," said Titania, " would you say Prince Florizel was untrammelled ? "

" Eminently," said Prince Charming. " Nice fellah."

" Well, look what happened to him."

" Indeed," said Prince Charming, " and what has happened to him ? "

" He's unhappy," said Titania. " Mother said so."

Prince Charming sat up. " Nonsense," he said. " Old witches tales. Florizel's the happiest man alive. No fuss and ceremonial, a place of his own, plenty of shootin', and the woman of his choice. What more can a fellow want ? "

That, thought Titania, is what I mean to find out. But aloud she said, " Darling, sing something to me."

Feeling that he had done well enough for one afternoon, Prince Charming obliged.

*   *   *

A lovely sunny day.

But in another of those impenetrable forests it was awfully dark. The woodcutter's children were trudging round in circles, while the birds behind them were having a lovely time gobbling up the crumbs they had dropped to find their way back.

Freshly made this morning. Delicious!

" We're lost," said Hansel with a little sigh. How he wished he had dropped white pebbles.

" Don't cry, dear brother," said Gretel. " Something is sure to happen soon."

She looked as though she were about to sing it.

" Wait for an audience," hissed Hansel.

They trudged on. And presently they came to a clearing. In it stood a dear little hut made of gingerbread with a roof of cake and windows of barley sugar. The chimneys were crystallised cherries and the doormat a piece of Turkish delight.

Hansel and Gretel licked their lips.

" Unrationed," they said.

They pounced.

*   *   *

A lovely afternoon in Goosefeather Land. Our monarchs were driving through it while Puss ran ahead to make his arrangements, and the Marquis of Carabas took a hot bath at the Palace.

" A lovely day," gloated King Gullible.

Just as though he had invented it, thought Old King Cole crossly. In his country, when he took monarchs round, it always rained.

" Is it tea-time yet ? " he asked.

They passed a cornfield, acres and acres of it, burgeoning with ripe corn the colour of ripe corn.

" Yours ? " asked Old King Cole, impressed in spite of himself.

" Can't remember," said King Gullible. He beckoned a reaper.

" To whom does this land belong, my good man ? " he asked.

" Why, don't you know ? " said the reaper. " It belongs to the Marquis of Carabas." He strolled off with the relief of one who has safely spoken his lines. Maybe they'd give him a bigger part next pantomime.

" Atchoo! " said the coachman.

They drove on.

In a meadow a herd of cows came to look on—cush cows, of course. Old King Cole lowered at them. All that beef!

" Who do these belong to ? " he grunted.

King Gullible beckoned and enquired.

" Who but the Marquis of Carabas," said the cowherd. " The kindest master in the world," he gagged.

" Atchoo! " said the coachman.

The carriage drove off.

" Man of substance," said King Gullible, brooding on it.

Presently they came to a field of waving colour. Peacocks! Hundreds of them. And each one with its tail spread.

" Mine," said King Gullible. " All mine," he gloated.

" Are you certain," asked Old King Cole.

" Of course I'm certain," said King Gullible. " Think I don't know my own peacocks ? "

A keeper, cap in hand, came up and bowed. " My master, the Marquis of Carabas, presents his compliments, sire, and will Your Majesty do him the honour of accepting a peacock ? "

Old King Cole looked darkly at King Gullible.

" Must have sold them," said King Gullible weakly.

They drove on with Old King Cole muttering " Trying to impress me," under his breath. He thought of something.

" Have you got an ogre ? "

King Gullible blanched. Why bring that one up ?

" What's an ogre ? " he said airily. " Any country might have an ogre. Sort of thing that keeps on happening all the time," he pointed out.

" Bad for tourist trade," said Old King Cole. " No good making an alliance with a country that gets no tourists. Never sell any postcards."

King Gullible changed the subject.

" This Marquis of Carabas," he said. " You know I've half a mind to give him the hand of my daughter—the Princess Thundercloud."

Now what had he heard about the Princess Thundercloud ?

" Ah yes," said Old King Cole. " She's got a taste for low company—ha, ha! "

King Gullible winced. " She's learnt her lesson," he said. " No more swineherds for her! And the Marquis of Carabas can't be called low. Look at the land he owns. I'll marry her off at once," he decided. " She's getting on my nerves," he added with a burst of candour.

Old King Cole was horrified. Was this the King with whom he was considering an alliance?

"You can't ignore tradition like that," he said. "He's got to prove his love first," he argued. "And survive it," he insisted.

"Certainly, certainly," said King Gullible, not at all pleased. "What sort of ordeal do you suggest?"

"Stands out a mile," said Old King Cole. "Let him kill your ogre for you."

"Um!" said King Gullible. He pondered. He saw an objection.

"Supposing he doesn't survive it?" he said.

"It would break my heart," snorted the merry old soul.

"Atchoo!" said the coachman.

The carriage trundled on.

*   *   *

A lovely summer's evening. Queen Mab is trying not to look astonished. For here is her son come to see her of his own accord.

"Remove Fanfaronade," she indicated.

The Fairies-in-Waiting carried the fainted Fairy out.

"Moother," said Prince Oberon, "I've got grand news for you. I want to wed."

"There's my own son," said Queen Mab, very much relieved. "I'm sure you will never regret your choice."

"Never," said Prince Oberon fervently. "Never. You should see her milk coo, moother."

Queen Mab took it in her stride. "I told you Titania would learn quickly, son."

"'Tain't Titania, moother," said Prince Oberon, who, whatever his limitations as conversationalist, at least came to the point quickly. "'Tis the Princess Dark Diamond."

"Really," said Queen Mab, and that was all. What a monarch!

"Ay, she's had a hard life, poor lass," said Oberon. "She's been telling me. But I'll make it oop to her," he promised.

Queen Mab decided to sit down. This needed thought. Do nothing in a hurry. Think of Florizel. No, don't think of Florizel.

"'Tis Princess Dark Diamond," gloated the besotted Oberon. "As purty as paint and as fine a housewife as any man could wish."

Queen Mab spoke.

" This person—this princess—you've known her quite a time, I suppose ? "

" Nay, moother, we met this morning," said Prince Oberon. " But it's this one and none other."

" I do not doubt her ability, son," said Queen Mab. " But what of her lineage ? "

" No call to worry about that, moother," said Oberon reassuringly. " She's royal all right. She told me so. Ay, she's had a hard life," he doted. " Both parents swallowed by the big bad woolf. Poor lass." He shook his head.

" And all records breathed on by a fire-breathing dragon, I suppose," said Queen Mab.

" How did you guess, moother ? " said Prince Oberon astounded. " But she's full of liveliness, and she tells the purtiest stories."

" I'm sure she does," said Queen Mab. She thought hard.

" Moother," said Prince Oberon, " how soon can we be wed ? " Queen Mab thought harder. She got there.

" I must meet your choice, my son, and welcome her to our Court. Where is she ? "

Prince Oberon beamed. " I luv you, moother," he said. " She be waiting outside. She was scared you wouldn't luv her. But I told her different." He chuckled.

" Bring her in," said Queen Mab quietly. " And she shall stay at the Palace with us so that I may get to know her better."

" I'll fetch her right now," said Prince Oberon. He made for the door. " You're not losing a son, moother. You're gaining a daughter."

He went.

" Peaseblossom," willed Queen Mab, " my smelling salts."

* * *

A lovely summer's evening.

" A nice strait you've got us into," snarled the miller's third son " Kill an ogre, indeed. Me! Why, I've never even killed a dragon."

" Leave it to me," said Puss. " I'll attend to everything. Just go on wearing the King's clothes and remember you're the Marquis of Carabas."

" Atchoo! " said the Marquis of Carabas.

* * *

Next morning the sun rose early. But no earlier than Queen Mab. Will her little scheme work?

Has that creature slept well?

The Queen put on her sensible dressing-gown. She summoned her Ladies-in-Waiting. They put on their sensible dressing-gowns. Accompanied by only three of them [" Moth will remain "] the Queen carried a cup of chocolate in her own hands to Fairy Dark Diamond's apartment.

Yes, she was sleeping soundly.

Naturally Queen Mab soon put a stop to this. Fairy Pease-blossom drew back the curtains with a swish, Fairy Mustard Seed pierced the canopy and shook the lily leaf, and Fairy Cobweb coughed.

Dark Diamond awoke. Heavens—it was the old hag herself! " Early to bed, early to rise," she was saying, and she'd caught her with her face cream on.

" Good morning, my dear," said Queen Mab. " Did you sleep well? "

" Beautifully, thank you, ma'am," said Dark Diamond. " So far," she could not resist adding.

" Were you quite comfortable? " asked the Queen.

" I love these old-fashioned beds," said Dark Diamond, making an effort. " Did you know," she said, " that I once slept in a bed-sitting-room in Bayswater and woke up to find myself folded inside a wall."

" I did not know," said Queen Mab icily.

False move! Under her breath Dark Diamond cursed.

" Still," said Queen Mab, " I trust you found it more comfortable here."

" I slept very well," said Dark Diamond. " Is that chocolate for me? Oh, thank you." She sipped it. Ugh!—sugar in it. Her poor curves. Still, delicious! She sipped again.

Was the Queen rubbing her hands? Just for a moment Dark Diamond thought so. She must have been mistaken.

" And now," said Queen Mab, " while you are breaking your fast I will tell you a little story."

Dark Diamond looked wary. The old hag was being nice to her. Why? But she must be nice back.

" Once upon a time," she prompted.

" Once upon a time," Queen Mab took up, " there lived an old Queen who believed in making sure of her facts and did not even take the weather for granted. She had an only son, and he was very dear to her, although he was impulsive."

Dark Diamond sipped her chocolate.

" Now the Queen was a widow and her dearest wish was that her son should marry a Princess—a real Princess," said Queen Mab.

Dark Diamond shot her a look. She decided to let it ride.

" A real Princess," Queen Mab repeated, " and lead as happy a married life as she had. For," said Queen Mab, " the Queen's marriage had been very happy."

" Very happy," said Fairy Cobweb sentimentally.

Queen Mab silenced her with a finger. " One night," she said, " there arose a fearful tempest."

" Fearful," said Fairy Cobweb. She shivered.

" The wind howled," said Queen Mab, raising an eyebrow. " And it thundered and it lightened . . ."

" And the rain poured down in torrents," said the Fairy Cobweb graphically.

" Cobweb," said Queen Mab, " you may leave us. So," she resumed, " while the tempest was at its height there was a knock at the front door. Who can that be ? said the old Queen and went herself to open it."

" I'll never do that when I'm Queen," said Dark Diamond.

" I don't suppose you will," said Queen Mab. " But the old Queen did. It was a Princess who was standing outside the door, and what with the wind and the rain she was in a sad condition. The water trickled from her hair . . ."

" And her clothes clung to her body," said Fairy Peaseblossom, carried away.

Queen Mab looked at her. She went.

" But," Queen Mab continued evenly, " she said she was a real Princess. Ah, thought the old Queen, that's what you say, but we shall soon find out. However, she said not a word of what she was going to do, and she welcomed her in, and she gave her supper, and she put her to sleep in her best bedroom."

Dark Diamond looked a little anxious. " Too kind, too kind," she said.

"It was a pleasure," said Fairy Mustard Seed. She put her hand over her mouth.

"In the morning," said Queen Mab, "the old Queen rose early, and, accompanied only by three Ladies-in-Waiting, none of whom spoke until they were spoken to"—she shot Mustard Seed a look— "she took the Princess a cup of chocolate with her own hands.

Dark Diamond's spoon dropped with a clatter. "Was it poisoned?" she asked.

"Good gracious no," said the Queen.

"She hadn't thought of that," said Fairy Mustard Seed.

"Mustard Seed," said Queen Mab. "You may leave us."

Now they were alone.

"As she sipped her chocolate," said Queen Mab, "the old Queen asked her guest a question. 'How did you sleep, my dear?' she said. "And the Princess looked at the Queen and there were dark circles of wakefulness under her eyes."

Dark Diamond listened intently.

"Oh, ma'am," said the Princess, "I did not close my eyes all night. I do not know what was in my bed but there was something pressing into my spine, and indeed, ma'am, I am black and blue all over." "And," said Queen Mab, "the old Queen kissed her, for now she knew that she was a real Princess."

"How?" asked Dark Diamond sharply.

Queen Mab looked round. Good heavens, she had dismissed her witnesses. She willed.

Peaseblossom . . .

Mustard Seed . . .

Cobweb . . .

They came hurrying in and ranged themselves expectantly behind their Queen.

"I'll tell you," said Queen Mab. "For when she had kissed the Princess she put her hand under the nineteen feather beds and the nineteen mattresses on which the Princess had slept and she pulled out a single dried pea. "I'm so sorry, my dear," she said. "I can't think how it got there."

"So, completely reassured, the old Queen sent for her son and the young couple were wed and lived happily ever after. For, my child," said Queen Mab, "you will agree that none but a real Princess could have had such a delicate sense of feeling."

" None," said Dark Diamond a little bleakly.

" To feel a dried pea under nineteen feather beds and nineteen mattresses," said Queen Mab, summing up, " was not this a lady of real delicacy ? "

" Indeed she was," said Dark Diamond. What else could she say ?

Queen Mab put her hand under one feather bed and one mattress. She pulled out a water-melon.

" Fanfaronade," she willed.   " Summon my son."

*   *   *

Serenading beneath his lady's window.   Got him first go!

*   *   *

Over the hills and far away and straight on till morning. Titania, riding barebacked on a white butterfly, made her way to the exile of Prince Florizel. Her heart was beating like a bumble bee, though how it managed this, sunk in the soles of her feet, she really didn't know. For she was not only thinking of a Name that was Forbidden, but actually going to see It, and if her mother ever found out she didn't know what she'd say.

The butterfly sighted a rose and touched down. It was a pink cabbage rose, and it started exploring it at once.

Titania jerked at the gossamer. " Oh, Dobbin," she pleaded, " do get up, or we'll never get to Morning till morning."

The butterfly looked wistfully at an unexplored recess. But it loved its mistress. It made a mental note to stop here on the way back and flew on till it came to an arum lily.

" Dobbin, please," said Titania.

The butterfly flew on. And on. And on.

*   *   *

On the green, in front of the Wheatsheaf and Wizard, a lephrechaun sat on an oaken stump reading a Doubloon Dreadful. As the butterfly drew up, he grunted and threw the book from him.

" Badly constructed," he said. " Spotted the murderer on the first page."

Titania looked at the title.

WHO KILLED COCK ROBIN ?

" I read that ages ago," she said.

But the butterfly was immersed.

The leprechaun looked at Titania. He was an Irish leprechaun. His eyes twinkled and charm radiated from him.

"The top of the morning to yez," he said. "Welcome to the Land of Kingdom Come."

"The top of the morning to you," said Titania, she dropped a curtsey, "and could you tell me where I may find," she looked round fearfully, "Prince Florizel," she finished in a conspiratorial hiss.

"Never heard of him," said the leprechaun with Irish gaiety. "None the worse for it," he pointed out with Irish complacency.

"But you must have heard of Prince Florizel," said Titania, unbelieving. "Nobody ever mentions him."

This pleased the leprechaun. "By St. Michael and all his angels," he exclaimed, "that makes as much sense as anything I've never heard. Yez might be an Irish Colleen yerself."

"But you must know Florizel," Titania insisted. "He's living happily ever after—has been for a long time—and never regrets his lost Kingdom."

Light dawned.

"Oh, you mean Scheherazade's sister's husband," said the leprechaun. "Hisself that opens the bazaar every year and never a smile on his face ever, not even when the three old men of Bosham put to sea in a boat," he went on with Irish loquacity. "No bigger than a cockleshell it was, and the waves as high as the hills of Connemara. Sure 'tisn't a very long story—might have been if the boat had been stronger—but if ye'd care to be taking a seat . . ."

"Prince Florizel," said Titania firmly. "Please, where does he live?"

The leprechaun stubbed his clay pipe over his shoulder. "Yonder," he said with Irish vagueness. "Left, past the Apple Tree and ask again."

"Thank you," said Titania. She detached the butterfly from the clue of the Tolling Bell, and the leprechaun helped her to mount.

"Happy landings to yez," said the leprechaun, "and could yez be lending me a fiver?" he finished with Irish charm.

Titania waved her wand and five pieces of gold fell into the leprechaun's outstretched hat.

"Beggorah!" said the leprechaun and vanished into the bar parlour.

Left, past the Apple Tree and ask again. . . .

"Does the road wind uphill all the way?" Titania enquired.

"Yes, to the very end," said the Ladybird.

" Can I get there by candlelight ? "

" That's a different road," said the Ladybird. She flew off like house on fire.

The road was long and dusty. Around a turn a man sat looking at a pile of stones.

" The top of the afternoon to you," said Titania, " and can I lend you a fiver and could you direct me to Scheherazade's sister's husband ? "

The man stood up. " I am he ? " he said. " What can I do for you ? "

Titania dropped a curtsey, as low as a blade of grass, as poised as though Wizard Sergeieff were supervising her. The man looked at her closely. It was a long time since anyone had made obeisance to him with anything but mockery.

"Who are you ? " he said. " And why are you here ? "

" I am Titania, daughter of the Widow Carabosse, and I have come to ask your advice, sire."

" My advice! " The man looked at her again. " Does my mother know you've come ? "

" Oh no, sire," said Titania. " Not even my mother."

" I see," said the man, and he seemed a little sadder, and a little older, and a little more lonely. " Then you are in some trouble ? "

" In great trouble, sire."

The man waved her to a primrose. He sat down beside her.

" What is his name ? "

What a nice question. How much time it saved.

" It is Prince Charming, sire," she said.

" Cinderella's husband," said the man. " I see. A mortal."

" And a married mortal." Titania avoided his eyes.

" I see," said the man again. " My poor child."

They fell silent.

" He sings beautifully," said Titania.

" I know," said the man.

They fell silent again.

" Then," said Titania, " your advice is for me to give him up ? "

" How can I tell you that," said the man. " You know what I have done."

Silence.

" And," said Titania.   " Would he be unhappy too ? "

" Yes, I'm afraid he would," said the man.   He patted her hand. The sun sank lower in the sky.

The man got up.   " Go home, my child," he said.   " Go home. Obey your mother and honour your Queen.   And don't think about me any more."

" And marry Prince Oberon," said Titania miserably.

" That too," said the man.   " Happiness comes in strange ways."

" You make it very difficult for me, sire," said Titania.

" It is difficult, yes," said the man.

Titania kissed his hand.   She turned to go.

" Titania," said the man, " tell me something.   Do they still plant wallflowers in the tiltyard on the south side ? "

" Yes, sire."

" And do they smell as I remember them ? "

" They do, sire."

" Go home child," said the man.   He put her on her butterfly and watched her flicker away into the distance.   Then he turned and trudged back to his castle.   He put on his uniform.   He went into his courtyard.

" Guard," said the man.   " Dismiss."

His occupation for the day was over.

He went back into the Palace.   He took off his uniform.   He gazed out of the window.

" Florizel," called a voice.   " Supper's ready.'

He went.

*   *   *

Meanwhile Puss had polished his boots and gone off to call on the Ogre, who stood in the way of the alliance between Gullible the Astute and Old King Cole, which in his opinion could not matter less, and, which in his view was most important, between his master, the Marquis of Carabas and the Princess Thundercloud, whom he had not yet seen.

The Ogre was very towering and very broad and very rich, and he received Puss as civilly as a rich man can, especially when he is an Ogre.

" G-rrr," he said.

" I could not pass this way without paying my respects to so well-known a citizen," said Puss.

He paid them.

The Ogre picked up a ring-purse marked " Respects" and dropped the coins into it. He became more affable.

" Siddown," he said, and went back to his supper.

" They say in the village," said Puss, " that you can turn yourself into animals."

" Wudge-wudge," said the Ogre, his mouth full.

" Of course," said Puss, " I don't believe such stories for a moment. Who would ? "

" Oh you don't, don't you ? " said Ogre. " G-rr-R-rrr." He was a lion.

Puss shinned up a marble pillar. Lions couldn't climb trees.

But this one could jump pretty high.

" They tell me in the village," said Puss between claws grabbing up at him, " that you can only change yourself into big animals. Stupid clumsy animals." He dodged.

" Oh, do they," said the lion. He was an Ogre again. He went back to his supper.

" Wonderful," said Puss sliding down thankfully. " Really wonderful. But if you could turn yourself into a small animal that," he gazed at the wudging hulk, " would be a miracle indeed. But, of course, you couldn't do it."

The Ogre stuck out a tremendous jaw. " You dare me ? "

" I dare you," said Puss, standing his ground. " I dare you to change yourself into a mouse."

The Ogre clasped his hands across his belly. " Ho, ho, ho," he roared. " Ho, ho, ho. Squeak." He was a mouse.

" Palooka! " said Puss. He pounced.

*　　　　*　　　　*

In sight of home the butterfly put on a spurt. One more delphinium and they'd be there.

In the bower window a light was burning. So mother was sitting up for her. Oh dear, she couldn't cope with mother to-night. Titania decided to fly in at her own lattice and face the resultant music in the morning. She slipped off her things in the dark, she omitted the rites laid down by Fairy Elizabeth Arden, she slipped gratefully into her lily. She was asleep.

Oh no, she wasn't.

" A nice hour to come home, I must say. Just like your father! Where have you been? I've been worrying and worrying. Never a thought for me. All you think of is pleasure, pleasure, pleasure. Get up and dress at once. The Queen has sent for you. What-are-you-going-to-wear?"

" The Queen?" said Titania. She sat up. She looked like a Fairy ghost. " Must I go now—this minute?"

" Of course you must go now. She said you were to go as soon as you arrived. It is not for me to criticise the Queen," said the Fairy Carabosse, " but it was a silly summons. Even the Queen should know that young girls these days come home at all sorts of hours. She's a mother herself, but she must have gone gaga. I hope you wake her up," she finished viciously.

Titania took out her plainest gown.

" At this hour of the night," snorted her mother. " No wonder you're looking worn out child. Come straight home the minute the Queen has finished with you and I'll send up your breakfast on a beach leaf to-morrow. You're wicked and ungrateful, and I don't know why I worry about you, but you'd better have your sleep out. I wonder," she mused, not for the first time, " what the Queen wants with you at this hour?"

" My butterfly is very tired," said Titania. " It seems a shame to wake her."

" Borrow my broomstick," snapped the Fairy Carabosse.

*   *   *

In her boudoir, her Court dismissed, Queen Mab, the sensible dressing-gown well in evidence, waited to receive the Widow Carabosse's daughter. She picked up her mirror. How badly the child sat a broomstick—not that it mattered now. Titania, however touching, was no match for her son. That was certain. She had disobeyed her Queen. It wouldn't do. Certainly not. Out of the question.

Still, better than Dark Diamond. She waved the thought away.

Her mother would have to be told. Queen Mab's mouth firmed. That would be an unpleasant interview. But unpleasant or not, told she must be. Though not till the spell was lifted, thought Queen Mab, diplomat uppermost. Certainly not until the spell that hung over little Aurora was well and truly lifted and for good and all.

And after that she would pass a new law, compelling all Fairies to submit their spells, in triplicate, for the royal approval and sanction before uttering them.

There was a timid knock at the door.

" Come in, Titania," said Queen Mab.

Titania looked at her Queen. She was almost too frightened to curtsey.

" Sit down, child," said the Queen. " Have a glass of milk. You must be very tired after your long journey."

Did she know ?

" I'm so glad you gave your butterfly a rest."

She did know.

" Forgive me, ma'am," said Titania. " I had to go."

" It is done," said Queen Mab. " There is nothing more to be said about it. Try to finish your milk."

Titania gulped.

" And did it help you, child ? " said the Queen. " Do you know now what you mean to do ? "

" No," said Titania. " It is all more difficult than it was."

Pretty manners. And, save to her mother, of course, truthful. Queen Mab decided to speak her mind.

" Give him up, child," she said. " Take an older woman's advice. Give the mortal up. Marry one of your own kind, even if he be only an honest elf."

Did this mean she wasn't to marry Oberon any more ? Or didn't it ? What difference!

" I don't know, ma'am," said Titania. " I'll try to do as you say, but I don't know."

" That's a good, dear girl," said Queen Mab. " Try, Titania, try hard. And now, go home. Obey your mother and do not disobey your Queen again."

" That's what he said," said Titania.

" Did he ? " said Queen Mab. She was silent.

Titania put down her glass. " Finish it up," said Queen Mab " Every drop . . . that's right. And now good night, Titania, and," she smiled a little sadly, " you're a good girl not to have vexed me with a scene."

Titania prepared to withdraw. She curtsied and backed a few steps. But the Queen had not quite done with her.

" Titania ? " she said.

" Yes, ma'am."

" How did he look ? " asked Queen Mab.

*   *   *

" Well," said the Fairy Carabosse, " what did the Queen want ? Great heavens, girl—What have you done to my broomstick ? "

" I'm so tired, mother," said Titania. " Please can I go to bed ? "

" But the Queen—What did she want ? "

" She was kind," said Titania. " So kind. I can't tell you any more."

She flew up the stairs.

" Tinny-minny-poof! " said the Fairy Carabosse.

*   *   *

Chop. Chop. Chop. But Chin-chin Chinaman was nowhere in sight. Only seven little nigger boys piling up the firewood for the cold winter nights to come. The stable yard rang with the merry rhythm of their axes and chips flew like snowflakes when Mother Goose turns her mattress.

Chop. Chop. Chop.

" Dat's right, chillun," encouraged Uncle Rochester. " Chop yo' kindlin' so dat dese old bones k'n warm theyselves come the blizzard of Oz. Swing ho! Swing ho! " he encouraged.

Six little niggers swung-ho, wielding their choppers with gusto. But the seventh little nigger boy had got hold of an immense pick-axe and kept swinging it right above his head.

" Eusebius," said Uncle Rochester with horror, " put dat instrument of de debil down. Or," he shook a finger, " you sho' will cut yo'self in half."

"What, me! " said the seventh little nigger boy, staggering stubbornly. . . .

CHAPTER IX   Can You Keep a Secret?

Boxing Night Land agog! Citizens running hither and thither, breaking into song, and making arrangements a full fortnight ahead. And the only man who was miserable was old Miser

Screwball, who had spent a great deal of money on a new mattress guaranteed to last a hundred years.

For rumour had it that the Fairy Carabosse was going to lift the spell and the Princess Aurora could hack herself to pieces without endangering any of them.

How nice to be living once more with only ogres, witches, state magicians and other normal perils around you.

"Hurrah for the Fairy Carabosse," they shouted.

And they hoisted triumphant banners to welcome her.

★   ★   ★

"Well, Peaseblossom," said Queen Mab, "by this time next hey-presto, the spell will be lifted and Boxing Night Land will be able to sew freely once more."

"All the more glory to you, ma'am," said the Fairy Peaseblossom.

"And yet, Peaseblossom, I am not happy. I am not happy at all. I know," said Queen Mab, "that a Queen can do no wrong, but letting the Widow Carabosse lift the spell and then not keeping my part of the bargain, would you call it . . ." She fought off the word.

"Sharp practice ?" said the Fairy Peaseblossom. "Oh no, ma'am. Just diplomacy. The dear King would have been proud of you."

"Would he ?" said Queen Mab, much relieved. "You're a good fairy, Peaseblossom."

Peaseblossom's ears went pink with pleasure. "Thank you, ma'am. And it serves the Widow Carabosse right, ma'am, for defying you."

"So it does," said Queen Mab. "You are right, Peaseblossom. There is nothing on my conscience."

"Nothing, ma'am," said the Fairy Peaseblossom firmly.

"I shall tell the Fairy Carabosse in my own good time," Queen Mab mused. "And meanwhile, Peaseblossom, remember—not a word to a mackerel."

"Not a syllable to a salmon," said Peaseblossom virtuously.

But the unaccustomed praise had gone to Fairy Peaseblossom's head.

D

" The Queen said I was a good fairy," she boasted to the envious Fairy Moth.

But, of course, such a claim had to be substantiated. How had it come about ? What had Peaseblossom done to merit it ?

" Remember," said the Fairy Peaseblossom, a delicious half hour later. " Not a word to a mackerel."

" Not a sentence to a sardine," swore the Fairy Moth.

. . . " And remember," said Fairy Moth. " Not a word to a mackerel."

" Not a syllabub to a cinnamon," wheezed Mother Goose . . .

" Not a hint to a hound," cackled Old Mother Hubbard.

" Not a tittle to a tattle," promised Tinkabell.

" Not a syllogism to a spratling," chuckled Puck.

" Not a breath to a candlelight," they were vowing all over Fairyland.

Four o'clock by the dandelion clock. It must be tea-time ? Fairy Ann's pantry was full. Everybody was talking. But at a table in a corner a couple hardly spoke at all.

Titania and Prince Charming.

Titania was pale and very sad. Prince Charming looked a little sulky. (A bottomless well and this on the top of it!)

All around them the babble swirled.

> " Good neighbour, I pray,
> What's the news of to-day ? "

> " They say a balloon
> Has gone up to the moon."

" A balloon! " they said. " All the way to the moon," they said. " O-oooh! " they said.

Puck flew in. He perched on a table, whispered something, put his finger to his lips and flew out.

" Not a mumble to a mare's nest," called the table after him.

And suddenly Fairy Ann's pantry was filled with a babble of

mackerel, salmon and sardines. It reached the silent table in the corner, swirled round it, and passed on.

"Did you hear that?" asked Prince Charming, suddenly hopeful again. "Queen Mab won't let you marry Oberon."

"I knew that yesterday," said Titania. "But I still can't marry you."

It was The End.

. . . "Not a whisper to the Chitling!"

As one head the whole room turned and looked at Titania.

"Is this thing true?" The Fairy Carabosse had caught Puck by his pointed ears and was tugging them alternately. "Is this thing true, you varmint?"

"See this wet, see this dry," said Puck, "it's true enough." He hit the floor and rubbed his ears.

"So she thinks she can do this to me," said the Fairy Carabosse. "The hag! The witch! The harridan! The double-faced, double-toothed, double-twister! The cheat! The two-timer!" She stopped for breath. "The cradle-snatcher! The widow-sneaker! The orphan grinder!"

Puck began to enjoy himself. This was more the sort of thing he had expected when he brought the news.

"The old bag," he suggested.

"The old bag," said the Fairy Carabosse gratefully. "The old basket! The windmill! The corkscrew Queen! But I'll show her! I'll show her!"

She paced the room.

"How?" asked Puck.

The Fairy Carabosse clawed the air, performing an evil spinning motion.

"The Princess Aurora has been awake long enough. I'm going to put her to sleep. I must act immediately. I'm going to draw that brat's blood with my own hands if it's the last thing I do. If the Queen thinks I'm going to remove the spell—she's crazy. And if you tell anybody," she rounded on Puck, "I'll claw your heart out."

"You know me," said Puck, hurt. "Not a hint to a herring!"

*   *   *

"Not a prattle to a prawn," promised the herring.

"Not a line to a lobster," swore the starfish.

"Not an inkling to an octopus," vowed the turtle.

"Not a mention to a mermaid," boomed King Neptune. He surfaced.

"Not a murmur to a molecule," beamed the Man in the Moon.

"Not a buzz to a bee." The birds of the air darted about.

And in Fairy Ann's pantry, though many people have left to spread the news they had already heard, many more had come in to tell the news they had just received.

"Your mother is putting the Princess Aurora to sleep," said Prince Charming. "Did you ever?" And was there just a hint of pleasure in his downcast demeanour at the prospect of another's misfortune?

There was. Never a quick thinker, Prince Charming had not yet worked out that he himself wouldn't be around much for the next hundred years or so.

But Titania got there quicker. "Never mind, darling," she said. "You will wake up every bit as young as you are now."

"Me!" said Prince Charming. The thought sank in. "My God!"

Put to sleep—and kept there! And here was Titania toying with a tea-leaf as though nothing was about to happen. He turned on her.

"Well!" he demanded. "Aren't you going to do something?"

"What can I do?" said Titania. "What does it matter?" She looked out of the window, past a hundred years, and on and on into a Charmingless future. "Nothing matters now," she reminded him.

Prince Charming did not agree. "I must flee the country at once," he said. He rushed out of the tea-shop and jumped onto his horse.

It was a roundabout.

"Not a whisper to a whirligig," wheezed the Wizard.

"Not an ogle to an ogre," cackled the old wife.

"Not a sibilant to a spider," said the seventh dwarf.

"Not a wink to a Nod," vowed King Gullible.

"Me! Never!" said Fairy Moth. "You know I'd never tell a soul."

"Oh dear, oh dear, oh dear," moaned Fairy Peaseblossom. She wrung her hands.

"Good gracious," said Queen Mab. "I must act immediately."

CHAPTER X   **A Matter of Time**

How long is immediately? If Einstein had lived in Fairyland he would never have worked the thing out. Roughly speaking, it comes somewhere between the twinkling of an eye and a flash in the pan, and it is well known that these cover anything from the bending of a twig to eternity. Thus it often happens that a seventh son setting out on a day's journey comes back to find his bride's wicked stepmother dead and buried and his new-born babe an old man with a beard. And he takes it in his stride. On the other hand, Puck can put a girdle round the earth in forty minutes, while Sindbad sails the seven seas twice over and comes home to find his supper still simmering. As for a forest it can grow up in no time at all, and, technically speaking, doesn't count.

For Time in Fairyland is as broad as it is long.

And so it follows that when Queen Mab acted immediately she paused only to change her gown, re-do her hair, select her jewels, enquire after her subjects [. . . "And what were you thinking of, Moth, to allow the Farmer's Wife to possess a carving knife?" . . .] change her mind, change her gown again, send Fairy Fanfaronade to fetch Prince Oberon, urge her to keep on looking, and take counsel of her soul before setting out on her journey to stop the Fairy Carabosse wreaking her vengeance : When the Fairy Carabosse acted immediately, she just straddled her broomstick and whizzed into the sky ; while to Titania the same space of time meant but yesterday when she had first met Prince Charming and the eternity since this afternoon when she had parted from him for ever ; and to the vertiginous Prince Charming, going up and down, and round and round and round on his roundabout while the steam organ warbled "Boomps-a-Daisy" and scalded him each time he passed the exhaust pipe, immediately meant the first possible moment the damn thing stopped. And while all these immediatelys were taking place in the same jiffy the Princess Aurora was passing her summers like lightning, and had romped through her schooldays before anyone could tell her they were the happiest days of her life, and was now sixteen years old and ripe for marriage, and all the suitors due to court her at the garden party in Act 2 the next instant were trying frantically to get themselves born in the nick of time.

It's really quite simple when you understand it.

And anyway, the citizens of Boxing Night Land, though the outlook for them had changed from ' Set Fair ' to ' All is Lost ' before they could say Jack Robinson knew full well what was to happen to them in two ticks. Their doom was upon them. In a brace of shakes they had cancelled their arrangements for yesterday—or was it to-morrow ?

Can you tell me the time, please ?

But though the Banners welcoming the Fairy Carabosse have been torn down in less time than it takes to tell, it is Aurora's sixteenth birthday, and the Garden Party in honour of it must go on. For the audience has paid its subscription to the lending library and is entitled to its 82,000 words produced in complete conformity with the authorized war economy standard in longer, far longer than the darkest hour before dawn.

And so in the Courtyard of the glittering Palace, four little kitchenmaids are knitting like anything. They had started this now once again permissible occupation the moment it had been permitted, and now that it was once again forbidden they had to finish in a trice or there would be trouble.

How soon is a trice ? Well, we can't go into that now. But you can take it that it is a great deal too soon, for here is the hedgehog, his spikes virtuously clipped again before they had properly started growing, catching them at it.

" Miserable wenches," he said. " Woe is you. For now you must be put to death before the sands run out."

The four kitchenmaids fell on their knees in next to no time.

" Spare us," they cried. " Oh, spare us."

But before you could bat an eyelid, the King and Queen appeared.

"Boil them in oil as the crow flies," he ordered, a muddled metaphor, but the best his exhausted authors could do for him right away.

"Spare us," cried the kitchenmaids. "Oh, spare us."

"Don't boil them in oil," said the Queen. "Just boil them," she suggested.

The King could refuse her nothing. "So be it," he said.

And the maidens fell on their knees again and thanked him for, as everybody knows, it takes three and a half minutes to boil a maiden, hardboiled or not, and everybody would be asleep for a whole hundred years before you could put a saucepan on.

* * *

Not in the bat! Not in the belfry! Not in the cuckoo's nest!

Where should she look now? Fairy Fanfaronade shook the cocoanut tree. Only cocoanuts came down.

Dangerous.

"Hurry," Queen Mab was willing her. "I must start immediately."

In the stable-yard the coachman, who had been a wicked uncle and was now a good frog, was harnessing the Unicorns. He was in a filthy temper.

The frog he would a wooing go.

And now he couldn't. All very well telling him to bring the coach round before the cows came home, but there were twenty-four hoofs to silver and six horns to polish. All that rubbing up! He spat.

In the royal room the royal foot was a'tapping.

"Cobweb," said Queen Mab, "this tiara is too tight and my pearls are choking me. Fetch Fairy Cartier."

. . . In Bond Street. In the Rue de la Paix. On Fifth Avenue. How the Fairy Cartier had got around! . . .

"I must hurry or I will be late," said Queen Mab. "Pease-blossom," she directed, "take a look in my mirror and tell me where the Widow Carabosse is now."

Fairy Peaseblossom peered. " Oh, ma'am," she said, " she's started."

" Shoot a star after her wherever she is," said Queen Mab, " and see to it that it knocks her off her broomstick."

*   *   *

A certain star shot madly from its sphere. But fast as it shot it couldn't catch up with Carabosse's broomstick.

Over hill, over dale, on and on, left by Banbury Cross, right by Gerrard's Cross, passing Charing Cross, on and on beyond Babylon, threading the mountains of the moon with the star panting behind her. Bringing the birds of the air and the beasts of the field to gaze at her wicked pilgrimage and causing three monkeys in a tree to break the habits of a lifetime.

See No Evil has opened the chinks in his fingers and is peering at the wickedness flying through the night. Hear No Evil has taken his hands from his ears to listen to the eerie swish of the broomstick in the sky. And Speak No Evil has quite forgotten what he stands for and is jabbering like anything. . . .

Time was flying. But Queen Mab was stationary. For anxious as the occasion was, the cares of a Kingdom could not be ignored.

" Moth," she indicated, " what is Scheherazade telling the Sultan to-night ? "

" Er," said Fairy Moth. . . .

*   *   *

It is the Princess Aurora's sixteenth birthday.

Every villager in the village has been out since the crack of dawn, gathering wild flowers in the meadows, which, as everyone knows, grow plentifully in Fairyland. Gay, sentimental, enchanting, and sometimes enchanted flowers, such as love-me, love-me-not, ring-a-roses, shepherd's purple, love-lies-bleeding, forget-me-not, forsake-me-never, please-come-back, sweet William, pussy-willow, buttercups, butter-fingers, cowslips, lion-tawny, dandelion, elder-berries, younger berries (and both in blossom), London pride and Canterbury bells, roses red, violets blue, and orchids all the colours of the rainbow, fair daffodils, pale-hands-I-loved, the primrose by the river's brim, and many, many others.

At the moment the Courtyard is smothered in them and there is scarcely room for the *corps de ballet* to dance an ensemble between the petals. And still the villagers come in, beaming under blossoms, until great banks surround the King and Queen, and you can only see the tips of their crowns above the foliage. And still the flowers come, and still the Conductor goes on waving his baton. Just like morning in Covent Garden Market or night at Covent Garden Opera.

In the vegetable garden, their posies clutched in their hot little paws, six little nigger boys have got themselves distracted. Picking flowers was a pretty occupation, and giving dem to de Princess might make dem all rich niggahs some day as Uncle Rochester dun promised, but in the meantime it was fascinating to watch the bees hiving. Specially dat little one at the bottom dat couldn't quite make it.

"Now den, chillun," said Uncle Rochester, "you dun forget your duty, your ambition, and "—his eyes grew large—" de Book."

"Six little niggah boys playing wid a hive," he intoned.

"A bumble bee dun stung one and den . . ."

"Dey was five," chanted the six little nigger boys naughtily.

Uncle Rochester wagged a finger.

"'Tis mighty dangerous to watch de bumble bees," he said, "but 'tis mighty more dangerous to inderfere wid dem. Oh no, you doesn't, Rastus!" And he smacked the little black paw of the sixth little nigger boy.

"Oh, dat's all right," said the sixth little nigger boy. "It likes being stroked. See! He stuck out a finger. . . ."

Then there were five.

It is the Princess Aurora's sixteenth birthday.

The Courtyard has quite overflowed with buttercups, daisies, and, of course, pansies. And now it is presently and soon the Princess Aurora must arrive and dance and the scene move inexorably to its climax.

But before this can happen, a young man in a polka-dotted dressing-gown is seen to cross the stage with his back to the players, and, without looking at her, address a little maid, who is turning over flowers in a flurry of desperation and howling her head off.

" Stop snivelling," he said.   " Explain yourself, little girl."

The little girl hiccoughed.

" Lucidly," said the young man in the polka-dotted dressing-gown.   " Lucidly," he insisted.

And now the Queen beckoned him over.

" What is the matter with Little Miss Muffet ? " she asked. " Why is she crying ? "

" All wrong," said the King.   " Can't have blotchy faces on a birthday.   Couldn't be more irregular."

" Well," began the young man in the polka-dotted dressing-gown confidently, " she's lost the tisket . . . the tasket . . ." His confidence ebbed.   Would he never rise above the idiom ?

" The tuffet," suggested the Queen.

" The basket," said the King.

*   *   *

It is Aurora's sixteenth birthday.

Six stately unicorns are pacing along a rainbow.   It is not the shortest way round, but the prettiest.   Habit dies hard.

. . . Not in the last resort . . .

Indeed, Queen Mab is travelling alone.

" Hurry, good Gilpin," she says, " or I shall be late."

But up on his box the coachman refuses to let himself be rattled. More haste, less speed, he reflects and he reins in his beauties.   No use hurrying a unicorn!

Time merges and Mr. Disney's young men are drawing like anything to keep up with it.

Here is the rainbow, all the colours of the rainbow, bridging the day with the unicorns high-stepping along it.   And here is midnight with the Fairy Carabosse astride her broomstick, riding madly through it, with certain stars shooting wildly all round her, missing her by hair's-breadths and tossing her broomstick like a shuttlecock

in a tempest. And as she journeys she sings a witches' song to the
wild winds :

> Tremble and go!
> First day day shiver and burn.
> Tremble and quake!
> Second day shiver and learn.
> Tremble and die!
> Third day never return!

A star whizzed by. Puck jumped from it on to the broomstick.
" Going my way ? " he asked chattily.
" I am the messenger of doom," said the Widow Carabosse
above herself. " I come to do justice to a defaulting Queen. My
staff is a righteous scourge and my mantle the mantle of sleep."
" Oh, come off it," said Puck.
But it was he who found himself dropping through space with
his heels in the air.
" My mantle of sleep," gloated Carabosse. " Let the Queen
dare to take it from me." She spat at a shooting-by star. " The
Queen and all her artillery." She spat again.
Ssschwish! A star passed over her.
Ssschwish! A star curled round her.
" My mantle of sleep," screamed Carabosse defiantly. She took
evasive action.

           *   *   *

It is Aurora's sixteenth birthday.
Prince Charming is spending it going up and down and up and
down and round and round and round on his roundabout. And
he never did care much for fun fairs, anyway!
" When, oh when," he cried with no consideration for the
children at the matinée, " will this bloody thing stop! "
" Daisy, Daisy, give me your answer do," ground out the steam
organ to the heaving, rotating, and unanswering sky.

           *   *   *

It is Aurora's sixteenth birthday.
And here she is standing in the portico of the Courtyard and
looking just like Margot Fonteyn.
The King and Queen are beaming with pride. She may not
have obedience but, by heaven, she's got school!

What is the conductor doing? How much longer does he think she can hold it? Ah, he's started!

With a sigh of relief the little Aurora sails through her adage as easy as grant-three-wishes and she takes the roses from her suitors with radiance and rapture, for all the world as though there were no single flower in the Courtyard. Or is it relief at having once again come through safely? Whichever it is, she has kissed the roses, and, in a beautiful arabesque, as natural as you please, given them to Mama.

" For me," says Mama, with as much pleasure as though she were not already banked in by them. Or is it relief that those boys in the *corps de ballet* didn't do so badly after all? Have to take what you can get these days!

And now for the variations. Aurora skips through them, as gaily as though they were a bunch of daisies. And so absorbed is the audience that they have not noticed that heaven has been raining certain stars, and that a black crouching figure has installed herself down by the parsley beds and is performing evil spinning motions in the air.

The Fairy Carabosse has arrived to fulfil her curse.

No one has noticed her save one.

The Princess Aurora.

And before anyone has realized what she is about she has danced over to the old crone.

" What are you doing, my good woman ? " she asked with all the charm of sixteen years at Sadler's Wells.

" I am spinning," said the Fairy Carabosse.

" Ooh," said the Princess Aurora, " can I try ? "

And even as the King and Queen arose and the entire Courtyard ran towards her crying ' Stop! ' she tried.

The Fairy Carabosse made a magic pass. Instantly the Princess Aurora pricked her finger.

And she looked at the red bead of blood and was frightened.

" Mother," she cried, and danced towards her.

" Blood," cried the Queen. And she tried to comfort her weeping daughter, but the words were difficult to find.

" There's nothing to be frightened of," she said. " Mother is here."

And even as she spoke the Princess Aurora reeled, sank to the ground and was asleep. All in two shakes of a cow's tail.

"Kill that cow," bellowed the King in a fury.

There was an evil cackle overhead. The Fairy Carabosse was legging it on her broomstick.

*   *   *

But at the seaside the world had none of these troubles. The sun shone on the sands, the sea was beautifully warm and smooth, and here was that dear old nigger with his naughty piccaninnies.

"I sho' got youse chillun' away jest in time," panted Uncle Rochester, "tho' if you was to sleep for a hundred years dis po' trash sho' wouldn't dun have so many worries." And he turned for sympathy to an old salt, smoking an old pipe, and leaning against an old boat.

"Nice day for a sail, sir," said the Old Salt.

Uncle Rochester looked the other way.

"Now, youse chillun' lie on de sands and don't youse gimme no mo' trouble."

"We want to go to sea, Uncle Rochester," said the four little nigger boys.

"No mo' wilfulness," said Uncle Rochester. "I had enough of yo' disobedience for one day. Poo' Rastus and dat bumble bee," he reminded them. "And pooh Ebenezer going in for de law and getting into Chancery on his way back just as though I never read de Book to him."

"We want to go to sea," said the four little nigger boys inexorably. They clambered into the boat.

Uncle Rochester turned to the Old Salt.

"Any herrings in dat sea?" he asked sternly.

"Only red ones," said the boatman, soothingly.

He pushed off.

*   *   *

Where does the rainbow end? To-night it is in the Courtyard of the glittering Palace of Boxing Night Land where Queen Mab is alighting from her carriage to find a group of grief surrounding the sleeping Princess.

"Too late!" she said. "Too late!" she repeated. It seemed as though she couldn't believe it.

"And she's never been late in her life before," said Titania, sweetly sorrowful.

" Except for her coronation," said Dark Diamond, sorrowfully sweet. She did not like Queen Mab very much since the episode of the melon.

Queen Mab surveyed the scene : the heartbroken parents, the weeping court, the stricken villagers, the withering flowers, and the Princess Aurora sleeping as peacefully as if she had been born yesterday.

" Good people," she said, " do not despair, for I am here to help you. The Princess shall sleep for a hundred years and you shall all sleep with her, and when you wake up everything shall be as it was."

The hedgehog looked hopeful.

" And you, my dear," Queen Mab turned to Titania, " shall have this little kingdom in your charge. For "—she waved her wand—" all this is no fault of yours, and I am sure that you will guard it well. I am not angry with you, child, but as for your mother . . ." Her mouth tightened.

Puck chuckled. Queen Mab looked round. Puck dodged. Queen Mab frowned at the hedgehog.

" And now," she said, " carry the Princess into the Palace. Carry her gently and settle her comfortably upon her couch of white satin, and," she advised sensibly, " settle yourselves comfortably too."

And as they carried the Sleeping Princess into the Palace, Queen Mab waved her wand and they all fell a-yawning. And she waved her wand again and their heads drooped. And she waved it a third time and the green trees grew all round the Palace, and all round the grounds, and all round Boxing Night Land.

And the curtain came down.

INTERMISSION

There was an old woman who was sweeping out her house, and she found a little crooked sixpence. So she went to market and she bought a pig and on the way back they came to a stile. And the pig was obstinate and he sat down and he refused to jump over it.

But the old woman was not easily discouraged. She had paid a crooked sixpence and she was going to get her money's worth. So she went a little further and she met a dog.

"Dog! Dog! bite pig; pig won't go over stile, and I shan't get home till morning."

But the dog shook his head. Every dog had his day, and this was his.

So the old woman went still further and she met a stick.

"Stick! Stick! Beat dog. Dog won't bite pig, pig won't go over stile, and I shan't get home till morning."

But the stick wouldn't.

So the old woman went a lot too far and she met a fire that refused to burn the stick that wouldn't beat the dog, who wouldn't bite the pig, who wouldn't go over the stile. "Oh dear," said the old woman, "I shan't get home till morning."

And she went on, and on, and on, and on, and on. And she met a lot of potential assistance and she asked ever so many favours. But the water wouldn't quench the fire, the ox wouldn't drink the water, the butcher wouldn't kill the ox, the rope wouldn't hang the butcher, the rat wouldn't gnaw the rope, and there seemed no chance at all of getting home before morning.

And still the old woman went on, her mouth set in a very determined line. And after a time she met a cat. And from that moment her prospects improved. For the cat did not turn down her plea on sight, as the others had done, but made a condition.

"If," said the cat, "you'll fetch me milk from yonder cow"—he pointed—"I'll kill the rat."

So away went the old woman to the cow. It was a cush cow.

"Tell you what," said the cow, "if you will go to yonder haystack," she flicked a tail, "and fetch me a handful of hay, I'll let down my milk."

And as soon as the cow had eaten the hay, she gave the old woman the milk and away went the old woman with the milk in a saucer to the cat.

And as soon as she had lapped up the milk, the cat began to kill the rat; the rat began to gnaw the rope; the rope began to hang the butcher; the butcher began to kill the ox; the ox began to drink the water; the water began to quench the fire; the fire began to burn the stick ; the stick began to beat the dog ; the dog began to bite the pig ; and the little pig, in a whale of a fright, jumped over the stile.

" And about time too," said the old woman.

They trudged on.

But presently they came to another stile.

The old woman sighed and picked up a pitchfork.

" Okay," said the pig.   " I'll come quietly."

CHAPTER XI   **Where the Snow Falls**

Now while the Princess Aurora lay sleeping and the Court of Boxing Night Land slumbered all around her ; while the neighbouring states were shrugging their shoulders and settling down to wrangle with one another ; while Queen Mab ruled over her Kingdom and the Fairy Carabosse bit her nails ; while Titania devoted herself to good works and Dark Diamond to sulks, and Puck was frankly bored with them both ; while Prince Oberon could never be found anywhere ; while Fairy Moth was on the verge of another indiscretion, and Gullible the Astute was wondering who to believe next ; while Jack Sprat, Jack and the Beanstalk, and Jack and Jill were behaving much in the way expected of them ; in short, while eighty-seven years passed like a flash and time stood still, over the hills and much further than that, in the great white land where it was always snowing, there lived a Moujik who had three sons.   As this was not enough he had four more.   That made seven.   He counted them.   Almost he might have been William Wordsworth.

And they all grew up with hearty appetites.

The first son was strong and clever.   The second son was not quite so strong, and nothing like so clever.   And when it came to the seventh son he was just simple.

" Aie," said the Moujik, " you'd better go out and seek your fortune."

" That's right," said the brothers.   " Seek your fortune, and when you've found it come back.   Not before," they insisted.

But Mamoushka wept and said, " What will become of him ? "

And Papoushka said : " He is the seventh son. Nothing but good can come to him. It is the tradition."

And hearing this Ivan brightened. And he rolled off the stove he had been lying on all his life, and he packed away the curd-cake his mother had baked for him, and he went out into the great white world, and the snow fell softly down.

Now the first good that came to him was a snowdrift. And when he had struggled out of that, he was very tired. And he came to the cottage in which lived the three sillies, and he knocked at the door.

" I am Ivan, the seventh son of Ivan, the seventh son of Ivan," he announced, " and I am on my way to seek my fortune."

" Come in," said the man, who had opened the door. " We are in great distress, but come in." And he shut the door against the snow and he began to weep.

And his good wife came hobbling in, and she wished Ivan the compliments of the season, and she gave him hot tea from the samovar. And then she sat down and cried too.

And presently Katya, their daughter, came in, and she was crying already. And after a while Ivan noticed this.

" You are weeping," he said. " God be with you." And he passed his plate for more rye-bread, for he had a hearty appetite.

" Alas," said Papoushka, " we weep because we are sad, and there is no rye-bread because Mamoushka has not baked any. For our Katya has lost her sweetheart and is inconsolable."

Ivan looked at Katya. " You are plump enough," he said. " Why did it happen ? "

" He said we were silly," said Papoushka.

" He said he was going out into the world to find three sillier people than we are," said Mamoushka.

" He said that if he could find three sillier people than we are he would come back and marry me," sobbed Katya.

" And this he will never do," said Papoushka with deep satisfaction. " It is impossible." And they all three fell a-weeping afresh.

I will never make my fortune here, thought Ivan. But he stayed on for it was nearly supper-time.

" Katya," said Mamoushka, " go down to the cellar and bring up the Kvas. For when we have drunk Kvas we will be merry."

And she cheered up at the very thought and slapped her thighs and laughed heartily.

And Papoushka cheered up too, and sang Otchi Chernia.

And Katya said there were other fish in the sea and went to the cellar tossing her plaits.

And Papoushka finished Otchi Chernia, and he sang Gaida Troika. And then he sang Two Guitars and the Volga Boatman, and Ivan sang with him. And Mamoushka said, " What is Katya doing all this time in the cellar ? " And she went to look.

And they sang Snegouritchka and the Song of the Flea, and nearly the whole of Boris Goudonov.

And the snow beat gently against the window panes.

And still Katya had not come up with the Kvas. And Mamoushka had not come up with Katya.

" We will see what has happened to them," said Papoushka.

And they went downstairs singing In Cellar Deep.

And deep in the cellar they stopped singing. For there was the Kvas running all over the floor and there sat Katya and Mamoushka clasped in each other's arms, crying bitterly.

" What is the matter with you ? " asked Papoushka astounded, for his singing had cheered him up very much indeed.

" It is a tragedy," said Katya. " A terrible tragedy." And she pointed to a hatchet which hung upon a grimy beam on the ceiling. " One day," she said, " it will fall to the ground, and I am powerless to prevent it."

" That is dangerous," said Ivan. " For if it falls on you it will kill you."

" But no," said Papoushka still cheerful. " For," he pointed out cleverly, " it may fall when you are not there. Also," he added, " it may not fall for many years to come."

" That is what is so terrible," said Mamoushka. She raised a tear-stained face. " For in the meantime our Katya will have married and she will have a son—such a strong handsome son, and so clever, just like you, my darling, just like you." And she fell to crying again.

" And what is there sad about that ? " asked Ivan. " My father had seven sons, but I cannot remember that he cried about any of them. Sometimes," he admitted, " the sons cried, but that was for a different reason."

" You do not understand," said Katya. " When my son grows up he will be thirsty. And," she caught her breath, " he will come down to the cellar."

" He will come down to the cellar," said Mamoushka, " and he will stand under the hatchet and . . ."

" Aie! " said Papoushka. He burst into tears.

*   *   *

While Ivan is taking his leave of the three sillies and setting out again to seek his fortune in the great white world ; while the three sillies have wiped their eyes, sung songs, and fallen to weeping afresh ; while Ivan's father has taken his place on the stove to lie there for the rest of his life while his six progressively less clever sons keep him ; while Mamoushka is cooking the supper and vowing ' I loved him best of all ' ; while the six brothers are planning how to spend the fortune Ivan will bring back and have fallen a-quarrelling, and while the snow falls gently down, the Fairy Carabosse has stopped biting her nails and gone into action.

Time, among other things, is a great healer. In Fairyland, as well as in other places, this was well known. And in time Titania would forget Prince Charming, and in time Queen Mab would remember Titania's good manners and forget her mother's bad ones. And in time all might yet be well. But meantime Prince Oberon had fallen in love again—this time a blonde—which threatened to spoil everything. Something had to be done. So Carabosse locked the blonde in a castle in the air.

Now the blonde was called Rapunsel, and her hair was the colour of flax. And there was an awful lot of it. And when she let it down it reached to the ground and a lot further. The Fairy Carabosse couldn't think of everything. She had thought of the Man in the Moon, and a place in the Sun, and how many herrings made ten, but she had not thought of Rapunsel's hair.

But Prince Oberon had.

So every night, while the Fairy Fanfaronade ran round and round the mulberry bush, a cowherd might be seen, straw in mouth, driving a cush cow down the long lane that had no turning. (Oh, impenetrable disguise!) And every night when he came to the castle in the air, he stood outside Rapunsel's window and sang :

" Lilies are white,
Dilly dilly,
Rosemary's green,
When I am King
Dilly dilly,
You shall be Queen.
Roses are red,
Dilly dilly,
Lavender's blue,
If you will have me,
Dilly, dilly,
I will have you."

And Rapunsel came and leant from the lattice and smiled down at him.

And when Prince Oberon had finished singing, and never before, he would address himself to the lattice and say :

" Let down your hair, Rapunsel."

And, after that, he settled down to wait, for when Rapunsel let down her hair, it took quite a time.

And after she had taken it down, and combed it out, and plaited it up, and let it down through the lattice, Oberon climbed up. And though the cush cow couldn't have been more bored, Oberon was happy ever after or, at any rate, till the crack of dawn when he had to climb down again.

*   *   *

While Prince Oberon is climbing up Rapunsel's locks, and, of course, down again ; while the Fairy Carabosse cannot understand why the girl with the flaxen hair looks so happy and is beginning to wonder if anything can be amiss, Ivan, seventh son of Ivan, seventh son of Ivan, has come to a seashore.

And he sat down to fish for he had a hearty appetite. But all he caught was a little golden fish, so small as to be hardly worth the frying. And the little golden fish was cussing like anything.

" Oh bother," it said, " this is the second time this has happened to me. Getting careless," it tutted.

In his surprise at hearing a fish speak, Ivan dropped it.

" Thank you," said the fish. " If ever you are in need come to this spot and I will grant you anything you wish." He darted back into the sea and the little green waves closed over him and the snow fell softly down.

"Hey," said Ivan. "Hey!"

The little golden fish bobbed out between the little green waves.

"You can't have thought of anything yet," he said crossly and vanished.

And Ivan sat down to think what he could wish for. "I am Ivan, the seventh son of Ivan, the seventh son of Ivan," he pondered, "and I am on my way to seek my fortunate. What more can I possibly wish for?"

Time passed. The Princess Aurora slumbered ten years away and Titania pulled the curtains more closely round her, and a ragged fisherman came and sat beside Ivan and fished. And though he caught a golden salmon, and a silver mackerel, and a nice fat turbot, he put them all back for, as he told Ivan, you can't be too careful with fish.

"You are right," said Ivan. "For I have just put back a little golden fish and I am being very careful what I wish for."

"Ah," said the fisherman, "if I could only lay my hands on that fish." He clawed his fingers.

And the sky went dark, and the sea swelled up, and the snow fell like anything.

"I mean," said the fisherman, "it's a very handsome fish and very intellectual, and I wouldn't hurt it for anything."

And the sun came out, and the sea subsided, though there was no noticeable difference in the snow.

"Very intellectual," said the fisherman. He bowed to the sea. But he put his finger against his nose and signed to Ivan.

"Step aside, my son," he said, "where the fish cannot hear us, and I'll tell you the truth of the matter."

"I've stepped," said Ivan.

"Not so far," said the fisherman, "or my wife will hear us."

And the snow went on falling.

"Very many years ago," said the fisherman, "when I was but a poor fisherman," he looked at his rags, "and doing nicely, I caught the little golden fish—drat him. And he pleaded with me to put him back. And he made me a promise to grant whatever I wished. And I put him back, and that night at supper, I mentioned it to my

wife. My son," said the fisherman, " never tell your wife anything
for then maybe she won't know."

" I'll remember," vowed Ivan.

" My wife," said the fisherman, " was very cross. She called
me an idiot. Did I want to remain a poor fisherman the rest of
my life, she asked me. I did, but how could I tell her this ? Go
right back to the sea, she said, and ask that fish for a decent cottage
instead of this wretched hovel. And though I pointed out that
the hovel had been good enough for my father it cut no grass with
her. ' And don't forget I want a sunflower in my garden,' she
called after me as I went."

" Sunflowers," said Ivan and looked wistfully at the bare patch
beside the fisherman's hovel. For when he had lain on his stove
he had done nothing but eat sunflower seeds all day long.

" So," said the fisherman, " I went down to the sea. . . . And
the sun shone, and the waves lapped the shore gently and there was
hardly any snow at all. And I said . . ."

> " O, fish of the sea
> Pray hearken to me
> My wife, the old hag,
> Does nothing but nag,
> And sends me to beg a boon of thee."

" And did the fish come ? " asked Ivan interested.

" It came," said the fisherman. " And it granted my wish.
And when I came home there was the cottage with four windows,
a chimney, a verandah and all that the heart could wish for."

" And the sunflower ? " Ivan prompted.

" And sunflowers grew all round," said the fisherman. " And
there was my wife, in a new shawl, looking very pretty and fifteen
years younger, and already she was grumbling.

" ' Here am I,' she said, ' in a new shawl, looking twenty years
younger and only a cottage to live in. Go to that fish at once and
ask for a palace, or,' she said, ' I'll never speak to you again.'

" But I knew she could not keep her word, so back to the sea
I went," said the fisherman (almost he might have been Mr.
Masefield). " And the sun was still shining, but the waves were a
little bigger and the snow was back to normal.

" ' Go back,' said the fish, a little curtly, I thought, ' and you will find your castle.' So I went back," said the fisherman, " and there was my wife, in silks and satins, surrounded by servants. And already she was grumbling. For now she wanted to be Queen."

" So you hit her with a knout," said Ivan.

" I did not," said the fisherman regretfully. " I went down to the sea and I called the fish again. And the sun had gone behind a cloud, and the wind had risen, and the little waves had got a little bigger and the little fish quite a lot snappier.

" ' Go back to your hag, you big fish,' he said, ' and you will find she is a Queen, Gold help you.' "

" And was she ? " asked Ivan.

" She was," said the fisherman. " And after that she was Empress. And then Monarch of all she Surveyed. And then she demanded television. And each time the sky got blacker and the sea got stormier and the little golden fish would hardly pass the time of day at all. And when I told him that my wife wanted to be Pope he just looked at me. I never knew a fish could look at you like that," said the fisherman. " But when I got home my wife was Pope."

" And I hope she was satisfied," said Ivan. And the snow fell gently down.

" Not she," said the fisherman, and he put a worm on his hook. " She wanted to rule the Universe, my wife did. The seas, the skies, the earth, and the waters under the earth."

" What about the stars ? " asked Ivan.

" The stars as well," said the fisherman. " And she nagged and nagged until I went down to the sea to ask for it."

" But why didn't you hit her with a knout ? " asked Ivan.

" How can you hit the Pope ? " said the fisherman. " I had left it too late. And I went to the sea and there was a great storm. And the wind howled, and the waves were as high as mountains, and the ships were wrecking themselves all over the place.

" ' Fish of the sea,' I shouted, with all my might, for I was afraid he would not hear me above the gale.

" But if the little fish heard my request it said nothing at all. It went a bright purple and swished its tail and disappeared into the green depths. And the sun came out and the waves went down and the little ships started sailing all over again."

"But when I came home," said the fisherman, "there was my old hovel, just as you see it now, and there was my wife in her old rags looking at me—just as you see her now.

"'Anna,' I said, 'let this be a lesson to you.' And for once she did not answer me back. And ever since then," said the fisherman with pride, "I have been master in my own house . . ."

"Piotr!" The old hag from the hovel was clawing the air in her rage. "Stop wasting your time with worthless strangers and bring me my faggots at once."

. . . "More or less," said the fisherman. He turned to the hovel. "Coming, my little love," he said.

He shuffled off.

She treats him like a servant, thought Ivan, looking after him. This gave him an idea.

"Fish," he called. "Hi—you!"

At once the little golden fish leapt out of a wave.

"I wish," said Ivan, "that I had a faithful servant."

The little golden fish smiled all over its face.

"Go on your way, my son," he said. "Your wish shall be granted." And he darted back into the green depths.

Was there just a flick of malice in his fins?

*   *   *

While Ivan is going off to find his faithful servant, the Fairy Carabosse has arrived at the root of her trouble. The exact root. Not to mince matters she has got hold of a large pair of scissors and is cutting off Rapunsel's hair.

"And now," she said, "off with you, baggage, to Red Riding Hood's grandmother." And she offed her.

Then she gathered up the flaxen tresses and settled down to wait till eventide. And she gloated quietly to herself at the shock Oberon was going to get. It did cross her mind that this might not endear his future mother-in-law to him, but she waved away the thought. Plenty of time for him to learn to love her later.

And meanwhile Boxing Night Land slumbered on. Half a dozen more years went by like the dip of a swallow's wing, and already Queen Mab was beginning to forget Carabosse's defiance and remember Titania's sad little face and dignified bearing the night she had talked to her in her boudoir, as the scent of the wallflowers came up from the tiltyard. Perhaps she would be the best wife for Oberon after all. Left to himself the silly boy might marry almost anybody. Thank goodness Carabosse was attending to the latest! The old hag had her uses after all.

And meanwhile Titania watched faithfully over Boxing Night Land and tried not to think of Prince Charming.

As for Prince Charming, he was dreaming a dream. He dreamt that he was going up and down and round and round and round on a roundabout.

*   *   *

Now while all these things were happening in Boxing Night Land, Ivan, seventh son of Ivan, seventh son of Ivan, was lost in a forest, impenetrable, of course, and smothered in snow to make it more difficult. And after wandering for many days and nights he came into a little cleared space where a bonfire was burning, and in front of it sat three men, weeping, wailing, and beating their breasts.

"Why are you weeping?" asked Ivan. "The fire is warm, you have eaten well," he looked enviously at the gnawed sheep's bones, "and the snow falls softly down."

"Aie," said the first man, "we weep because we have lost our master." And he looked tall and noble in his grief. Or, at any rate, tall.

"The finest master in the world," said the second man. "How he used to beat us when we would not work." And he sobbed afresh and looked æsthetic and gaunt in his grief. Or at any rate gaunt.

"He taught us all he knew," sobbed the third man. "The best cut throat in the district." And he looked round and red-faced in his grief. Or, at any rate, round.

"We have no master," they all sobbed together. "Aie! Aie! What is to become of us?"

"If we had our master now we'd be cutting your throat this very instant," said the tall servant.

"And going through your pockets," said the gaunt servant.

"And maybe cutting off your ear," said the round servant wistfully.

"Those were the days," they agreed. And they fell a-sobbing all over again.

" What will become of us ? " they asked Ivan.   " Three faithful servants without a master."

Ivan thought it over.

" I am Ivan," he said, " the seventh son of Ivan, who was the seventh son of Ivan.   I will be your master.   Follow me, for I am on my way to a great fortune."

The three servants brightened.   " How great ? " they asked.

" I do not know," said Ivan, " but remember I am the seventh son of a seventh son, so it must be all right."

" It is the tradition," agreed the three servants gravely.

They jumped to their feet and bowed to the ground.

" I," promised the tall servant, " will run ahead of you and burn all the villages."

" I," said the gaunt servant, sharpening his knife on the sole of his boots, " will cut the throat of all your benefactors, for then," he pointed out, " you will owe them nothing.

" I," said the round servant, " am the hunter.   When I am with you, you will never be short of food."   He picked up a catapult.

" You're hired," said Ivan.

He only meant the round servant, but all three knelt down to kiss his hand.

" Little Master," they said, " you have chosen well.   We will serve you as faithfully as we served our old master."   And at the memory, tears came into their eyes.

" You are good souls and faithful," said Ivan.   " I will," he vowed, " repay you for your faithfulness and comfort you for your loss.   How," he asked, " did your master come to die ? "

The three faithful servants wept afresh.

" We killed him," they said.

And far away, in the silver sea, a sprat, setting out to catch a mackerel, passed a little golden fish, who was grinning like anything.

*   *   *

While Ivan is making his way through the nameless terrors of the forest and his three faithful servants, skulking well behind him, are stepping in his footsteps as though it were the Feast of Stephen ; while a two-headed giant is looking out of a pair of windows to mark their progress and shouting across to himself to tell himself what to do about them ; and while the snow falls gently down ;

far away in Fairyland a cush cow is hurrying down the lane. But hurry though she may, she cannot go fast enough for her cowherd.

Prince Oberon has never been more eager. And when he has arrived beneath Rapunsel's lattice he can hardly wait until his own song is over.

"Let down your hair, Rapunsel," he cries, even before the last note has died away.

And here it comes, as long and as beautiful as ever. And as strong.

Hand over hand, he starts on his climb. Higher and higher. Higher and higher . . .

"What large eyes I've got," said Red Riding Hood's grandmother, gloating into her mirror.

"Beautiful, I'm sure," said the shorn Rapunsel absently. Oh dear, where was her Oberon now?

"What lovely sharp ears I've got," said Grannie. And she put a large pearl stud into each of them. "How do I look?" she asked.

"Beautiful, I'm sure," said Rapunsel. If she had to be banished, why here?

"What fine teeth I've got," said Grannie.

Rapunsel gritted hers.

Red Riding Hood's grandmother glared. This was no audience for a grandmother of eighty-seven, the story of her sensational rescue from the wolf's belly barely off the front page and destined to become immortal. And anyway, fair hair was insipid, especially so little of it.

Grannie put on her new mob cap, pulled her fleecy shawl more closely round her shoulders and looked at herself in her new mirror, a present from a reader who had no further use for it:

"Mirror, mirror on the wall
Who is the fairest of them all?"

she asked. And she waited confidently for the answer.

* * *

Have you ever seen a dream whizzing?

While Princess Aurora and her court have slumbered away an oak tree, though it was but an acorn, Ivan, son of Ivan, and his three faithful servants have come to a glade. Now in this glade

was a silver lake and it was playing Tchaikovsky. And even as
they watched a covey of tough old swans changed into enchanted
Princesses dancing like troopers. Just like troopers.

"Look, little Master," said the tall servant. "Here comes the
Swan Queen."

"Look, little Master, she is in distress," said the gaunt servant,
noticing her distraught *pas de chat*.

"Little Master, little Master, aren't you going to rescue her?"
cried the round servant.

But even as Ivan pondered there came a purposeful flutter of
wings and the Fairy Ninette jumped down from a snowflake.

"Leave this to Robert Helpmann," she said. "He'll be back,"
she assured Ivan crisply.

So Ivan and his three faithful servants went on their way, and
after they had journeyed seven days and seven nights they came
to a craggy height on the top of which stood a craggy castle.

"Little Master," said the tall servant, "here is your opportunity.
In yonder castle lives a giant."

"Oh, does he?" said Ivan.

"And he has in his power a beautiful Princess," said the gaunt
servant. "You must scale the heights and kill him."

"Oh, must I?" said Ivan.

"And when you have killed the giant and married the Princess
we will share your fortune. It is in the tradition," said all three.

"Oh," said Ivan.

"On your way, little Master," said the first faithful servant.
"Git up dem craggy heights. I," he promised, "will wait down
here for you." And he took Ivan's knapsack from him and made
a pillow for his head.

"I," said the second faithful servant, "will light a fire to guide
you on your return." And he lit one and warmed himself in front
of it.

"I," said the third faithful servant, "will weep for you if you
do not return, and I will always treasure this cloak in memory of
you." And he took Ivan's cloak and wrapped himself in it.

"Off with you, little Master," they cried. "See, we will start
you on your journey." And they led him to the bottom of the
craggy heights.

" Hie to high fortune," they cried and waved their arms like windmills.

But Ivan was firm. " You must help me to kill the giant," he said, " or you will not share my fortune."

The first faithful servant looked sullen, the second faithful servant scowled ferociously, and the third faithful servant said something under his breath and it wasn't ' bother.'

" Onwards! " cried Ivan, seventh son of Ivan. And he took four steps forward and the faithful servants took two. And Ivan took four more and the faithful servants took one. So after that he made them walk in front of him.

Up the craggy heights they climbed while the Princess Aurora slumbered on and the oak tree became a ship and put to sea and carried Robinson Crusoe. Higher and higher climbed the gallant four, with one of them prodding the other three, past lizards basking in the sun and rabbits burrowing in the snow. Until at last they came to the gates of the giant's castle and guarding them was a dog with three heads, each fiercer than the one before.

" Woof."

" Woof."

" Woof."

The first faithful servant dodged himself behind his master, the second faithful servant shinned up a tree, and the third faithful servant ran like anything.

But Ivan was not frightened. " It is a dog," he said. " I have seen them before."   And he went confidently forward.

But when he patted the first head, the second head growled with jealousy, and when he patted the second head, the third head squealed with rage, and when he tried to pat them all at once, he found he hadn't enough hands. So he bethought himself of stroking the dog's back and at once all was well and the tail wagged welcomingly.

So, leaving the dog to look after his three faithful servants, which he could do admirably, for he had a turn of speed that would make a Totalisator's mouth water, and one set of teeth for each clean heel, Ivan strode to the castle door. " Fee-fi-fo-fum, I smell the blood of a Russian man," floated out to him in somewhat divided harmony, but this did not deter Ivan and he thundered again on the door. It was like a gnat knocking at a skyscraper. But the door opened, all the same, and there stood the two-headed giant.

" Come right in," said the first head.

" Stay where you are," said the second.

They glared at one another.

Ivan took a deep breath.

" I am Ivan," he said, " seventh son of Ivan, who was the seventh son of Ivan, and I have come to kill you."

" Wassat ? " said the first head.

" Wassat ? " said the second.

" And rescue the Princess," Ivan finished manfully. " They tell me," he said, " that she is beautiful."

" Divine," said the first head. It kissed its fingers.

" Insipid," said the second head. It snatched its hand away.

" But rich," the heads remembered and . odded happily.

" And now," said Ivan, " I must kill you.' And he tried to draw his sword, but his three faithful servants had borrowed this from him while he slept (and omitted to return it) long ago. So Ivan had to rely on his wits.

Meanwhile the giant was holding a conference with himself.

" Boiled," said the first head. " With onion sauce."

" Grilled," said the second head. " Yum-yum."

And while Ivan was collecting his wits which by this time were all over the place, the giant picked him up and carried him to the kitchen. And when he had been put in a dish the heads fell to quarrelling again over how to season him.

" Not too much pepper," said the first head.

" Highly spiced," said the second.

" Atchoo! " said Ivan.

But the sneeze cleared his mind. And as he listened to the two heads wrangling an idea came to him.

" The trouble with you," said Ivan, " is that you've got two heads."

" Trouble! " said the first head.

" Trouble! " said the second.

" No trouble at all," they assured him.

" You're always quarrelling," said Ivan, " so you never get anything done."

The giant was definitely impressed.

" That's true," said the first head.

" Too true," said the second. It sighed. " John," it said, " we mustn't quarrel any more."

" Very well, Jack," said John. " We won't."

They shook hands on it.

" Let us sit down and eat him amicably," said the first head.

" Like two minds with but a single thought," agreed the second head, and Ivan began to fear that his little plan might miscarry.

" No pepper, of course," said the first head.

" On the contrary," said the second head. " Highly spiced."

They stuck their chins out.

Ivan heaved a sigh of relief. " What did I tell you," he jeered. " There you go—quarrelling again."

The giant looked crestfallen. Both faces fell.

" You'd be much better off if you only had one head," said Ivan. " What use are two heads to a giant, anyway ? "

But the giant, though wavering, was not convinced.

" We're company for one another," said the first head.

" A giant gets so little company," said the second head. It looked lonely.

" It's very hard for a giant to make friends." The first head drooped.

" Got to face it, people don't like us." The second head rested itself sadly on an arm.

" Not popular," said the first head. " Only got each other."

" Alone against the world," agreed the second.

They embraced.

" And when someone does call," said the heads almost sobbing at the injustice of it, " he only wants to kill me." And with that the giant rounded on Ivan.

" Pepper or no pepper," said the heads with one voice, " I'm going to eat you at once."

" Sliced and fried in butter," said the first head.

" Chopped into mincemeat with onions," said the second.

They were at it again.

" If you only had one head," said Ivan craftily, " you could eat anything you liked, and," he clinched it, " cook it any way you wanted to."

The giant stopped growling. The two heads purred.

" So I could," said the first head.

" That's a very fine idea," said the second.

" Get along nicely with only one head," they discovered.

Ivan rubbed his hands. And Papoushka had called him the simple one!

"Then all you've got to decide now," he told the giant, " is which head you want to chop off."

It was enough. The two heads fell a-brawling. And Ivan gave to each hand an axe and left them slashing. Then off he went to look for the captive Princess . . .

              *   *   *

Not in the first impression. Not in the last ditch. Not In Town To-night. Oh, dearie, dearie her!

              *   *   *

. . . And after he had searched the giant's castle high and low, Ivan found the Princess White Carpet in a turret and she was as beautiful as the day and as kind as the night. And Ivan loved her at once.

" I am Ivan," he said, " seventh son of . . ."

              *   *   *

While Ivan is introducing himself to the Princess White Carpet and she is wondering if he will ever finish, far away in Fairyland, Queen Mab is dressing for dinner, and once again her ladies-in-waiting are gathered round her.

Fairy Peaseblossom is looking anxious. She has been high in the royal favour for some time now, but how would the Queen react to the news she had for her to-night. Courage, Peaseblossom said to herself, maybe the Queen will enquire after someone else, Goody Two Shoes, for instance, or Little Jack Horner. . . .

" Well, Peaseblossom," said Queen Mab with an indulgent smile, " and how is Humpty-Dumpty ? " . . .

Closing time at the Zoo in Fairyland. And what a wonderful Zoo it is. And small wonder, for, with spells two a penny, the proprietors, Long John Silver and Sailor Sindbad, can exhibit any specimen they like without the trouble of bringing it back alive from whatever country it happens to be born in.

" Now youse chillun', come away from dem Polar bears," said Uncle Rochester. " Time to say good night to all God's creatures."

"Good night, big bear," fluted two little nigger boys sadly, " and we'll be back with a bun for you to-morrow," they promised.

But the third little nigger boy was back with a bun right now.

"Ananias," called Uncle Rochester shocked. "Didn't youse tell me yo' had eaten yo' bun for tea."

"Me!" said Ananias. "I nevah!"

"Niggah, niggah," said Uncle Rochester, "you dun forget de Book."

' " Three little niggah boys walking in de Zoo
    A big bear hugged one and den," '
Uncle Rochester shook a warning finger,
' " Dey was two." '

"Dat'll be one ob de odders," said the third little nigger boy.

He pressed himself against the bars.

. . . "And now," said Queen Mab, as the distraught Fairy Peaseblossom rushed away to call out all the King's horses, " let us go into the matter of the seventh sons. Time is passing," she reminded them, "and Princess Aurora will be ready for her awakening soon. Who," she enquired, "is in charge of the seventh sons ? "

"Moth, ma'am," said Mustard Seed.

Queen Mab controlled her eyebrows. "Come forward, Moth, and read your report."

Fairy Moth stepped forward. She unrolled no parchment. The Queen's eyebrows allowed themselves to rise a little higher.

"Well ? " she said.

Fairy Moth gulped. She had no very pleasing news to relate. The trouble with seventh sons was that modern parents seemed to lose interest after five, and become definitely sated when it got to six.

"Well, ma'am," she said. "Five hundred and forty of them haven't been born yet."

"Not born!" The eyebrows reached ceiling. "Cobweb," said Queen Mab, "tell Fairy Stopes to present herself to me to-morrow without fail, and," she added, "without her books." She turned back to Moth. "Proceed," she said.

But Moth was silent.

"Come, Moth," said Queen Mab not unkindly. "Unborn

E

seventh babes are not your fault, my dear. Tell me about the born ones. There should be quite a number of them on their way to the Princess Aurora by now."

"There were, ma'am," said Moth in a very small voice. "Twenty-three of them. All seventh sons of seventh sons. I started them off on their journey from all the quarters of the globe—the travelling I had to do, ma'am!" At the memory all the fatigue came back into her voice. "And they were all on their way, ma'am, but," she faltered and stopped.

"Well?" said Queen Mab.

"Oh, ma'am," said Moth almost inaudible, "they have fallen by the wayside." If only the Queen were content to leave it that she might escape with little more than a reprimand.

"Details," said Queen Mab. "Full details, if you please. And speak up."

Moth braced herself. If the Queen insisted on a full account, she should have it. All that travelling and not even a thank you. Not even an you must be tired!

"Twenty-three seventh sons set out," said Moth distinctly. "Eleven of them rescued damsels in distress and are living with them happily ever after."

"Eleven?" said Queen Mab on a rising note.

"So many damsels are in distress these days," said Fairy Moth defiantly. "It is almost impossible to stop a seventh son from meeting one. And quite impossible to stop him from falling in love with her."

"It is in the tradition," said Fairy Cobweb sentimentally.

Queen Mab looked at her. "No one," she said, "is better aware of tradition than I." Fairy Cobweb wilted. "Proceed, Moth," said Queen Mab, "there are still twelve seventh sons left. And don't shout," she added.

Defiance ebbed.

"Well," said Moth, "one of them got himself turned into a frog and must find a Princess to do his bidding for a day and a night before he can be turned back again."

"And when he does find her," said Mustard Seed, "he'll have to marry the girl, so we might as well write him off."

"Quite," said Queen Mab in tones of ice. It was no use fighting the inevitable. "Proceed, Moth. Where are the other eleven?"

" Three of them," said Moth, " took the wrong turning." She blushed.

" The other eight," said Queen Mab quickly.

" Well," said Moth, " Thamar flung her scarf at one of them, and the Big Bad Wolf met another, and two of them got into hot water. A cauldron of hot water," she amplified.

Queen Mab sighed. " The other three," she said resigned.

" Two of them," said Moth, " have stopped to admire flowers, and somehow I don't think they'll ever be quite the same again."

" Neither do I," said Queen Mab darkly. " What about the last one ? I suppose," she said with irony, " he has sold himself for a mess of potage."

" Oh no, ma'am," said Moth. " He's quite all right." She brightened. " He is Ivan, seventh son of Ivan . . ."

" I know," said the Queen, resigned. " Seventh son of Ivan."

" Just so," said Fairy Moth radiant. Why, the Queen was practically smiling at her.

" Well," said Queen Mab, " since Ivan is our one hope, I had better take a look at what he is up to now. Cobweb, my mirror."

But when she looked into it, and the mists had cleared, and the images consolidated, she got a shock. In fact, if she had not been Queen Mab, you would have said that she staggered. For Ivan, son of Ivan, was sitting beside a beautiful Princess and he was definitely making love to her.

" You are plump," he was saying, " and they tell me you can cook."

Another moment and they would be betrothed.

" Moth, Cobweb, Peaseblossom, Mustard Seed," willed Queen Mab in a frenzy, " my long-distance wand." She waved it.

And when she peered into the mirror again the Princess White Carpet was a white carpet and Ivan was looking at it in a bewildered manner.

Queen Mab relaxed. " Moth," she said, " see to it that from now on Ivan, son of Ivan, is well guarded."

Fairy Moth glowed with virtue. How nice to have anticipated the Queen's wishes for once.

" I have seen to it already, ma'am," she said. " He has three faithful servants."

" Oh dear," said Queen Mab. She gazed earnestly into the mirror.

There were the three servants in a huddle outside the castle, faithfully awaiting their young master. No doubt they were discussing his many virtues. The Queen bent an ear to listen.

"The little master has overcome the giant," gloated the tall servant.

"The little master has rescued the beautiful Princess," beamed the gaunt servant.

"The little master has made his fortune." The round servant rubbed his hands.

And the three faithful servants rejoiced together.

"Let's kill him," they said.

"Moth," willed Queen Mab, "attend to this at once."

And while Moth rushed away to deal faithfully with the three faithful servants, Queen Mab wafted a Vision Beautiful to Ivan.

*   *   *

And so Ivan, son of Ivan, stopped staring distractedly at the white carpet and stared distractedly at the stone wall opposite. For there, where the stones ought to be, was the Princess Aurora, the fairest maiden that Ivan had ever seen, standing on one toe and smiling at him. And Ivan rose to go towards her.

The vision faded. Once again Ivan was looking at the grey stone wall. And beside him the white carpet had become the Princess again and was tugging at his sleeve.

Eventually Ivan looked at her.

"You are plump," he said. "But I have seen one who is plumper. She smiled at me. It matters nothing," he said still in a daze, "if she cannot cook."

And the Princess White Carpet knew when she was beaten.

So Ivan, son of Ivan, went on his way as a seventh son should, out of the castle of the two-headed giant, still locked in mortal combat with himself, past his three faithful servants now three weeping willows, down the craggy heights, slipping and slithering and saving himself at the last moment, with the Fairy Moth, vigilant but imperceptible, hovering above. On and on he went through forests and valleys, over the steppes and across the plains, up hill and down dale, and sometimes just in a circle, until he came to a spot where many roads met. And though of course in the long run they all led to Rome, Ivan did not know this. And he stood and gazed at the branched sign-post and could not make up his mind.

To the Land of Nod.	Seven leagues and more.
To the Land of Hope and Glory.	Three Rules Britannia and half a league onward.
To El Dorado.	To travel hopefully is better than to arrive.
To Goose Feather Land.	Is your journey really necessary?
To Boxing Night Land.	Follow your nose to Toyland and ask again.
To the Never Never Land.	?

Ivan stared and stared, and, though the directions were clear enough, he could not make up his mind. So Fairy Moth made it up for him. But Ivan did not realize this and imagined that it was of his own free will that he chose to follow his nose.

CHAPTER XII   **Toyland**

On and on went Ivan. And the sun came out and rocking-horses roamed the meadows, and little blunt ships with giraffes sticking their necks out of them sailed the frothy seas, and the birds in the trees sang like clockwork. And suddenly Ivan noticed something most unusual and it took him a long time to discover what it was. And when he found out he could hardly believe his eyes.

It had stopped snowing.

And as Ivan marvelled at this, a shiny scarlet roadster, streamlined and glittering, whizzed round the corner, whizzed up to him, whizzed round him, and stopped. The owner climbed out. He took off his goggles, he lifted the dickey seat, he took out a key as big as himself, he turned the car over, he inserted the key somewhere in the back axle and he wound and wound and wound. And when he could wind no further he let go and the wheels revolved in the air.

" Jump in if you're coming," shouted the motorist, and he turned the car over and he hopped in himself. And Ivan gave a great leap and landed beside him. And as the clockwork car ate up the miles, he introduced himself.

" Pleased to meet you," said the motorist absently, and concentrated on the steering wheel.

And after a while they came to Hamley's corner, and there were many other cars and omnibuses and mail vans and even trams, all with big keys sticking in their sides and going round and round. And there was a traffic light, which never changed colour, so there was also a policeman who never dropped his arm, but the hand of destiny—a very chubby hand, with a gurgle somewhere above it— came down from time to time to swivel him at right angles. And then the trams clanged and the motor horns tooted and the released lanes of traffic would flow forward, at least those of them that did not need winding up again.

But as Ivan's car did, Ivan got out and walked.

And he walked down the high street of Toyland and he thought that he had never seen anything so grand. The butcher's shop with its joints of meat so shiny they might have been painted wood, the coal merchant with baskets of black glass in his window, the greengrocer—heaven knows what he didn't stock—and the pastry-cook in a large white cap with delicacies that made your mouth water. And, thronging the pavements, the beautifully dressed women of Toyland, many of them wearing shoes and some saying " Papa " and " Mamma " according to which string you tugged.

And Ivan marvelled at it all. So this, he thought, is what a big city is like. Why did Mamoushka warn me against it ?

And even as he wondered a bell clanged furiously and the citizens scattered all over the place and the cars skipped on to the pavements and the policeman fell down as a fire engine, with firemen in beautiful golden helmets standing all over it, came clanging round the corner.

I wish I had a hat like that, thought Ivan. I will get one for myself as soon as I have made my fortune, he promised himself.

And he followed the fire engine till it stopped at a house on fire. And Ivan saw the tall flames, like long paper streamers, roaring out of the chimneys and rushing out of the windows. And all around people stood wringing their hands and shouting " Fire!

Fire " And here was a ladybird hurrying home like anything.

This, thought Ivan, is more exciting than the time Papoushka
lay on the stove when it was too hot. And he put his hands in his
pockets and wondered what the fire brigade was going to do.

And the firemen ran up and down ladders and to and fro with
hoses. And presently they unrolled a white handkerchief and
held on to the ends of it, and they called to a doll, leaning out of
the highest window, her hands outstretched and her hair on end, to
jump. And the doll jumped. And they bounced her up and
down on the handkerchief, and they carried her into the house, and
made her do it all over again.

Then they wound up their hoses and hooked up their ladders,
and they drove away, and they left the house with orange streamers
drooping out of the window like forgotten flames.

So Ivan walked up to the house and breathed on them, and the
flames fluttered out all over again, but no one shouted " Fire! "
and no fire brigade came clanging back. And a Jack-in-the-Box
bobbed out and told Ivan that this house never had more than one
fire a day now that it was no longer new and sometimes not even
that.

And Ivan thanked him and walked on and marvelled at everything he saw. Here was the theatre with Punch and Judy showing.
And here was the cinema with magic lantern slides all about a girl
being rescued from a burning house. And the flames shot up the
chimney, and the fireman ran up and down the ladders, but,
thought Ivan, it was not so good as the real thing.

And as he came out of the cinema and wondered where to go
next, a tin soldier, with a puffed out scarlet chest and black Busby
hat and a little tin trumpet, smiled at a Dutch doll standing outside a
windmill while behind her a stuffed Dutchman with a patch on his
breeches smoked a calico pipe. And the Dutch doll smiled back
at the soldier and marched off with him every bit as stiff as he was.
And the stuffed Dutchman sagged and said, " You've got no chance
against a uniform," but he did not take his pipe out of his mouth.

" She was not so plump," said Ivan consolingly, " so I should not
grieve too much."

Then a hobby horse went prancing by. On it sat the town
crier.

" Oyez, Oyez, Oyez," he shouted.

> " Go to the Zoo.
> At half-past two
> To the Zoo
> At half-past two."

For it was Nannie's afternoon off, and there was no one to keep the town crier quiet.

So Ivan went to the Zoo. And it was not like any Zoo that he had ever seen. Not that he had ever seen one. And Ivan marvelled at the Teddy Bears, so tame and tubby, and the kindly calico elephant, and the lion, all mane and tail but no roar and only a squeak if you pressed him. And the pin-cushiony zebra and the little lead gardens, with their glass birds. A friendly Zoo and not at all frightening.

And Ivan marvelled.

" What time do they feed the animals ? " he asked.

" It varies," said the keeper. So Ivan hung about and as nothing seemed to be happening he wandered out and on.

And after a time, having seen much and marvelled more, Ivan came to a village green and on it stood a maypole—as it does to this very day—and, round it, danced Kate Greenaway children.

Indeed, the green is full of Miss Greenaway's merry brood. And the little boys are spinning tops or bowling hoops, and the little girls are skipping, either by themselves or three at a time, and the bigger boys and girls are flying kites or trying to, and the fat boy stands benevolently by, his cheeks as rosy as the apple he has taken from the howling Toddy or Budge beside him. And further away the wind has blown Donald Duck's yachting cap into the pond and he is jabbering at Pluto, who won't jump in to bring it back.

And Ivan watched it all, and he forgot he was no longer a little boy, and he tried to join in. But when he flew a kite it wouldn't rise into the sky, and when he spun a top it wouldn't sing, and when he bowled a hoop it broke and the little girl howled like anything. And the fat boy kicked Ivan in the pants and Donald Duck jabbered at him, and Ivan couldn't take it, so he pretended he didn't care, and he said " Sucks to you " (in Russian, of course), and he wandered off the green and went to look at the houses.

And what lovely houses they were! Ivan marvelled at them—all built in shiny red brick that glistened like new paint, and every one of them two storey's high, with scarlet chimneys and a static wisp of smoke coming out. Aie! thought Ivan, how elegant the rooms must be inside, and he wished that he could see into them.

And even as he wished, chuckling destiny toddled that way and a chubby hand reached for the hooks, and after a lot of fumbling every house swung open and Ivan could see all the rooms simultaneously; the kitchen and the dining-room on the ground floor, then the stairs that led up to the two bedrooms, and all spotlessly clean, and all shining as though they were swept and polished every other minute, as, of course, being new, they were.

A good way to build a house, thought Ivan. When I have made my fortune, my palace shall be built like this, and then I shall know when supper is ready without coming back to ask.

So Ivan watched the happy families inside the houses and envied them. For here was the Mamoushka, with glasses on, sewing, and there was the Papoushka, his work finished for the day, taking off his apron and settling down to read the paper. And there were the son and daughter sitting on footstools and pulling faces at each other. How united they all were, staying at home as happy families should, and even in those houses where some member was away, you felt that this was unavoidable and that he would be back soon and indeed his supper was being kept warm for him.

And as Ivan stood watching, a young man in a polka-dotted dressing-gown came striding across the green and rat-tat-tatted at a window. And the Mamoushka took off her glasses and poked her head through the window and said, " Who do you want ? "

" Is Mr. Bung, the brewer, in ? " asked the young man.

" Not at home," said Mrs. Bung, the brewer's wife. She went back to her rocking chair and from the heavens above came jeering laughter.

" Hell," said the young man in the polka-dotted dressing-gown, " I'll have to take to gin-rummy! "

And Ivan stood and gazed and marvelled, but at last he tore himself away and wandered on, for, he reminded himself, he was a man with a mission and must continue his search for the vision beautiful, and, of course, his fortune.

Soon it grew dark. Then it grew darker. Then it grew very dark. In fact, it was Harlem, where the golliwogs lived. Golliwogs with white eyes and grinning mouths, bright blue coats and red trousers. Golliwogs sprawling on pavements and hanging out of windows, and their babies with black china faces and curly china hair and still in their long clothes, propped against door-posts, or laid out upon window-sills. And costly coal-black mammies, the absolutely newest thing in toyland, their hair done up in bright bandana handkerchiefs, real brass ear-rings hanging from their ears, and bosoms encased in bright striped gingham, akimboing in corners and all of them singing. If the ten little nigger boys, now only two, had chanced this way, Uncle Rochester, bless him, would have lost both of them at once, for there was nothing in De Book to deter either.

"I am Ivan," said Ivan, "seventh son of Ivan, seventh son of Ivan, and I am on my way to find the vision beautiful."

The coal-black mammies patted their hair and fluttered their eyelids.

"White man," they said, "youse come to de right place."

But when Ivan had considered this he shook his head.

"You are plump," he said, "and your smile is like great-Aunt Elisavetta's the day Katinka danced the polka, but the Princess in my vision was plumper and she smiled like Katinka."

And he swept them a bow and they sang him good-bye and he promised to remember them all to de old Folks on Swannee Ribber, should he pass that way, and a sweet chariot swung low and he got in it, and the sweet chariot swung high and he was off.

And their voices followed him into the sky and he wished he had time to stay and teach them the song of the Volga Boatmen.

And when Ivan alighted from the chariot, there he was at the railway station. And the little locomotives were puffing to and fro, and round and round, and stopping at signals, and coming off the rails, and all of them moving like clockwork. And somewhere up above was the voice of a sobbing destiny and a gruffer voice of a higher authority saying, "Let Daddy show you."

And Ivan marvelled.

"I am Ivan, son of Ivan," he said to the porter, "and can you tell me where all these splendid trains are going?"

And the porter looked at him.

"This is Toyland," he said pityingly. "Our trains don't go anywhere. They just go."

And he trundled a milk van bigger than himself down the platform and was busy for quite a while.

And Ivan stood and watched. And an engine whizzed past him and fell off. And Ivan stooped and put it back again and it whizzed on.

And Ivan felt fine.

*   *   *

. . . "Go on, Cobweb," said Queen Mab deeply interested. "And what did the littlest bear say?"

Once again the Queen of Fairyland was dressing and once again her ladies-in-waiting were gathered round her. What a lot of time a Queen spends before her mirror!

For the past half hour Fairy Moth had been trying to catch the royal eye, and almost hopping up and down to do it. But though if she had been hopping for any other reason, Queen Mab's eye could have been relied upon to quell it instantly, to-day the Royal Eye, when it was not scanning its own coiffure, was, as it were, hanging on the well-being of the subjects.

"Go on, Cobweb," said Queen Mab. "What did the littlest bear say? Tell me the worst." She faced it bravely.

"Someone's been sleeping in my bed," said Fairy Cobweb in a little bear's voice. Certain of her audience now she paused for a fuller effect. "And there she is," she finished with a very creditable little growl.

"Dear me," said Queen Mab. "And what did Goldilocks do next?"

And while Fairy Cobweb told her in detail, Fairy Moth hopped up and down and thought how tiresome Goldilocks was, and how glad she was the Queen had removed the little wretch from her charge even though she had cried herself to sleep at the time.

But at last the wretched Goldilocks arrived at her happy ending and Queen Mab tried on a tiara. But the cobweb was too heavy and the dew-drops too gaudy.

"Oh dear, my son won't like me in this at all," she said. "By the way," she remembered, "where is he?"

With a heavy sigh the Fairy Fanfaronade trailed out of the room.

Fairy Moth hopped forward hopefully.

" In due course, Moth," said Queen Mab and turned to Fairy Peaseblossom. " You look pleased with yourself to-night Pease-blossom," she said, and indeed, Peaseblossom was glowing all over. " Well—tell me your good news."

" Your Majesty will be delighted," said Fairy Peaseblossom, " Ali Baba has got the forty thieves where he wants them ? "

" In oil ? " asked Queen Mab doubtfully.

" Boiling oil," said Fairy Peaseblossom enthusiastically. She rubbed her hands.

But Queen Mab was not pleased. " You know very well, Peaseblossom," she said, " that I like all oil to be kept for pouring on troubled waters. A jar here and there for a traitor I don't mind, but forty of them . . ." She pursed her lips. " Don't let it happen again."

Fairy Peaseblossom retired crestfallen.

Fairy Moth pushed herself forward. On second thoughts she pushed herself back. Clearly this was not the moment.

" Moth," said Queen Mab instantly, " something has been on your mind all evening. Let's hear what it is."

" Oh, ma'am," said Fairy Moth, " it's a locomotive."

For an instant the Queen regretted that she had allowed her eyebrows to soar over Ali Baba.

" A locomotive," she said. " How quaint ! " And even with the eyebrows static the effect was quite paralysing.

" Yes, ma'am," said Fairy Moth. " A clockwork locomotive. It goes round and round on rails," she explained flustered, " and sometimes it falls off."

" I am aware how a locomotive behaves," said Queen Mab coldly, and the chandelier shivered at the ice in her voice. But not more than poor Moth.

" 'Tisn't so much the locomotive, ma'am," she said, " as the man's who's playing with it. Mind you, it's an awfully nice locomotive," she babbled fairly, " and I don't a bit blame him for being fascinated with it, but it's very worrying when he won't leave it, never, ever."

" Who ? " asked Queen Mab, and the chandelier, which had just relaxed started shivering all over again.

" Ivan," said Moth with a little gulp. " Son of Ivan." Her

voice shook. " Son of Ivan." Her shoulders shook. " And I can't get him away from it," she burst into tears.

With superb self-control Queen Mab sat down and tore a lace handkerchief to shreds.

" Really, Moth," she said, " you are not fit to be trusted even with Simple Simon. You are unable to execute the easiest task. Whatever you do there are complications to follow. First," the Queen went into past history, " there was Peter Piper and the pickled peppers. Then that dangerous accident to Jack and Jill. A child could have foreseen it. And after that—entirely your own carelessness again, Moth—there was that awful time at St. Paul's . . ."

" We *were* in the dumps! " remembered Fairy Peaseblossom.

> " We're all in the dumps
>   For diamonds are trumps.
>   The kittens are gone to St. Paul's,"

sang a voice lustily and Fairy Fanfaronade, hearing it, abandoned her fruitless search of the cypress grove and hurried in the direction of the tilt-yard.

> " The babies are bit,
>   The moon's in a fit,
>   And the houses are built without walls."

But it was only the gardener thinning out the wallflowers against the south wall.

Who did he think he was ? Prince Oberon ? She tutted off.

" . . . and after that," said Queen Mab, emerging from past history into the present, " there was Georgie Porgie, and then little Polly Flinders. And now there is this seventh son. Why in the world," said Queen Mab exasperated, " did you let him get into Toyland ? "

Moth stifled her gulps. " Well, ma'am," she said, " it was the shortest way."

" The shortest way! " said Queen Mab, stunned. " The shortest way! " She looked at Moth unbelievingly. " How many more times am I to tell you, Moth, that the shortest way round is the longest way home. Or vice versa," she alibied.

And Moth blushed all over and the ladies-in-waiting pursed their lips and shook their heads. The shortest way! Why even the bats in the belfry knew better than this.

" Ah well," said Queen Mab recovering, " what's done can't be undone so we'd better see what we can do without it."

" Oh ma'am," said Fairy Moth, " if only we could distract his attention. If only we could tempt him away . . ."

" That is precisely what I was about to suggest," said Queen Mab. " But before I give you my views on how it should be done," said the cunning old bag, who had none, " let us hear yours."

" What about the vision beautiful again ? " said Fairy Moth. " Last time it worked like a charm."

" You must be mad, Moth," said Queen Mab coldly. " Last time it did not have to compete against a locomotive."

Fairy Moth looked rebellious. She still thought it was a pretty hot idea.

" How could it be," mused Queen Mab, " if I appeared to him myself to remind him of his duty ? In my lilac gown," she said, tempted.

" You must be cra——" began Fairy Moth. She caught it back just in time. " Careful," she altered it. " The North wind," she reminded her.

" Remember the Book," warned Fairy Peaseblossom.

> " The North Wind doth blow," she intoned.
> " And we shall have snow
> And what will poor Robin do then, poor thing ?
> He'll go to the barn
> To keep himself warm
> And tuck his head under his wing, poor thing.
> And tuck his head under his wing."

Almost she might have been Uncle Rochester.

" Nonsense," said Queen Mab briskly. " Never felt better in my life."

Almost she might have been the ninth little nigger boy.

*   *   *

Chug-chug. Tnck. Plonk. Whirr-whirr-whirr.

This time it is not Rumpelstiltskin, turning flax into gold.

It is another engine at the Toyland terminus fallen off the rails.

Ivan picked it up, put it back on the rails, gave it a cautious little push, and off it went again, round and round and round.

And Ivan laughed ecstatically and the signals went up and down with uncanny precision and the voice of destiny howled louder than ever.

And now Ivan became ambitious. I will, he decided, build a loop-line, and I will pull the switch at the right moment and the engine will leave the main line and go on to it, and that will be wonderful.

And he fitted some lines together until they formed a loop, and he fitted the loop to the points, and he wound up the engine and he started it on its run towards the loop.

And just as the engine had got up speed and was rushing towards the points and rattling like anything, a ring of seed pearls surrounded by the royal cipher appeared in the sky and an elderly lady in lilac smiled charmingly down at Ivan. One hand held a wand pointed in the direction in which his duty lay, the other was extended as though in blessing.

It was a vision that could not fail to influence anyone except an engine driver. Or possibly a signalman.

It was perhaps a pity that at this very moment, with the vision smiling every bit as benignly with perhaps just a suspicion of strain round the corners and the clockwork engine coming nearer and nearer to the loop-line, Ivan was both. Watching the points keenly he threw over the switch—at just the right moment.

Clnk. Whmph. Plonk. Whirr. Whirr.

The clockwork engine had jumped into the air and fallen over on its side.

" Ah well," said Ivan, " as Papoushka always says, ' if the rolling stone will not roll up the mountain, snow, snow again.' "

And he picked up the engine, and encouraged it with tender pats, and he put it back on the line a little nearer the loop.

The vision faded. It was no longer smiling. In fact, if ever there was a vision in a paddy this was it.

The clockwork engine chugged up to the loop. It balked a bit. It fell off.

A pleasure garden swung overhead, its orchards a sea of blossom, its pergolas agog with roses, its trees shady and born to be sat under, its waterfalls tinkling like a thousand musical boxes. Just the sort of place Fairy Fanfaronade might delight in searching.*

But Ivan did not look up, let alone wander off into it. He was winding the engine again.

" This time," he warned it, " wait for it! "

With a disgruntled swish the fairy garden was wafted into the sky, so suddenly that Fairy Fanfaronade was left fluttering distractedly around nothing and disappeared after it wailing " Wait for me! " But Ivan did not look at her either.

After that, in rapid succession, there came a flutter of three butterflies, a sleigh with bells and three horses, and a circus with three elephants and a performing sea-lion. But though at any other time Ivan would have been enraptured by them all, right now he was oblivious to the lot for the clockwork engine was still chugging up to and falling down at the loop.

" I've a good mind to turn him into a turnip," said Queen Mab viciously, and she could not have meant it more if she had been the Fairy Carabosse. " Moth," she turned on her, " are there no other seventh sons at all ? Think, Moth," she urged. " Think."

Moth thought. " Well, ma'am," she produced, " there's the seventh dwarf."

Queen Mab was so angry that she actually gave this match her serious consideration.

" Won't do," she decided regretfully.

Meantime, in another part of Fairyland, another fairy was giving another match her serious consideration. The Fairy Carabosse was remembering her daughter's age.

Titania, she was thinking, is getting a big girl. A hundred and seventeen by one way of reckoning, though not a day older by others. A few more centuries like this and, though still not a day older, she would be an old maid and fit only to be lady-in-waiting to Queen Mab, drat her!

Something would have to be done, decided Carabosse. With Boxing Night Land due to wake up again at any moment and Prince Charming about to stop rising and falling and going round and round and round on his roundabout, with Titania given over entirely to good works and not even putting on red-berry to do them in and not giving her mother a moment's anxiety for nearly

* . . . Not in the Gazebo! . . .

a century—tut-tut, what were young girls coming to?—with Prince Oberon recovered from Rapunsel and his eye ready to rove anywhere and alight, Puck knows on whom, the situation called for immediate action.

But immediate action meant making her peace with Queen Mab, tar and feather her! Nothing for it but to placate the old bag, shrivel her wings!

Fairy Carabosse pursed her lips. It went against the grain to placate Queen Mab, steep her in treacle! It went against every grain Carabosse had in her, but it had to be done.

Above everything, she reminded herself, she was a mother.

That seventh son lingering by the locomotive—what a triumph to leave him there! How nice it was to think of her own spell working out to the tick of the clock with Queen Mab's counter-spell a flop and several centuries late. What a triumph to keep him there tinkering with that engine while all Fairyland laughed at the puerile efforts of the Court to lure him away. Queen Mab in lilac! What a vision! She threw up her hands.

But what if she came to their help with some really practical suggestion to detach him from his loop-line! Queen Mab could not bear to be beholden to anyone ever since the Beast had picked up her handkerchief. And the only way she could get unbeholden to Carabosse was to let Titania marry Oberon. Carabosse would see to that. No fobbing her off with three wishes or any of that nonsense. Revenge was sweet, but success was sweeter, the more so as this way she could have both.

All that she needed now was to think out some way of prising Ivan from his loop. Carabosse considered. Ha! She had an idea already.

But the Court of Queen Mab was full of ideas.

" Send him to Coventry," suggested Fairy Cobweb brightly.

" In what?" asked Queen Mab.

The chandelier quivered.

" Sweep him off his feet," said Fairy Mustard Seed.

" The Princess Aurora shall do that," said Queen Mab. " And no one else," she finished firmly.

The chandelier shook.

" Come hail, come snow," said Fairy Moth.

The chandelier nodded. But Queen Mab glared.

"Don't be a simpleton, Moth," she said. "He's a Russian."

Silence settled on the Court. Everyone was thinking furiously.

And as they thought the windows flew open, and the curtains blew out, and a gust of wind caught the chandeliers and clashed the crystals, and a broomstick flew in and circled the room and dropped its load at Queen Mab's feet. Then it flew out through the windows, and they closed, and the curtains drooped, and the chandeliers stopped clinking and everything was as it had been before, except that there, before the Royal Mirror, stood two shiny black brainwaves.

"Seven league boots," breathed Fairy Moth. "Now why didn't we think of that?"

It almost made you believe in magic!

*   *   *

The clockwork engine chugged up to the loop for the seventh time, hesitated, wobbled a little, but made it. Then puffed out with pride, it chugged round the loop. Almost it might have been the London, Chatham and Dover and London, Brighton and South Coast Railway.

And Ivan lay back and kicked his heels in the air with delight. And when he lowered them again he noticed that he had new boots on. Beautiful new boots, black and shining. And he promised himself that he would admire them later. But for the moment there was work to be done.

"Rest my little one," he said to the run-down engine, "for now I will build you a bridge across a river."

And he got up and took a step forward.

Fwhoop!

CHAPTER XIII   **Over the Border**

F whoop!

Ivan blinked. Where was he? How had he got to the outskirts of a forest seven leagues from his railway engine—lying there not even wound up?

It must be those boots. He kicked them off and glared at them. Black and shining they might be, but as Papoushka always said : "All is not cabbage that comes to the Bortsch."

And as Ivan, son of Ivan, glared at the boots the sun came out and the birds sang and the green grass grew all round. And the spell of the engine was broken, for Ivan had suddenly remembered his vision.

"How plump she is," he thought, "I must go to her at once."

And he looked for the boots which he had flung from him and he saw a strange creature, like a huddled old woman with long ears with its young in a pouch in its tummy, shuffling up to the boots, and it snuffled around them and so did its young, and Ivan watched and laughed. But suddenly the huddled shape inserted a leg in one boot and then another leg in the other.

"Hi!" cried Ivan, but he was too late.

Fwhoop!

The shape had gone. And so had its young.

And that, O Best Beloved, is how the Kangaroo got its hop. Just so.

*   *   *

Thus it came to pass that Ivan, seventh son of Ivan, seventh son of Ivan, on his way to seek his fortune, entered the forest that had sprung up around Boxing Night Land. And the first thing he saw was a lion, and he shinned up a tree, but the lion slept peacefully on. So he slipped off the tree and tiptoed away for he did not wish to wake the dove that was sleeping on it, and he trod on a snake and it didn't even hiss, and he stroked a monkey and it didn't jabber, and he leant against an elephant and it did not budge.

"Why," said Ivan, "I do believe these animals are sound asleep."

And now, from the other side of the forest, he heard music, and it was the same sort of music he had heard when the circus had come to the village in the year that Uncle Vanya had not grown cucumbers. And when he got near enough to see it wasn't a circus at all but only a roundabout. And instead of bears and dragons prancing up and down there were only horses and ostriches, and instead of merry moujiks drinking from hip flasks and lolling in all directions, there was only Prince Charming, going up and

down and round and round and looking just as though he had
been doing it for a hundred years or more.

And something told Ivan that he was nearing the end of his
journey.

*   *   *

A seventh son has reached the borders of Boxing Night Land!

The news was out, and Fairyland was agog with excitement.
Except, of course, for the citizens of Boxing Night Land.

A flurry of preparations burst out for the Awakening.   Customs
officers hurried back to their frontiers, long-term policies were
rapidly shortened, and people who had borrowed books were
regretfully resigned to returning them any day now.

All the fairies were delighted.   Though at first it had been nice
to have most of your charges safely asleep, leaving you quite a lot
of time to yourself and Queen Mab with very little to carp at,
ennui had soon set in ; for few fairies had the right psychological
approach to loafing.   Fairy Peaseblossom, for one, had never
thought she would find herself hankering after one of Simple
Simon's curious questions, but now she found she simply couldn't
wait for the next one—even if it should be ' but why a gooseberry
bush ? ' again.   And Fairy Moth was simply longing to get her
hands on Polly Flinders and brush her down.   Better inspect the
clothes brushes at once.

As for Puck, he was aglow with delight.   He had kept a record
of what everybody outside Boxing Night Land had said about
everybody inside it for the last hundred years, and he proposed to
spend the next hundred happily repeating it.

As to Carabosse, she ordered a whole new wardrobe for Titania
before the rush started, full of the kind of frocks that only a mother
could order, for the chitling was much too listless to think of these
things for herself.   But after the Awakening all would be different.
Titania should snap out of it if she had to snap her into it herself.

As for Dark Diamond, she had passed through a very thin time.
The story of the watermelon had got around, and a hundred years
was not long enough to live it down.   But the Awakening, with
its attendant celebrations, would bring many new faces to Fairyland
and give the old ones something else to talk about, and maybe,
among them all, there might be just one face with a bank balance,
who had not heard her story and could be married before it did.

He must be young and handsome, thought Dark Diamond. Or not so young but still handsome. Or not handsome. Or rich with a tummy. Who cared, thought Dark Diamond.

Even Queen Mab, under her enamelled calm, was much relieved. It would be nice to have this regrettable incident over and forgotten. She had carried the thing off with an air, but it had done her prestige no good. And neither had Oberon with his obsession for farming and his unfortunate affairs. Nobody had dared say anything to her face, of course, but she knew that behind her back people were talking. They were saying she was getting past it. They were saying how could she manage a kingdom when she couldn't even manage her own son though, small consolation, they all admitted she had managed his father.

Queen Mab's mouth tightened. She'd show 'em! The moment the Awakening was over, Oberon should marry. She would find a suitable match at once and instruct Fairy Fanfaronade not to let him out of her sight till the honeymoon. Varicose veins—stuff and nonsense!

Titania? No, not Titania. The child was all right—but the mother! Beholden? Fiddlesticks! Not Titania. Though she liked the chit well enough, indeed she liked her very well. But not the mother. That was final. Still, she didn't like being beholden . . .

The Queen turned to pleasanter topics. Now what should she wear for the Awakening?

But while the whole of Fairyland purred with pleasure, one fairy leant against a hedge and sulked.

With all this awakening business, thought Oberon, there's bound to be a ball of unrivalled splendour and Mama will make me wear buckles on my shoes again.

He kicked moodily at a stone.

But if the fairies were in a state of delight, the mortals were more businesslike. A Kingdom that had slept for a hundred years would be needing a lot of things when it woke up. First come—first sold! So it was up to the wide-awake Kingdoms to beat each other to it.

Old King Cole was a merry old soul. . . .

" Get to hell out of here," he roared, " and get busy on those tourist leaflets. I want one in every letter-box in Boxing Night Land the morning after the Awakening.

" They'll need a change of air after a hundred years," said the Chamberlain.

" So do I," said Old King Cole. He swung on his three fiddlers. " You're fired," he said.

But Gullible the Astute, King of Goose Feather Land, was not going to do anything so silly as to wait for Boxing Night Land to wake up before selling them anything. No! His tourist leaflets were going to be lying beside every one of the sleeping but potential trippers. The first thing they should see on awakening was ' How Green is my Goosefeather ' and a picture of a valley.

Wait for the Awakening—tcha! These leaflets should be delivered right away if he had to do it himself. And it looked as though he would have to do it himself for every one he summoned had found urgent duties elsewhere.

So, with his faithful mule staggering beside him, he took the leaflets to the fringes of Boxing Night Land. But once across the border the mule lay down.

" Dear me," said King Gullible, " he seems to have fallen asleep."

And he fell asleep beside him. And the wind blew the leaflets all over the place.

" A pity," said the Chancellor, tidying up, well his side of the border, " but he won't be asleep for very long."

And he took a patchwork quilt and he judged the distance nicely and he threw it and it floated through the air and alighted to cover the whole of the faithful mule and quite a bit of King Gullible.

" It won't be for long," the Chancellor repeated, " so we must do the best we can before he wakes up."

* * *

Now, though Ivan felt he was nearing the end of his journey, he did not know what path to take. And as he stood and wondered, Fairy Moth made an impressive entrance on a bee's back. She harnessed the bee to a blade of grass, and, though her knees were trembling, spoke graciously to Ivan.

" O mortal," she said, " I have come to help you. And if you bungle this, Moth, my girl, she thought, Queen Mab will knock your blasted block off!"

Ivan swept her a bow.

"I am Ivan," he began, "son of Ivan . . ."

"I know," said Moth, "and you have come a long way and faced many perils but," she finished thankfully, "you have arrived. So be of good cheer for good fortune awaits you."

"It is the tradition," said Ivan, with simple faith, "but where?"

"In yonder palace," said Moth, and she pointed to the Palace that was glittering as brightly as it had at the beginning of this story, but this time it was not Aladdin who had polished it but hordes of pressed-in fairies. Though why the old hag couldn't have done it herself, thought Moth, whose back still ached, with a wave of her wand . . . wilfulness, she supposed.

Ivan looked at the Palace. "It is not very far," he said, "God be praised." He strode off.

Fairy Moth leapt on her bee and caught him up.

"It is not so easy as that, Ivan," she warned him. "For there are as yet many barriers that you must pass before you can penetrate to the Palace. And unless you speak the right password each time you will never overcome them.

"What am I to say?" asked Ivan. And he puckered his brow and prepared himself to make a great effort to remember the words no matter how difficult it was. For, as Papoushka always said, a bad sieve is better than a bad memory though not so bad as a bad egg. And he would pick up the egg and throw it at Mamoushka, and Mamoushka always wept, though he was a kindly man and never meant to hit her, except once and then he had hit the money-lender and they ate black bread all winter. "What must I say?" he repeated with determination.

And Fairy Moth knew that he would never remember and that Queen Mab would blame her for it.

"You must bow three times and the words will come into your head," she said. It meant an awful lot of whispering, but it was better than the Royal Eyebrows. "And now," said Fairy Moth, "onward, Ivan, and remember, I shall be watching over you."

"It is the tradition," said Ivan. "Go with God."

And he swept her a bow and the bee buzzed off. And Ivan hoisted his knapsack and strode bravely forward.

*   *   *

Now outside the glittering palace there grew a thicket hedge. It was sharp and twisted, for it had taken a hundred years to grow, but it was not quite so twisted and not nearly so sharp as the little old woman who sat spinning outside it, for she had taken much more than a hundred years to grow and will go on for many centuries yet. Round her was a ring of attentive faces, gazing up at her with the fascinated concentration of children listening to a fairy story, which, of course, they were. Nice little girls and boys, in sun bonnets and rompers, and very glad their parents were to have them off their hands for a time and know that they were where they would not hear anything but what was good for them and might even make them behave better when they got home.

" And so," Old Mother Goose was saying, " they lived happily ever after."

" Ever after ? " piped a treble.

" Ever after," said Mother Goose reassuringly. " As for the wicked stepmother, she was put in a dark dungeon and fed on bread and water."

" I don't like the dark," piped a treble.

" I don't like bread and water," piped another treble.

" Oh, Mother Goose," a very little girl burst into tears, " couldn't the wicked stepmother be forgiven ? She did love her daughter— the bad one," she reminded her.

But Mother Goose shook her head.

" Evil-doing has to be punished," she said. " And as long as I am telling these stories, it will be," she finished firmly.

One saw what the parents meant.

" And now," said Old Mother Goose, smiling benevolently again, " the sun is setting behind the hill, so off with the lot of you and don't let's have any argle-bargle."

But a disappointed wail went up.

" Oh, Mother Goose, not yet."

" Oh, Mother Goose, you promised."

" Oh, Mother Goose, it's too early to go home."

" Oh, Mother Goose, I hate home."

" Oh, Mother Goose, just one more story."

" A teeny weeny one."

" Just a nursery rhyme."

Mother Goose held up a bony finger.

" Very well," she relented, " I'll tell you a nursery rhyme, but only one mind you. Now which shall it be ? "

A shriek of suggestions prickled the air.

" Jack and Jill."

" Dickory-dickory."

" Hey-diddle-diddle."

" Oh, Mother Goose—Simple Simon—*Please!* "

" Oh no, Mother Goose—Cock Robin. Takes longer," the treble elaborated.

" Quiet all of you," said Mother Goose. But the shrieks went on.

" Boys and girls come out to play."

" London Bridge is falling down."

" There was a young lady of Gloucester."

The shrieks stopped suddenly.

" Certainly not," said Mother Goose outraged. " The idea! Georgie Porgie, I'm ashamed of you. And at your age."

" I'm seven," said Georgie Porgie defiantly. " Next year," he swanked, " I'll be nine. Big boy soon." He puffed out his chest.

" Go home and tell your daddy to whip you," said Mother Goose. " Wherever did you hear this "—she hesitated—" this nursery rhyme ? "

Georgie Porgie considered. But how could he give the little girl with the little curl away! Nothing for it but to perjure himself.

" Fairy Moth," he said.

Somewhere in Fairyland an Eyebrow lifted.

" Ah," said Mother Goose darkly, and tucked away the information in her capacious memory to be brought out when suitable. Then she smiled at her flock.

" Rub-a-dub dub," she began.

" Three men in a tub . . . "

" What sort of a tub ? " piped a treble.

" A large tub," said Mother Goose. She resumed.

" And who do you think they be ? "

" Don't tell me," piped a treble. " Let me guess! "

A long shadow fell across the spinning wheel. Mother Goose looked up to see a handsome youth standing beside her.

" Young man," said Mother Goose, " this is the children's hour. What do you want ? "

" Good grandmother," said Ivan, for the handsome youth was none other, " I am on my way to the Palace and could you tell me if there is a way through the thicket ? "

" There is a way," said Mother Goose, " but not all can pass through it."

They seemed to have arrived at a deadlock.

" Well," said Mother Goose, " is there nothing you have to add ? "

" Please," suggested a treble helpfully.

" Thank you," piped another.

" Ask her nicely," hissed a third.

Then Ivan remembered his instructions and he bowed three times to Mother Goose, and, as though whispered in his ear, the words came to him.

" Once upon a time," said Ivan, son of Ivan.

Mother Goose relaxed. " The most blessed words in the English language," she said. " I do not know what we should do without them. Go your way, my son."

And she spun her wheel and the thicket parted. And Ivan swept her a bow, and he hoisted his knapsack on to his shoulder and he strode bravely forward.

" Oh, Mother Goose," piped a treble, " where is he going ? "

" Oh, Mother Goose," piped another treble, " can I go with him ? "

" Me too! Me too! Me too! "

" Once upon a time," shouted Mother Goose above the din. . . .

*   *   *

Now beyond the thicket was a great stone wall that ran all round the glittering palace. And in the stone wall were two high wrought-iron gates, locked, bolted, and barred, and the keys long lost. And before the gates sat a stiff little circle of girls and boys, with powdered hair and rich brocades, and in front of them sat one little boy in even richer brocade and they were all listening with fascinated concentration to a kindly courtier who was telling them a fairy story. It looked like the children of the Court of le Roi Soleil listening to Charles Perrault telling them all about " La Belle au Bois Dormant," as, of course, it was.

" And some day there will come one, a Prince, braver than all the rest," said Monsieur Perrault, " and he will penetrate the Palace and he will waken the Princess with a . . ." He looked up.

Approaching him was a handsome youth with a mob of children at his heels. And as they came nearer the children pulled faces at the little Dukes and Duchesses of the Court of Versailles and very soon they were fighting.

" Monsieur," said Charles Perrault, politely because he was a Frenchman, but curtly because he wished the children would stop pulling the hair of Monsieur, the brother of the King, " what do you wish ? " And he tapped his snuff-box with impatient fingers, while the handsome youth bowed three times.

And as Ivan, for it was none other, came up from the third bow, the words came to him as though someone was speaking them slowly and clearly into his ear.

" Eh ? " said Ivan, for Monsieur, the brother of the King, was howling and it was difficult to hear. And the words came to him again as though someone was speaking them more loudly. And Ivan heard them perfectly.

" Il-y-avait une fois," he said, which is French for " once upon a time."

" Parfait," said Monsieur Perrault, and the bars fell down, and the bolts flew up and the great iron gates swung open. " Allez, allez, je vous en prie," he urged Ivan, for Monsieur, the brother of the King, was at that moment collecting a black eye.

And Ivan swept him a bow, and hoisted his knapsack on his shoulder, and strode bravely through the gates. And all the little boys and girls ran shouting and kicking after him, all except Monsieur, the King's brother, who ran kicking and shouting at Monsieur Perrault.

" And they lived happily ever after," soothed Charles Perrault warding him off. . . .

★   ★   ★

Now beyond the thicket, and inside the grey stone walls of the palace was an ornamental lake ; fountains played and lilies floated on it. And by the side of the lake sat an old man with tears in his eyes and round him sat a circle of children sobbing. For the fairy story that he was telling them was very sad.

"And so," said the old man, "the little tin soldier stood in the fire in a blaze of red light. He looked at the little wax dancer and she looked at him, and he felt that he was melting away, but still he managed to keep himself erect, shouldering his gun bravely.

"And the wind seized the little wax dancer and, like a sylph, she flew straight away into the fire, to the tin solider; they both flamed up in a blaze—and were gone."

The old man wiped his eyes.

"Oh, Uncle Hans," piped a treble, "why are the stories you tell us always so sad?"

"They come to me like that," said Hans Andersen. "Perhaps to-morrow," he tried to convince himself, "I'll tell you a merry one." He wiped his eyes and resumed.

"And when the maid took away the ashes the next morning, she found the remains of the little tin soldier in the shape of a little tin heart. All that was left of the dancer was a spangle, and that was burnt as black as coal."

There was a loud sniff at his elbow. Hans Andersen looked up. In front of him stood a handsome youth in tears, and behind the youth stood a lot of little boys and girls, some in simple cottons and others in rich brocade, with blackened eyes and scratched knees, and all of them crying.

What an audience, thought Hans Andersen gratified. But aloud he said: "Who are you, my friend, and what do you want?"

Ivan bowed three times, and, as though hammered into his ear, which was tweaked too, the words came to him.

"En gang var det," he said, which is Danish for "Once upon a time."

"Bravo," said Hans Andersen. "A happy beginning—though I rarely use it myself. To the real craftsman it is not indispensable. For the brothers Grimm, of course . . ." he waved them away. "Go your way, my son, and may God bless your journey."

And he pointed to where a little boat had suddenly appeared. And Ivan swept him a bow, and hoisted his bundle on his shoulder, and stepped bravely into the boat. And the little boat unfurled its sails and carried him across the lake, and the boys and girls who were Mother Goose's charges, and the powdered Dukes and

Duchesses from the Court of Versailles, and the sobbing little rabble around Uncle Hans, all jumped into the lake and hung on to the sides of the boat.

"Ah well," said Hans Andersen, watching the splashings fade into the distance, "I tell these stories for myself as much as for anybody."

*   *   *

Now across the lake and before the palace there was a moat. And it was dank and deep and could only be crossed by a draw-bridge, and this was always up. And before the moat was a stone bench and on it sat two professors of the Berlin University, and they were deep in argument.

"And I think, Wilhelm," said the first Professor, "that the maiden must guess his name soon,"

"Ach, Jakob, you are crazy," said the second Professor. "What sort of a reward is it for our poor Rumpelstiltskin if, after all his spinning of the flax into gold, he does not get his bride?"

Clatter-clatter. Whirr-whirr. Chink.

"It is you who are crazy, Wilhelm," said the first Professor, "and also wicked to suggest such a thing. He is a goblin and she must not marry him." He set his lips.

"But he has done no wrong," said the second Professor, "and a bargain's a bargain."

"Not with a goblin," said the first Professor firmly.

The Grimm brothers glared at one another.

Clatter-clatter. Whirr-whirr. Chink.

"Ach, Jakob, let us not quarrel again," said Wilhelm presently. "Was it not enough that we did not speak for three days when we were deciding Snow White's destiny?"

Jakob sighed. "You are right, my brother. It is unintelligent to quarrel over what we both love. Though, mind you," he said obstinately, "it should not have been an apple that Snow White bit, for the apple has been bitten into for all time in the Bible. A poisoned cherry would have done just as well and looked much prettier in the illustrations.

"Jakob, you are a numbskull," said Wilhelm not unkindly. "A poisoned cherry the mädchen would have swallowed in one gulp and been dead for ever—and no stumbling Prince could have shaken it from her mouth."

" A doctor could," said Jakob fiercely.

" Would you have our Snow White marry a sawbones," said Wilhelm pained. " Jakob Grimm, I'm surprised at you."

Jakob looked ashamed of himself. " I am sorry, Wilhelm," he said, " I know you are right—it is just for that I get so cross."

Clatter-clatter. Whirr-whirr. Chink.

" It does not matter, Jakob," said Wilhelm. " Let us forget Snow White and Rumpelstiltskin and work on our dictionary of the German language. We do not quarrel over that."

" Ach! " said Jakob without much enthusiasm, " what a great work that will be when it is finished."

" When it is finished," agreed Wilhelm wanly.

The two old gentlemen pulled out their notebooks.

Clatter-clatter. Whirr-whirr. Chink.

" All the same," said Jakob suddenly, " to think of a lovely maiden—well a maiden, anyway—marrying a goblin. It is not like us, dear brother, it is not like us! "

" We must not always write the same thing," said Wilhelm. " People will notice." He made an effort to concentrate on his notes. " How," he asked, " would you define ' Lebensraum ' ? "

" Anyway you please," said Jakob carelessly. He closed his notebook with a snap. He produced his last weapon—logic.

" Wilhelm," he said, " above everything, we ourselves must believe our own stories. Now I put it to you, as a professor of Berlin University, who may shortly be offered another Chair, is it logical for a young, intelligent girl, whose whole existence is at stake, to spend all night thinking of names without guessing the right one ? "

But Wilhelm had closed his notebook and fallen back on logic too.

" It is more than possible, it is inevitable," he argued passionately. " For what chance has a young girl to guess in one night what it took us, two Professors of the Berlin University with I cannot remember how many Chairs between us, four days to invent. Had we adopted your first suggestion," he said scornfully, " we would have had no story for she would have guessed it at once. Adolph! Ha! "

" It was no worse than your suggestion," said Jakob incensed. " Groucho! Tcha! "

They turned their backs on one another.

Clatter-clatter. Whirr-whirr. Chink.

And presently the two old gentlemen started edging round, catching each other's eye, looking quickly away and turning back for another look. Presently they were face to face.

" Ach! Wilhelm, you are right," said Jakob. " The maiden shall not guess the name, and she shall marry the goblin."

" No, Jakob," said Wilhelm, " I have been thinking, and you are right. She shall guess the name and shall not marry the goblin."

" But she cannot guess it," said Jakob. " You have just proved it to me. I am convinced. Rumpelstiltskin," he said. " No one could guess it."

" Alas, Jakob, you are right," said Wilhelm. " We have invented too well. But also," he said, " she must not marry the goblin. So what can we do ? " He thought.

" Wilhelm," said Jakob tentatively, " how would it be if the maiden should learn his name by some chance ? "

Wilhelm brightened. " Excellent," he said. " But by what chance ? "

" We must find a chance," said Jakob.

Their notebooks dropped unnoticed on the grass.

" It will not be easy this," said Wilhelm, " but it should not be beyond us to find the happy ending."

Jakob nodded. " To be sure," he said. " For we are not Hans Andersen."

The Brothers Grimm glowed at one another.

And as they sat in pride and amity, a handsome youth surrounded by a rabble of scampering children came up and bowed three times. And, as though they were being dinned into his ear, the words came to him.

" Es war ein mal," said Ivan, which is German for " Once upon a time."

The Brothers Grimm bowed at him, benevolently but vaguely, for they were both working out how the maiden might learn Rumpelstiltskin's name.

" Go forward in peace, my son," said Wilhelm.

" And leave us in peace also," said Jakob, kind but firm.

And the drawbridge came down. And Ivan swept the brothers a bow, and hoisted his knapsack on his shoulder, and stepped

bravely on to the bridge, and all the little boys and girls, in
rompers and rags and rich brocades, ran shouting on to the bridge
after him, and a lot more little girls and boys, in spectacles and
plaits, came up out of nowhere and ran after them, shouting,
" Ach! wait for us."

And the drawbridge flew up after them, and the two Professors
sat alone again pondering their problem, and the two notebooks,
full of learned definitions, lay forgotten on the grass, as had often
happened before and would certainly happen again. For though
all the world has. read " Grimm's Fairy Stories," the publisher
waited in vain for the complete manuscript of " Grimm's
Dictionary."

Which is as it should be.

*   *   *

Now beyond the drawbridge stood the glittering Palace, with
its great doors closed to all who came. And before the doors
sprawled a huge man, with fierce whiskers all over his face. On
his right hand stood a great bowl of kvas from which he refreshed
himself frequently, while on his left hand stood a samovar from
which he drank tea when he was not drinking kvas. In front of
him was a table covered with papers, and whenever he had a hand
free from either glass, he picked up a quill pen and wrote. And
before him, charm well to the fore, stood a middle-aged young
man in a polka-dotted dressing-gown.

" Ah, Poushkin," said the young man. " Nice to see you."

" Zo," said Poushkin. He went on drinking and writing and
drinking.

" How do I get into this Melville Brothers Mausoleum, old boy,"
asked the young man, pointing to the glittering palace.

" Thou dost not know," said Poushkin shocked. " The English! " He went on drinking.

Up the hill came Ivan with the rabble of children jumping all
round him. The young man paled, drew his polka-dotted
dressing-gown protectively around him, and retreated.

Ivan bowed three times and he rose from the last bow he did
not have to be told the words that Fairy Moth was at this moment
frantically hunting up in the dictionary.

" Raz Kogdata," he said. which is Russian for " Once upon a
time."

" My son," said Poushkin, " it gladdens my eyes to see you and my ears to hear you, for it is many years since I have heard our language spoken properly. Sit down and let us talk a little." And by this, of course, he meant till dawn, and later, as every Russian does.

But the doors of the palace had swung open and the children were tugging at Ivan's belt and swinging from sleeves and pulling at his pockets.

" I will come back, little father," promised Ivan over his shoulder as they dragged him through the doorway and the great doors closed behind him.

" Nitchevo," said Poushkin, and he went back to his writing and his drinking. But presently he looked up again for the young man in the polka-dotted dressing-gown was clearing his throat.

" Pfui," said Poushkin, " it is thou again. What dost thou want ? "

The young man looked furtively round. All clear. Then he leant forward.

" Once upon a time," he said in a conspiratorial but brittle whisper.

" Oho! " said Poushkin.

The great doors swung open and the young man, after a nervous glance round, dived through them.

If they should hear of this at the Ivy!

CHAPTER XIV   **The Awakening**

And so Ivan, the rabble of children all around him, their voices suddenly hushed, stepped out of the sunshine and into the sleeping depths of the palace. And he found himself in the vastest hall he had ever seen, with ceilings branching up like great trees in the forest, and a marble staircase going up and up like the snow-covered steppes. Why, it must belong to the Tzar himself, thought Ivan, though, of course, the Imperial Guard would never dare to fall asleep like these two rascals on duty.

And he strode across the great shining floor and the children

F

tiptoed after him, and he walked through the portals into the most magnificent room he had ever seen—no doubt the throne room—and there was a man in magnificent robes with a chain around his chest—no doubt the King himself—raising a crystal goblet with a drop of wine in the bottom, and there all around him were sumptuously dressed ladies and gentlemen, in liveries and aprons—clearly the courtiers—raising their goblets with drops of wine in them too. All except one man, and he was tilting an empty decanter and looking disappointed. He was the knife-boy. For, had Ivan but known it, he was in the servants hall, and these were the butler and his staff drinking the toast they had started a hundred years ago, before sleep had overtaken them.

"Uncle Ivan," piped a treble. "They're all asleep."

"Uncle Ivan," piped another treble. "Why are they all asleep?"

"Uncle Ivan," piped a third treble. "Why are they all asleep with their clothes on."

"Uncle Ivan," confided a fourth treble. "My mother won't let me go to sleep with my clothes on?"

"Mamoushka does," said Ivan. And he strode up the largest marble staircase he had ever seen, quite a lot larger than the one he had seen a minute ago, and he looked out the windows and he saw a gardener asleep among his own roses and a butterfly motionless above a flower. And he rounded the staircase and looked out into the courtyard and it was full of people who had fallen asleep even as they swept their curtsies. This is strange, thought Ivan, but already the children took it to be the most natural thing in the world, and they would not let Ivan linger to look and wonder but pulled and tugged and bobbled him up the stairs until he was like a large blonde cork in a rainbow of waves.

"Hurry, Uncle Ivan," they said. "Hurry. For in one minute it will be a hundred years."

*   *   *

"In one minute," said Queen Mab, blowing at the dandelion clock, "it will be one hundred years. Where, Moth," she said, with all the quiet of a waterfall holding itself in check, "is your charge?"

"Twenty-seven steps to go," said Moth, "and being bobbled up all of them."

A ripple of expectation passed among the fairies assembled in the

Chamber of the Sleeping Princess. The moment was at hand—and Queen Mab in time for it, though with nothing to spare. How beautiful the Princess Aurora looked, breathing peacefully as she lay on her quilted bed. Almost a pity to disturb her. Though quite a relief to disturb the King, straddled across the armchair with a handkerchief rising and falling across his face.

" Ten seconds to go," said Queen Mab. " I trust he will be punctual, Moth."

" Oh, bobble faster," prayed Moth. " Faster."

" Time," said Queen Mab.

The door opened. A horde of children burst in. They ran round the room, they pulled off the King's handkerchief and tugged at his beard, they stroked the Queen's velvet gown, they swung from the curtains and tumbled all over the room and pricked themselves on the hedgehog, and they stood and gazed at the sleeping Princess, lying there in a dress their great-grandmothers might have worn.

" Moth," said Queen Mab in tones too terrible to describe. " What is the meaning of this ? "

But before Moth could explain Ivan had entered and all eyes were fixed on him.

Ivan looked round the snow-white room of the Sleeping Princess. But he did not see the slumbering courtiers, he did not see the King and Queen, he did not see the Fairies, he did not even see Queen Mab dressed in lilac and smiling at him encouragingly. He saw only the Princess Aurora asleep, and he crossed to the bed and bent over her. And there he stayed gazing at her. And his cheeks grew red and he did not know what to do next.

" Once upon a time," he faltered, " Il-y-avait une fois . . . I am Ivan, seventh son of Ivan, seventh . . ."

But the Princess went on sleeping, as though she had only just this moment closed her eyes. And the fairies began to nudge one another, and Ivan went on standing there, and poor Moth was almost in tears. Oh dear, she did have the stupidest charges!

Ivan thought of something. He bowed three times. And, as though shouted at his elbow, the words came to him.

" Kiss her, you fool," urged Georgie Porgie. " Go on. Kiss her."

Ivan looked round. And for the first time he saw that there were others in the room. He looked at Queen Mab and the smile on her face reminded him of Mamoushka when she was just about to get her own way.

"Proceed," said the Queen. "Kiss her."

But Ivan still hesitated, for when he had kissed the girls in the village there had been no one to see or else it had been at the fair when everyone was doing the same, even Papoushka. And a fairy flew down from the canopy and alighted on his shoulder.

"Oh please, please kiss her," said Titania. "She wants to be woken up."

And Ivan hesitated no longer.

The conductor heaved a sigh of relief. He brought in his cymbals.

And so, to the music of Tschaikovsky, the sleeping Princess woke up, and the whole Court awoke two bars behind her.

"Nonsense," said the King. "Fall asleep! Me! Ridiculous!"

*   *   *

Ding-dong. Ding-dong. Oyez! Oyez!

Yawn-Stretch-Blink-Yawn. Turn over and try to snooze again. . . .

The village is waking up.

Ding-dong. Ding-dong. Oyez! Oyez! Hear ye!

It is the Town Crier going on his round.

"Oyez! Oyez! hear ye! ding-dong. Take warning. The Princess Aurora is about to prick her finger, and, the consequences of such being well known, all law abiding citizens are requested to make their beds in advance and lie on them. Ding-dong. Oyez! Oyez! Hear ye! Ding-dong. Take warning."

He has taken up where he left off.

Poor dog Tray rises from a doorstep, shakes out a hundred years dust, and trots off behind him. Breakfast?

Yawn. Stretch. Yawn. And now Whp!

Blinds have flown up windows as though by magic. Shutters are pushed open and tousled heads are thrust out of casements and peer at the sun.

"What is the time?" asks Jack Sprat alarmed. He wonders if he has overslept himself.

His neighbours have no doubt of this. From every house in the village comes a cloud of dust as the good housewives get to work.

Ding-dong. Ding-dong. Oyez! Atchoo!

The butcher, the baker and the candlestick-maker are attending to the customers, who have woken up in their shops with them.

" There you are, Mrs. Mulberry," says the baker. " A nice cottage loaf fresh from the oven this morning."

" Feels a bit hard," says Mrs. Mulberry sharply.

Across the way, surrounded by his guttered stock, the candlestick-maker is shrugging his shoulders and spreading his hands at the pools of wax. Night's candles have burnt out.

And now the children, with shining morning faces, creeping like snails unwillingly to school. A hundred years and never a holiday!

And then, outside the barber's shop, the soldier, bearded as the leopard—as several leopards. But he'll have to wait. The barber is cutting his own hair.

" Oyez! Oyez! Ding-dong. Hear ye! Take warning. The Princess Aurora is about to prick her finger."

How lucky he knows the text of his proclamation by heart for the parchment has crumbled away in his hand.

*   *   *

" I'm for ever blowing bubbles."

Prince Charming has woken up from his nightmare of going up and down and round and round on a roundabout. He snaps out of it in an instant, all his wits about him, ready to take stock of the situation. He gets it in a flash. He is going round and round on the roundabout. He couldn't be more alert.

But he hasn't the least idea what to do about it.

" Hee-haw! Hee-haw! "

On the fringes of the forest the faithful mule wakes up. He nuzzles the breathing bundle beside him. But King Gullible slumbers on in the sunshine.

Resigned the faithful creature shoulders the sack and gallops off to distribute the pamphlets himself.

In the Royal gardens the flowers are blooming as though to make up for a hundred springs, and the Royal gardeners, without waiting to straighten out their hundred-year cricks, are bent double among them already. The blue butterfly has dropped a couple of inches and is balanced on a petunia—what a long day she has had, and what a pity she does not know it.

In the Courtyard the guests are coming up from their curtsies and little Miss Muffet is crying again. She has found her tuffet, but it isn't as new as it was.

And inside, the Palace has sprung to life.
Swish. Swish. Swoom.
The serving wenches have got hold of new brooms and are sweeping the place clean.
Glugle-glugle.
The butler, back to normal, is swilling the port.
Ouch!
Someone has clouted the knife-boy. Very back to normal.

> STIR!
> Stir!
> STIR!
> Stir!

Upstairs, in the Princess Aurora's chamber, all is love and happiness and not a little emotion. The King and Queen are beaming fondly at one another.

" A hundred years and never a cross word," said the King proudly.

" That's right, dear," said the Queen. " Never a word."

And the Court clustered round to offer their congratulations.

" How would it be," said the King, " if we had a ball of un-rivalled splendour or," he waved a genial hand, " unsurpassed elegance, to celebrate the Awakening ? "

" Wait my love," said the Queen. " We may have a better excuse soon." And on her face was the smile of a mother about to marry her daughter off at a hundred and seventeen.

On the dressing-table another Court was clustering. Queen Mab had esconced herself on a quilted pin-cushion and was receiving the congratulations of the fairies.

How happy they all are, thought Titania and wondered why she felt a little lost.

" Punctual to the starling's supper," said Peaseblossom.

" Passed off without a hitch," said Cobweb.

" Marvellous," said Moth.

And Queen Mab bowed and beamed and lapped it up. And when at last the congratulations had run out she stood up on the cushion and held out her wand.

" Good people," she said, " it has been as I promised. You have slept for a hundred years and now you are awake and everything is as it was."

How they cheered!

The hedgehog crossed to a mirror to look at himself.

He was still a hedgehog. He sagged.

In an alcove the Princess Aurora and Ivan, son of Ivan, were standing hand in hand and smiling shyly at each other. Another minute and they would be engaged.

" You are pretty," said Ivan, " though you are not as plump as you were in the vision."

" Aren't I ? " said the Princess Aurora. She seemed worried.

Ivan gulped. " It does not matter," he swore. " I do not like them to be fat."

*   *   *

And far away in Cobweb Cottage, Fairy Carabosse was preparing for her only child's return. The chitling would need a little coseting after a hundred years vigil in that draughty palace.

Things were going well enough, though there was still plenty of intriguing to be done. She waved it away. She could look after Queen Mab when the time came, she could look after Oberon, she could look after Prince Charming—she cackled—but right now she was going to look after her own child.

She peered out of the window. A white butterfly was skimming over the kitchen garden. Only three cabbages to go.

Carabosse put the milk on to warm.

CHAPTER XV   **Ring, Ring the Bells**

" We will ring a merry peal,
Say the bells of Bakewell."

All over Fairyland bells are ringing like a month of Sundays. Boxing Night Land is awake once more—here's reason for rejoicing!

" Pitchem and patcham,"
Say the bells of Old Atcham.

" Wrissle and wrastle,"
Say the bells of Bishop's Castle.

" Poker and Tongs,"
Say the bells of St. John's.

In the old days, when London Bridge was lined with shops and
salmon swam under the arches, and bells were ringing everywhere,
no bell was heard at the village of Swaffham, which is in Norfolk,
for the old church had fallen down and there was no money to
raise it again.

" Buttermilk and whey,"
Say the bells of Hopesay.

" Lay a bottle in the wood,"
Say the bells of Leebotswood.

" You're too fond of beer,"
Say the bells of Elsemere.

And the villagers of Swaffham cocked their ears to catch the
distant chimes and sighed.

Clunton and Clunbury,
Clungerford and Clun
Are the quietest places under the sun.

" But," they shook their heads, " they have a church and we
have none."

" Hop, skip and run,"
Say the bells of Clun.

" Axes and brummocks,"
Say the bells of Clungunnus.

" There they go," said the villagers wistfully. And they
drowned their sorrows in mugs of ale.

Now in this village of Swaffham, which is in Norfolk, there
lived a poor pedlar, and he lived in a cottage with a canary in the
window, and a cat on the porch, and a dog at his heels. And he

had as many children as there were sparrows in the garden, and though it was easy to feed the sparrows, he found it very difficult to feed the children. He'd much ado to make his living, trudging with his pack on his back and his dog at his heels, selling oranges and lemons to local yokels. For, they said, how can we afford oranges or even lemons for ourselves when we cannot even afford to build a church to the glory of God. And the poor pedlar could not but agree with them and trudged away with empty pockets, and at the end of his day's trudging was only too glad to lie down and go to sleep.

> " Trundle a lantern,"
> Say the bells of Northampton.

And, with the sound of the bells in his ears, it fell out that the pedlar dreamt a dream. And therein he saw the great Bridge of London Town, lined with magnificent shops and houses, some of them two storeys high not counting the attic, with customers on every floor. And he dreamt that if he went and stood on the Bridge he would hear joyful news.

> " Why don't you ring louder ? "
> Say the bells of Hope Bowdler.

And they did and the pedlar awoke from his dream. " I must go and stand on London Bridge," he said to the cat, and he kissed his children good bye, and he whistled his dog, and he set hopefully out on his journey.

> " Two slippers and trash,"
> Say the bells of Moneyash.

" Peaseblossom," said Queen Mab, " close the windows." The bells were giving her a headache. " The din is deafening me."

" Deaf-initely," said Peaseblossom. She waited for the laugh. But Queen Mab didn't get it.

" Thank you, Peaseblossom," she said quite normally. " No— not the Imperial Emeralds, Mustard Seed. The family pearls."

For she had granted the Fairy Carabosse an audience and must not appear too resplendent for that would be construed as conciliating. On the other hand, it would not do to wear her kimono! Moderation in all things. The family pearls would do nicely.

G

" And now," she said as Mustard Seed snapped home the clasp, " tell me—what has happened to the two sisters ? "

" Well, ma'am," said Mustard Seed, " the gentle one is doing very well indeed. De Beers are paying her handsomely to keep her mouth shut."

" Just as I expected," said Queen Mab. " With diamonds dropping every time she opens it, it was inevitable."

" Quite so," said Fairy Peaseblossom.

" But what of the other sister ? " asked Queen Mab. " The selfish one. If my memory serves me aright, toads drop from her mouth when she speaks. What has happened to her ? "

" Works in an aquarium," said Mustard Seed tersely.

Satisfied, Queen Mab turned back to the mirror.

" If you please, ma'am," said Fairy Moth, " the Widow Carabosse waits without."

" Keep her waiting till she starts looking at the photographs," said Queen Mab. " Then show her in and leave us together."

> " Two sticks and an apple,"
> Say the bells of Whitechapel.

On the mossy bank, among the flowers of the forest, shaded by tall green fronds, a little deer lay. There was nothing the matter with his flesh and bones but his heart was breaking. He was to have posed for an immortal picture. He should have hung in the National Gallery with daily groups gasping at his courage and weeping at his plight. But, at the last moment, Mr. Landseer had changed his mind and painted a stag. And from that day the little deer had pined away and refused to be comforted. And now he lay on the bank and gazed into his reflection in the pool beneath and thought how different everything might have been if he had grown antlers.

> " We must all die,"
> Say the bells of Ledbury.

Over the pond fluttered a butterfly, and the ripples reflected its wings and the shimmer of a fairy on its back. To-day it could fly where it would, for the blades of grass which threaded its snaffle never tugged, and no urgent little voice pleaded " Dobbin, do hurry." It had been a lovely outing for the butterfly. A dog

rose here, a lotus there, and a whole field of golden mustard somewhere else. For Titania had only come out because Mama had
said she must get some colour in her cheeks, and she did not care
where she went.

The butterfly skimmed rapidly over the pond—it had sighted a
lotus flower. But Titania's firm little hands checked it in full
flight.

"Whoa, Dobbin, whoa! There's a little deer by the bank and
he's crying."

And Titania tethered the butterfly to a bluebell and sat down
beside the deer.

"Oh pretty deer," she said. "Why are you unhappy? You
should be leaping and skipping in the forest and proving yourself
the fleetest of all little deers."

A large tear trickled out of the deer's eyes and fell with a plop in
the pond.

"Don't cry," said Titania, for that tear told her everything.
"It was mean of Mr. Landseer to change his mind, but you mustn't
let it get you down."

Another tear plopped into the pond.

"Come, come," said Titania. "Have a mulberry."

The deer nuzzled at the outstretched palm, he did his best to
swallow the mulberry but he just couldn't manage it.

"See," said Titania. "The sun is shining, the flowers are
growing, and so should you be. You'll laugh about it in a few
years time, really you will." Her voice broke as she remembered
Prince Charming. "Listen! Someone is singing a song just
because it is a lovely day and he is glad to be alive."

A joyous baritone was singing strongly :

> "Cromer crabs,
> Runton dabs,
> Beeston babies,
> Sheringham ladies,
> Weyborne witches,
> Salthouse ditches,
> And the Blakeney people
> Stand on a steeple
> And crack hazel nuts with a five-farthing beetle."

"See," said Titania, " he is singing just because he is happy."

" And crack hazel nuts with a five-farthing b-e-e-e-tal," sang the baritone rising to a high note and holding it.

The ferns parted and the baritone came into view. He took in the little group by the bank and he crossed to the deer at once.

" Sick," said Oberon. " What's wrong ? What's that you've got in your hand ? "

" Mulberries," said Titania. " But he won't eat them."

Oberon looked at her with pity. " Poor lass," he said. " Mulberries to a deer! Watch this." He put his hand in his pocket and pulled out some oats.

But the deer could not eat them either.

" That's bad," said Oberon. " Mortal bad. I'd best carry it home and give it a nice bowl of milk from a cush cow."

But the deer still looked listless.

" It won't help," said Titania. His feelings are hurt. Mr. Landseer," she explained.

" Is that the trouble ? " said Oberon. And he stooped down and stroked the deer's snout.

" There's nothing to be upset about," he said. " We can do better than Mr. Landseer any day."

The deer cocked an ear. It wasn't a very hopeful ear but it cocked.

" You come home with me," said Oberon, " and drink a nice bowl of milk, and when you've plumped out a bit I'll have a word with Walt Disney. Maybe he'll let you play Bambi."

The deer stood up. He nuzzled the oats. He gobbled them up. He snuffled gratefully at Titania's palm. He even ate a mulberry.

" Oh, sire, you're wonderful," said Titania. " You've cured him."

" Wouldn't think much of myself if I couldn't cure a sick deer," said Oberon. He picked the creature up in his arms. " You should see me with calves."

" Should I ? " said Titania wanly.

Oberon looked at Titania and saw her for the first time.

" What," he said accusingly, " did you have to eat before you came out ? "

" Nothing," said Titania. " But it's all right. I never eat breakfast now—haven't for a hundred years."

Oberon frowned. " Seems to me you could do with some

plumping out yourself. Come with us," he patted the deer, " to my farm and you shall have a nice egg. A goose's egg."

Titania looked a bit like the little deer when first it was offered the mulberry.

" I'm not hungry," she said.

" Come and eat your nice egg," said Oberon in much the same voice as he had cajoled the deer, " and I'll show you a little foal born this morning."

And Titania reacted much as the deer had done.

" A foal!" she said. " I've never seen a foal on the day it was born. What does it look like?"

" Where were you brought up?" said Oberon.

" At Court, sire," said Titania.

" All legs," said Oberon. " Such silly legs. Come, I'll show you."

They wandered down the lane together, Titania leading the butterfly and Oberon carrying the deer. And as they walked through the forest Oberon told Titania about his farm.

" The trouble with you good fairies," he said, " is that you don't begin to understand animals. You think that if you are kind to them that is enough."

" Isn't it?" said Titania.

" Not by a long chalk," said Oberon. " It's no use being kind if you don't know what you're doing. Many's the animal that's been made miserable by a mort o' kindness and a short weight o' skill.

" I'm sure my butterfly isn't unhappy," said Titania. " Oh, do come away from that honeysuckle, Dobbin." She tugged.

Oberon clicked his tongue. " Gee up, Dobbin," he said, and flicked the butterfly's rump with a blade of grass. " See," he said as the butterfly ambled amiably on, " a little firmness and there you are. Mind you," he said gravely as they walked on, " butterflies were never meant for hacking. They're meant for racing."

" I'm sure Dobbin wouldn't care for racing," said Titania.

" That's because you feed her too much," said Oberon. " She's out of condition."

" You mean I'm too kind to her," said Titania doubtfully.

" Got it in a bag of barley," said Oberon. " Did you know," he asked, " that you can kill people by too much kindness?"

" Can you really," said Titania.   She blanched.

Oberon kicked open a gate, and the deer jumped right out of his arms, ran across the meadow, and circled hopefully around the cush cow.   And at the sight of him Titania laughed like Canterbury bells.

" Wait for it," said Oberon to the deer.   " Our breakfast first, then yours."   And they wandered on through a kissing gate and into the goose yard.

" Do you know," said Titania, " I think I'm hungry."

" Then coom, lass, and look for your breakfast," said Oberon nearer to normal on his home ground.

" I'm cooming," said Titania with a twinkle.

And they went towards a nest and a goose came out of it and strutted past them cackling importantly.

" He's laid an egg specially for you," said Oberon.

They went to the nest together and there was the egg lying in it. They peered down.

" Drat it," said Oberon, " it's golden.   Coom lass.   Let's look somewhere else.

> " Pancakes and fritters,"
> Say the bells of St. Peter's.
>
> " Where must we fry them ? "
> Say the bells of Cold Higham.
>
> " In yonder land thurrow,"
> Say the bells of Wellingborough.

Right glad was the pedlar of Swaffham when at last, after much trudging and many nights on haystacks, he stood on London Bridge itself with his faithful dog at his heels and saw the tall houses on the right hand and left and had glimpses of the water running and the ships sailing by.   All day long he paced to and fro across the great thoroughfare and watched the shoppers going into the shops empty and coming out laden and looking none the happier for it, and he saw the rich merchants ride past with their money-bags clinking from their saddles and not one of them was singing, and he saw the prentice boys jeering at him from the attics : but he saw no sight that might bring him comfort save for the river sights.   Nor did he hear anything to give him pleasure save the bells of London Town.

" Oranges and lemons."
  Say the bells of St. Clement's.

" You owe me five farthings,"
  Say the bells of St. Martin's.

" When will you pay me ? "
  Say the bells of Old Bailey.

" When I grow rich,"
  Say the bells of Shoreditch.

" Pray when will that be ? "
  Say the sweet bells of Stepney.

" How do I know ? "
  Says the great bell of Bow.

And the pedlar of Swaffham enjoyed the chimes and thought how they might be talking about himself, and determined not to abandon his dream so easily.   And he came back again and stood on the bridge the next day.

" Gay go up and gay go down
  To ring the bells of London Town."

For the sun had come out and a fresh breeze blew up the river and the little ships puffed out their sails and tacked joyously across each other as though they were swans, and the swans puffed out their chests and sailed majestically past them as though they were ships.   And the citizens of London peered down from over the parapets between the houses and their chests swelled with pride, not for the first time, because they were citizens of London.   And they gathered in ale houses, and passed the time of day in barber's shops, and stood in little groups on the pavements reciting sonnets at one another, but nobody spoke a line to the pedlar of Swaffham and his faithful dog, though he had a quatrain all ready to bestow on anyone who might ask for it.

" Your pockets lined with silver,
  Your barrels full of beer,
  Your pantries full of pork pies,
  I wish I had some here."

" Woof," said the dog.   So did he!

And now an old man with a long beard came hobbling along the bridge, and, at the sight of him, all the citizens waved a greeting and beat it to the cellars or ducked into alleys before he could catch up with them.   For he was Rip Van Winkle and he never tired of telling his story.

So the pedlar of Swaffham was left alone on the Bridge with his dog and Rip Van Winkle came up to him and said, " God be with you stranger on this lovely sunny morning."

And by the time he left him the sun had gone down and the shopkeepers were putting up their shutters.

> " Good night and sleep soundly,"
> Say the bells of Bermondsey.

Now the third day being come as the pedlar still stood on London Bridge and gazed, a shopkeeper hard by spoke to him.

" Friend," said he, " I wonder much at your fruitless standing. Have you no wares to sell ? "

" No indeed," quoth the pedlar.

" And you do not beg for alms ? "

" Not while I have strength to stand."

" Then what I pray dost thou want here and what may thy business be ? "

And the pedlar looked at the shopkeeper's rosy cheeks and his spat-upon hair and his fine striped apron, and he wished that he too had been a butcher.   But he answered him without bitterness.

" Well, kind sir," he said, " to tell the truth, I dreamt that if I came and stood on London Bridge I should hear good news."

> " Kettles and pans,"
> Say the bells of St. Anne's.

Right heartily did the shopkeeper laugh.

" Nay," he said, " thou must be a fool to take a long journey on such a silly errand.   Poor silly country fellow," he said, for he was much too polite to say ' bumpkin,' " I tell thee I too dream o' nights."

" Do you now," said the pedlar.

" Last night I dreamed I was in Swaffham."

" Did you now," said the pedlar.

" Swaffham it was," said the shopkeeper convulsed. " A place clean unknown to me. But in Norfolk, they tell me."

" Did it have no church ? " asked the pedlar.

" None that I noticed," said the shopkeeper. " And methought that I was in an orchard behind a pedlar's house."

" Did it have a canary in the window ? " asked the pedlar.

" Come to think of it, it did," said the shopkeeper. " And a cat up the chimney."

" And were there any children ? "

" Why bless my soul," said the shopkeeper, " there were as many children as there were sparrows in the garden."

" Were there now," said the pedlar. " And was the eldest called Ann ? "

" That she was," said the butcher, " for I heard her little brother call her."

The pedlar fetched a deep sigh. It seemed to be his house all right. How strange life was.

" Now in the orchard," said the shopkeeper, " was a great tree."

" Had a blackbird its nest in it ? " asked the pedlar.

" It sang all the time," said the shopkeeper.

The pedlar nodded. He had identified the tree. " And what happened then ? " he asked.

" Then," said the shopkeeper, " it seemed to me that if I digged I should find beneath the tree a great treasure."

" A great treasure," said the pedlar, as though in a dream himself.

" So it seemed to me," said the shopkeeper. " But think you that I am such a fool as to set out on a long and wearisome journey and all for the sake of a silly dream ? "

" Oh no," said the pedlar. " Not a busy man like you." And he hoped with all his soul that he was right.

" No, my good fellow," said the shopkeeper, " learn wisdom from a wiser man than thyself. Go home and mind thy business."

" That I will do at once, kind sir," said the pedlar, " for there is no place like it." And he whistled his dog and he hurried off.

And he was exceedingly glad,

" White bread and sop,"
Say the bells of Kingsthorpe.

" A nut and a kernel,"
Say the bells of Acton Burnell.

" A pudding in the pot,"
Say the bells of Acton Scott.

" If you please, ma'am," said Fairy Peaseblossom, " the Widow Carabosse has arrived."

" Show her in," said Queen Mab. " Why are you keeping her waiting ? "

Behind her back the fairies-in-waiting raised slight eyebrows at one another. This was the seventh day in succession that Queen Mab had received Carabosse, each time a little more promptly, and the conversations were fast obliquing themselves to a dénouement— a happy dénouement, judging by the Queen's temper.

" Ah, Carabosse," she said. " A pleasant journey I trust. Are they rubbing down your broomstick ? Sugar ? I know—two lumps."

" Too kind, too kind," murmured Carabosse almost overcome. The fairies filed out marvelling.

" Hold up your shield,"
Say the bells of Battlefield.

" It is indeed gratifying," said Carabosse, sipping her tea, " that the difficulties in the little story we started a century ago seem to be ironing themselves out."

" Quite so," said Queen Mab. " I too am not displeased with our progress. Indeed," she said, " I cannot see now why our little story should not have a happy ending."

This was surrender and Carabosse knew it. But not by a quiver of a claw did she show it.

" Indeed, ma'am, you are right," she said. " The humble subject's dutiful daughter has learnt that mother knows best and will make an admirable wife for the gracious Queen's impetuous and quite-time-he-settled-down son. There are, indeed, no crumpled rose-leaves in the yew walk."

" Not even a melon seed," said Queen Mab.   She smiled.

" That," said Carabosse, " was quite another and beautifully executed story."

At this flattery Queen Mab blushed with pleasure.   " I got it from Hans Andersen," she said.   " Credit where credit is due."

> " Under and over,"
> Say the bells of Condover.

" But the melon was your idea," said Carabosse.

" Ah well," said Queen Mab.   " These little touches."   She waved them away.   But she still looked pleased.   " I think," she said, " that our gracious Queen and her humble subject now understand one another perfectly."

" Perfectly, ma'am," said Carabosse.

" There have been misunderstandings in the past and perhaps a little wilfulness."

" But the humble subject has done her best to atone," said Carabosse quickly, " and the gracious Queen has never been slow to recognize true repentance."

> " You're a rogue for sartin,"
> Say the bells of St. Martin.

" Though she would not be so quick to forgive if it happened again," said Queen Mab.   " No more spells, Carabosse," she said firmly.

" Certainly not, ma'am," said Carabosse.   " And," she looked meaningly at the Queen, " no more backsliding."

The bells repeated themselves.

" Then that's settled," said Queen Mab, coming right out of obliquity as deftly as she had stepped into it.   " Oberon shall marry Titania and it shall be Wedding Day in Fairyland."

The Fairy Carabosse relaxed in her chair.   Mother of the Princess Royal with the Court bowing and scraping to her and hating her guts.   A consummation devoutly to be wished! She had vowed she would achieve that if it took her a hundred years—and it had.

" Thank you, ma'am," she said.

" Three naked lads,"
Say the bells of St. Chad's.

" Three silver pickles,"
Say the bells of St. Michael's.

" Three gold canaries,"
Say the bells of St. Mary's.

" Why don't you ring louder,"
Say the bells of Hope Bowdler.

" I shall build them a palace," Queen Mab was saying. " Ivory
and peacocks," she decided.

" Most suitable," cooed Carabosse.

" Or amethyst and chalcedony," said Queen Mab. " Anyway,"
she said, " not emeralds. Ostentatious," she explained.

" Oh," said Carabosse.

" The Bride's establishment," said Queen Mab with great
firmness, " shall be left in my hands and you can visit your daughter
on fête days and feast days, and on Walpurgis."

" And Mothering Sunday," said Carabosse quickly.

" And Mothering Sunday," Queen Mab conceded.

" That is just enough," said Carabosse, for, she reflected, she had
many ways in which she could defeat justice.

" Up seven down Garth,"
Say the bells of Bridge North.

" An owl in a tree,"
Say the bells of Norbury.

" There is just one thing," said Carabosse, " though I don't know
that it matters. I don't think our children like each other very
much."

" Neither they do," said Queen Mab. " I had forgotten that."

" Roast beef and be merry,"
Say the bells of Shrewsbury.

" Roast beef and marshmallows,"
Say the bells of All Hallow's.

" Roast goose and gander,"
Say the bells of Longor.

" Why don't you ring louder ? "
Say the bells of Hope Bowdler.

" What a pity," said Titania, " that our two mamas do not like one another." But she said it lightly as one who feels that this is but a slight obstacle to be overcome.

" Aye," said Oberon. But he said it gloomily as one who has had much experience of what happened when mama did not like his bride.

They were lying on the bank above the pond where they had found the deer, gazing at their reflections in the water, while, hard by, Titania's white butterfly was sharing a foxglove with Oberon's black admiral. This was the seventh day in succession that they had shared the foxglove and the white butterfly was hopeful and the admiral resigned.

And not a mama on the horizon.

" It seems strange," said Titania, " that only a little while ago we didn't like one another either."

" Aye," said Oberon. " Must have been daft."

" And it seems ages," said Titania, " since we began to like one another very much indeed."

" Not like," said Oberon. " Luv."

They held hands.

From the foxglove two butterfly heads peered forth. No hurry. They settled down again.

" This time we're sure," said Titania. " It's for ever and ever."

" Aye," said Oberon almost absently. He seemed to be meditating something. " And if mama doesn't like it," he produced, " she can loomp it."

The Queen loomping it! " Can she ? " asked Titania impressed.

" Aye," said Oberon more confidently, " she can loomp it." He sprang to his feet. " Coom, lass, and I'll teach thee to milk coo."

They untethered their butterflies.

" Race you! " cried Titania and was off like a white streak.

" Faster, Dobbin," she cried, her hair streaming out. " Faster! " she urged, for she could feel the powerful wings of the black admiral thundering up behind. " Faster! Faster, dear Dobbin, we must get there first! "

" Gently, my pretty," whispered Oberon into the ear of the black admiral. " Take it easy, now—let the ladies win! "

> " All of God's chilluns,"
> Say the bells of the Chilterns.

> " I gotta shoe,"
> Say the bells of Port Looe.

The sun is shining on the sea. Shining with all its might. Two little nigger boys in little striped loin-cloths are lying on their backs basking in it.

" Now youse chillun come out ob de sun," called Uncle Rochester from the shade of his covered deck chair, well back from the water's edge. " Come out ob de sun or yo' sho' will be as black as niggahs."

One little nigger boy put up his striped umbrella and sat demurely under it. But the other little nigger boy scooped some sand over his toes and went on basking.

With a sigh Uncle Rochester left the shade of his deck chair, and putting a large bandana handkerchief over his head, went down to reason.

" Now see here, Erasmus," he said, " ain't I dun see enough sorrow already, losing all de family one by one—jest as De Book said." He opened it and read :

> " Two little niggah boys, sitting in de sun.
> One got frizzled up, and den,"

his voice broke.

> " Dere was one."

" Oh nuts in May," said the ninth little nigger boy and stretched out his arms to the sun. Already he was sizzling slightly.

Uncle Rochester sagged. " Nobody knows de troubles ah sees," he said, wiping his eyes and overcome with self pity.

> " Up the ridge and down the butt,"
> Say the bells of Smethycote.

> " Ivy, holly and mistletoe,"
> Say the bells of Winstanton.

Meanwhile the pedlar of Swaffham, with his dog at his heels, had returned home, and, putting London Bridge and its marvels behind him, he retired to his cottage and took up his old plain aptly named spade. And he digged underneath the great oak tree and the blackbird looked down through the leaves and sang to him. And he found a prodigious great treasure and waxed exceedingly rich. But he did not forget his duty in the pride of his riches. For he built up again the old Parish Church that had fallen down and the people in the village could hold up their heads once more come Sundays.

> " Three loaves in an oven,"
> Say the bells of Swaffham.

And he lived to a ripe old age and when he died they put up a statue of him in the Church, with a sack on his back and his dog at his heels, and all in stone. And there it stands to this day to witness if we lie.

> " Haystacks and stiles,"
> Say the bells of St. Giles.

" Oh, mother," said Titania, looking very small under her goosefeather, " I'm so happy."

" So you should be, daughter," said Carabosse, seating herself on the foot of the bed for it was that hour of truce when mother and daughter exchange confidences. ` " So you should be."

" Has the Queen really given her consent ? "

" She has," said Titania's mother. " And to-morrow she will send for you to indicate her wishes. You will be the Crown Princess, child, and some day you will be Queen of Fairy Land, and then you will have to remember what your mother has taught you and take care not to dream on a midsummer's night."

" Oh, mother," said Titania stanily, for she had not been listening, " I owe it all to you."

" Silly goose," said Carabosse. " What else are mothers for but to fight their daughter's battles when they are too green to win them for themselves. Now," her voice vibrated with gratification, " the whole world will realize that Titania has a mother."

> " Love them and leave them,"
> Say the bells of Bredon.

" Good night, son," said Queen Mab, rising from the foot of Oberon's bed, for it was that hour of the night when mother and son exchange confidences, " and here is a book for you. Read it all the way through," she advised, " and don't skip."

" A book," said Oberon doubtfully.

" A very important book," said Queen Mab, belting herself more
tightly into her sensible dressing-gown.   " And if there is anything
in it you don't understand, ask the Chamberlain."

She kissed him on the forehead and sailed serenely out.

Oberon picked up the book.

THE FACTS OF LIFE FOR FAIRIES.

He concentrated.

> " Peacocks are proud,"
> Say the bells of Stroud.

It was the hour of confidences.   Sitting on Highgate milestone,
Dick Whittington turned to his cat.

" Oh, Puss," he said, " they told me the streets of London were
paved with gold, but they are only paved with good intentions."

" Meow," said Puss, and rubbed himself against his master's leg.

And the clouds blew away and the stars came out and Dick
Whittington sat and looked at them, and listened to the bells that
seemed this night to be ringing all over England.

> " Toadstools and dew,"
> Say the bells of Kew.
>
> " We will ring them down,"
> Say the bells of Tidwell Town.
>
> " That will be ample,"
> Say the bells of the Temple.
>
> " Hurry—you're late,"
> Say the bells of Aldgate.
>
> " All for a horse,"
> Say the bells of King's Cross.
>
> " A brown honeybee,"
> Say the bells of Torquay.
>
> " Cockles and corn,"
> Say the bells of Eastbourne.
>
> " Pease pudding and porridge,"
> Say the bells of Norwich.
>
> " Lark pudding and pie,"
> Say the bells of Wye.

" Five beans and a cherry."
Say the bells of Canterbury.

" Pie crust and pork,"
Say the bells of York.

" Why don't you ring louder,"
Say the bells of Hope Bowdler.

" That would be tellin',"
Say the bells of Helvellyn.

" Fire and hearth,"
Say the bells of Bath.

" Scissors and smiles,"
Say the bells of Seven Dials.

" Scissors and rings,"
Say the bells of Seven Kings.

" Silver and gold,"
Says Stow-in-the-Wold.

" Gulder and doubloon,"
Say the bells of Troon.

" Coin and cash,"
Say the bells of Saltash.

" Give us some money,"
Say the bells of Bermondsey.

" Why don't you ring louder ? "
Say the bells of Hope Bowdler.

" Money and rank,"
Say the bells of the Bank.

" Money and power,"
Say the bells of the Tower.

" Money and Pride,"
Say the bells of St. Bride.

All the bells in England, ringing and ringing. All that we have sounded and many, many more. But to Dick Whittington it seemed that they were all saying the same thing.
"Hear that," he said to Puss. . . .

CHAPTER XVI

Wedding day in Fairy Land.

Titania is marrying Oberon.

Princess Aurora is marrying Ivan, son of Ivan.

And all the lived-happilies-ever-after are following their example.
It takes one to make a happy ending.

It is the hour before dawn and all is grey and still in a sleeping
world. The lilies on the pond are closed coloured cups and the
branches of the trees shadowy cradles for sleeping birds. A baby
bear has curled himself up under a Christmas tree and a bunny's
ears can be seen peering above his burrow.

But now a glow comes over the sky and over the world beneath,
and the greys and the mauves turn slowly into greens, pinks, blues
and yellows, and every other colour on Mr. Disney's palette. The
birds awake, shake off their sleep and preen themselves in the early
sunshine. The baby bear yawns deliciously and bunny's ears
disappear into his warren. The water-lilies open, a water-baby in
each. They stretch and test the water with their toes.

Oooh!

Mother Earth is stirring. Brownies roll out of leafy hammocks,
goblins hop out from hollow trees, elves unroll themselves from
under toadstools, and gnomes come tunnelling out—ready for the
day's activities.

For it is Wedding Day in Fairy Land and Mother Earth must
look her best.

And so the little workers get busy.

The elves to the flowers, washing down the petals and one
another and seeing that each dew-drop falls on the right place and
in time with the music.

Plink! Plonk! Plop!

The brownies to the squirrels, their tails must be good and bushy to-day. Brush. Brush. Brush. Sit still, Sammy, plenty of time to nibble that nut later.

To the gnomes a sterner task. They are responsible for every leaf that falls in summer or stays on in winter, and now it is summer and there must be no mistake. All that is allowed to flutter to-day is hearts. So up into the branches for a stern inspection and a green thread for every waver.

As for the goblins, they are the polishers. Here are two of them, one at each end of large pieces of seaweed, to-ing and fro-ing across the trunk of a fir tree and dodging the fir cones that drop with the shaking. And here is a swarm of them in the orchard, washing down the apples and rubbing up the cherries, bronzing the apricots and standing back from the peaches to make sure they have given them just the right touch of bloom.

And under their ministrations Mother Nature shines out and knows she is looking her best.

If only it doesn't rain!

" If only it doesn't rain! "

A thousand and one brides turn back from a thousand and one windows and turn round before a thousand and one mirrors and a thousand and one mamas.

" How do I look ? " they ask.

" As pretty as a picture," say a thousand and one mamas.

Mr. Norman Hartnell has come into his own!

And a thousand and one brides sweep curtsies and practise walking down aisles.

" It reminds me of the time I married your father," say a thousand and one mamas, and they dab their eyes with a handkerchief and become irrelevant.

" It reminds me," said Fairy Carabosse, " of the day I married your father, drat him! Never find your husband out, Titania," she counselled.

" Oberon is different," said Titania blissfully. " I'd trust him anywhere."

" H'm," said Titania's mother, and made a mental note that she wouldn't.

In front of her mirror, Queen Mab was rotating like a royal

pigeon on the weathervane on the dome of St. Paul's, only somewhat slower. No need for her to ask how she looked in her new
dress of lilac bombazine, as assorted coo-ing, as from the pigeons
assembled at the steps of St. Paul's, rose from the assembled fairies-
in-waiting.

" Superb! "

" Majestic! "

" Wonderful! "

" Breath-taking! "

" Charming! Absolutely charming! "

" Not a day over two hundred," said Fairy Moth above herself.
But not even an eyebrow was raised. What a good humour the
Queen was in!

" Fanfaronade," she said. " Go and see if the bridegroom is ready."

Not in his dressing-room! Sob. Not by the lily pond! Sob.
Not in a month of Sundays. . . .

Fairy Fanfaronade broke down and cried like a child. To think
this was the last time she wouldn't find him.

In front of a mirror the tenth little nigger boy was rotating with
the best of them. He had put on his cleanest cottons, he had
polished his boots, and he had tried to comb his hair. Uncle
Rochester, coming in from the cotton fields, stopped short in the
middle of a song about his Little Piccaninny and gazed at his
strutting nephew with a sinking heart.

" Lochinvar," he said accusingly, " what be you doing wid mah
top hat ? "

The tenth little nigger boy looked obstinate.

" I sho' be tired of libing all alone," he said. " I dun planned to
marry Topsy dis morning."

He fluffed out the carnation in his buttonhole and strutted off.

Uncle Rochester picked up De Book and threw it out of the
window.

" Might as well nevah have bought yo'," he shook his fist,
" fo' all de good yo' done."

" Now Ivan," said the Master of Ceremonies, " what do you say
when the preacher says ' Will you ? ' "

Ivan pondered. "I am Ivan," he said hopefully. . . .

"Darling," said Prince Charming. "Do come to the wedding. You'll have the smallest foot there."

"I'm tired," said Cinderella. "But you trot along. You like these society merry-go-rounds."

Prince Charming winced.

One thousand and one marriages. One thousand and one brides picking up their trains and descending staircases. Yet here is Fairy Dark Diamond gazing at her reflection in a pond and not even rotating to get a better angle on it.

One thousand and one bridegrooms gazing into mirrors and sprucing themselves up. Yet on the other side of the pond a man, born to be a bridegroom, tall, dark and handsome and clearly rich, is gazing moodily into the depths.

One thousand and one best men, dipping anxious fingers into waistcoat pockets. Yet here is Puck, without any waistcoat at all, lying on his tummy and laughing hoarsely at the two figures by the pond. Time he got busy.

He throws a pebble into the pond. Dark Diamond looks up. So does the born bridegroom. They notice one another. The born bridegroom signs and looks back into the green depths of the pond. But Dark Diamond is edging round as fast as she can manage it casually.

From all around them comes the silver peal of wedding bells.

"The whole world seems to be getting married this morning," said the born bridegroom, looking taller and handsomer then ever. "Excepting me," he sighed.

"And me," said Dark Diamond. She sighed.

They gazed into the pond.

In his lotus leaf Puck kicked his heels in the air.

"Why aren't you getting married to-day?" asked Dark Diamond. "It's General Wedding Day. Don't you want to live happily ever after?"

"Nobody wants to marry me," said the born bridegroom. And he looked taller and handsomer and richer than ever. "Why aren't you getting married?"

"Nobody asked me, sir," she said. And she looked prettier than ever.

And, as Puck crammed his fists in his mouth, they gazed at each other with dawning hope.

Is it possible he hasn't heard ?

Is it possible she doesn't know ?

" Dearest lady," said the born bridegroom, " will you marry me ? "

" Oh—yes! " said Dark Diamond.

She could have hugged him.

*　　　*　　　*

The church bells are ringing more urgently, bluebells, harebells and Canterbury bells. Down the path leading to the porch come the radiant, hopeful, well-matched couples—Kings and Queens about to step into their kingdoms.

Inside the church the pews are filled to overflowing. Here are all the earlier Happy-ever-Afters, obviously all the happier for it, come to welcome the About-to-be-Happies, though, of course, not so happy as they are. Never a cross word these twenty-five, fifty, or sixty years—and they are divided into pews accordingly, the silver jubilees at the back, the golden jubilees nearer the centre, and the diamonds well to the front, for they are getting a little hard of hearing.

The choir is in its place and looking up angelically at its conductor. Is it the light that makes him look like Mickey Mouse ?

The organ is playing in spurts, and, from time to time, an angry jabber floats out above the scandalized Archbishop's head. Donald Duck is having trouble with the stops.

" Here come the Brides! "

The organ greets them triumphantly—not a false note all down the aisle, and Donald Duck is crooning his content. He has forgotten that his little nephews are singing in the choir.

" Ready, Uncle Donald! "

The organist strikes a note and the Voice that breathed o'er Eden quacks o'er the Church, while Mickey Mouse runs to and fro, subduing the altos.

And now the couples are lined up before the Archbishop. But they must wait for the Brides of Honour. " I wish they'd hurry," thinks Dark Diamond, clutching her born bridegroom. So many cups—so many slips.

And now at last the Princess Aurora, as beautiful as the day is long, in a gown like ice when the sun is shining on it, and, at the sight of her, Ivan throws out his chest and all the Darbies and Joans hold hands. And they stand together in front of all the other couples, and wait for the last Bride of all.

She is Titania, and here she comes, floating on air, with the Widow Carabosse, almost affable, arranging her train in her wake. And here is Oberon, buckles on his shoes and wearing them without any fuss.

But what can be keeping the dear Queen ? Surely she will not be late to-day ! Why she has not been late since the last time.

Nothing for it but a walk in Paradise Garden. But Delius is difficult, especially when the organist is a duck. Who can blame Donald if, after one or two attempts, he plays it safe with The Wedding of the Painted Doll.

The Queen at last ! And not a hair out of place. The congregation rises as the lilac figure, followed by her Court, progresses to her place.

" What are you waiting for," she eyebrows to the Archbishop.

The organ wells up.

From the gallery a very old lady and five very old gentlemen beam down at the Happy Endings.

Mother Goose, Charles Perrault, the Brothers Grimm, Hans Andersen and Poushkin are well pleased with their work.

" I now pronounce you men and wives," says the Archbishop thankfully. He mops his brow.

The bluebells, the harebells, and the Canterbury bells peel out again.

One thousand and one brides raise their faces. One thousand bridegrooms lift the veils and kiss their brides.

" Darling," says Oberon.

" Krassavitza," said Ivan.

But nobody has raised Dark Diamond's veil and nobody has kissed her cheek, and nobody has called her my beautiful in any language whatever. Can she have married a cold frog ?

And this precisely is what she has done. For when she lifts her own veil she has to look down to see her husband, and there he is, green and perky, hopping up and down by the hem of her gown.

" Who," said Dark Diamond livid, " who has dared to turn you into a frog ? " And she glares at Carabosse.

"You've got it wrong," croaks the frog blissfully. "I am not a Prince turned into a frog. I am a frog turned back from a Prince. I used to be a very wicked frog," he cast his eyes up, "so they turned me into a Prince to punish me and the spell could not be lifted till I found someone to marry me. Thank you, dearest lady," said the frog, "for marrying me."

"Don't mention it," said Dark Diamond tautly.

"And now," said the frog, "I am a frog again." And he hopped out of the window and splashed happily in a puddle.

"Darling," said Titania.

"Dearest," said Aurora.

"Oh Hell," said Fairy Dark Diamond.

*   *   *

Aurora's Wedding.

Mendelssohn has given way to Tchaikovsky. The Church has dissolved into the reception. And here we are in the Ballroom of the glittering palace, just as Diaghilev and Bakst were to imagine it. There was to be, of course, some doubt whether the scenery would arrive in time, or indeed at all, and it seemed beyond all hope that the costumes could be ready.

To-night all Fairy Land has come to the ball and there are more sequins to the square inch than in other scenes of this production. As the King of Boxing Night Land remarks to his amiable Queen, "I have seen many balls of unrivalled splendour, m'dear, but never one so unrivalled as this."

"I hope they'll be as happy as we are," says the Queen, and if she had not been a Queen she would have mopped her eyes. As it is, she squeezes his hand.

The guests are pouring in, a parade of walking candelabra, and the air is full of coos of admiration and enquiries after dressmakers, for all the world as though they were not standing, blackcoated and thinly smiling, in the wings.

But two of the guests are not impressed. They are standing aloof from the throng, stroking their beards disparagingly. Almost they might be Sir Thomas Beecham at a different kind of Promenade.

"These weddings!" says the first guest. "Fuss and fiddlesticks. When you've been married as many times as I have, old man, you won't give that for it." He flicks his fingers. "I'm Henry the Eighth," he explains.

"Pleased to meet you," says the second guest. "I'm Blue-
beard."

Henry the Eighth bows his head.

*   *   *

And now twelve plump little girls, dressed as twelve plump
little boys, sound a fanfare. The guests part, shimmering, to left
and right, and down the gangway progresses Queen Mab and her
Court, smiling greetings and pausing for a pleasant word with
Titania's mother.

"It's going nicely, Carabosse," she indulged. "Just as we
planned it."

"To the last particular," says Carabosse, bowing low. A
hedgehog tugs beseechingly at her drooping chiffons. She does
not notice him.

Queen Mab takes her place on the dais. She motions to Carabosse to sit below her. Her Court groups itself round her in
attitudes of respectful ecstasy.

"Let the revels begin."

The Conductor swoops into it.

On come the Fairies led by Oberon and Titania. "Point your
toes and keep your hips in," whispers Titania lovingly. What a
little helpmate she will prove. The besotted Oberon beams at her
and does his best. "Wait till I get thee in peascods, lass," he is
heard to observe and pats her on the rump—a motion Petipa could
certainly never have intended.

Queen Mab and her Court look graciously on as, one after
another, the Fairies go into double turns on pinpoints. "Not
what it was at the Maryinski," she says, "but quite creditable for
Covent Garden."

The dance continues. Now the Fairies begin their variations.
From the buffet a couple of Kings, arm in arm and a bottle under
the other, come staggering into the ballroom. They are Old King
Cole, in ermine and purple, and King Gullible of Goosefeather
Land in nothing at all. They have been celebrating Aurora's
wedding and an agreement to share the tourist trade. King
Gullible stumbles on his imperceptible train. Both Kings lie
sprawling on the floor and raise their bottles instead of each other.

"Tell you somshing," said King Gullible with a confidential
hiccup. "Somshing I haven't told a shoul."

" Yesh," said Old King Cole.

" You know my invishable clothes ? "

" Yesh."

" You know that only the worthy can shee them."

" Yesh," said Old King Cole warily.

" Tell you somshing," said King Gullible. " Can't shee them myself." He wept.

Old King Cole was a merry old soul. He took a swig out of his bottle. Thus braced he embarked on a confidence on his own.

" Tell you somshing," he said. " You know your invishable clothes."

" Yesh," said King Gullible sadly.

" Can't shee them either! " said Old King Cole.

And far away in Goosefeather Land the tailors gathered up their earnings and rode quickly away. It had been good while it lasted. . . .

The Fairies have found their places in their final tableau. Now the Children's Tales take the floor, dancing with gay abandon. Beauty and the Beast, Puss in Boots, and Little Red Riding Hood strewing flowers from her basket all over the place.

Goody Two Shoes, unable to take her gaze off her feet, longs to join in the revels. For, so far, nobody has asked her. But here comes Donald Duck, head in the air and very proud of himself in his white starched front with diamond stud in centre. The trouble he has had to get into it and the number of times it has jumped up to hit him under the chin only Mr. Disney knows!

"Why, Donald," cries Goody Two Shoes, " do come and dance with me."

But Donald shakes his head.

" Oh, Donald, be a duck," she coaxes. . . .

While the Nursery romps, the Fairies are refreshing themselves. In the Conservatory, Titania is waiting for Oberon to bring her back an iceling.

" My wife," says a voice from the deepest shadows, " doesn't understand me."

Titania starts.

" You poor thing," says a softer voice.

" Of course, she has the smallest foot in the world," says the first voice, " but," it faces it, " that isn't everything."

The blood flies to Titania's cheeks. How could she have ?

And now the children's tales have given way to three Moujiks, stamping and jumping and leaping over one another. They are the three Ivans, and one of them is our Bridegroom. This spot has been promised him for he has been a good boy and learnt his entrechats, though he is by no means strong enough technically yet to take the Prince in Giselle. What a pity, thinks the Princess Aurora, a momentary cloud upon her bridal horizon. Ah well, she blows it away, Dolin will do!

Still, at jumping, beating and leaping, Ivan has no equal, and the room rocks with applause. But even amidst the applause dubious heads are being shaken.

" A trifle farouche to marry the Princess Aurora," pursed lips are murmuring behind fans.

" What would you! " Shoulders are raised. " He is the only seventh son not under contract."

The three Ivans roll themselves off the stage. " Bravo! " cries the ballroom. " Well danced! Bis! "

But suddenly the applause falters and dies away. For at the top of the marble staircase stands a new guest.

" His Highness, Prince Florizel," announces the major-domo and his voice is a little shaken.

Queen Mab puts her hand to her heart and half rises from the throne. The Court leans anxiously forward ready to catch her in case she swoons.

Very much his mother's son, Prince Florizel descends the stairs. He is a little pale but his dignity is unshakable. He crosses the floor and kisses Queen Mab's hand.

" I have come," he says, " to offer my congratulations."

You could have heard a lupin drop. Fairy Moth turned scarlet and fussed with her bouquet.

" Welcome, son," said Queen Mab. " And where is your wife ? "

" She sends you her loyal greetings," said Prince Florizel, " and regrets that she could not make the journey."

" What a pity," said Queen Mab beaming. Her eyes searched

his face. Not drinking enough milk. " Come and sit beside me, son, and tell me all about yourself."

And suddenly the room seems full of the scent of wallflowers.

*   *   *

The revels are over. The party is breaking up. One thousand and one horseshoes have been fixed to one thousand and one types of conveyances. And one thousand and one departing couples have been showered with rice, confetti, spangles and rose petals.

And, as though just to please Ivan, the snow falls softly down.

Now only one thousand and one dressed-up mothers and five thousand and five unmarried aunts are left, dabbing their eyes all over the glittering ballroom.

The Fairies gather round their Queen and wave their wands.

" A beautiful wedding day," says Fairy Peaseblossom, her wand quivering with emotion.

" A triumph of organization," says Cobweb, her wand well under control.

"Not a hitch anywhere," says Mustard Seed, disengaging hers.

" Happy ever after," says Moth dreamily, and spins it.

Only Fairy Fanfaronade seems listless and her wanding has no animation whatever. Glancing at her, Queen Mab unerringly diagnoses the cause. Othello's occupation gone.

" Fetch me," says the Queen crisply, " the Scarlet Pimpernel."

And with the fairies waving their wands and the conductor laying down his,

CURTAIN

MORAL

. . . "And you shall visit her on fête days, and feast days, and Walpurgis.
And Mothering Sunday. . . ."

It was Mothering Sunday.
"Oberon! Oberon!" Titania, fluttering frantically alighted on the foot of her husband's bed. "Oh darling, there's a lion in mother's room."
"Can't help that," said Oberon firmly. "He'll have to get oot as best he can.